Sophie Duffy has an MA in Creative Writing from Lancaster. Her first novel, *The Generation Game*, won the Yeovil Literary Prize and the Luke Bitmead Bursary. She has also published short stories in a range of literary journals and anthologies. Having taught in primary schools in inner-city London with a special interest in early years and emergent writing, Sophie now leads life-writing workshops at Teignmouth Library. She also works as a book reviewer, and has been a judge for many writing competitions.

You can discover more about the author at www.sophieduffy.com

BETSY & LILIBET

They named me Elizabeth Sarah Sunshine, after the brand new princess, born at the exact same time as me, only across the other side of the river, to posher parents, with a swankier address. The princess was given a string of names that would grow ever longer so that in some ways she would always have more than me. But she didn't get the sun-shine . . . London, 1926: Two baby girls are born just hours and miles apart. Both will grow up in very different families; each will carry the burden of responsibility, service, and duty. One will wear the Crown of the Commonwealth; the other will bury the bodies of the dead. Over the course of ninety years, their paths will cross three times. This is the story of Betsy and Lilibet.

Books by Sophie Duffy
Published by Ulverscroft:

THE GENERATION GAME
BRIGHT STARS

SOPHIE DUFFY

---◆---

BETSY & LILIBET

Complete and Unabridged

CHARNWOOD
Leicester

First published in Great Britain in 2018 by
Legend Press Ltd
London

First Charnwood Edition
published 2019
by arrangement with
Legend Press Ltd
London

A catalogue record for this book is available
from the British Library.

ISBN 978–1–4448–4051–3

For Johnny, Eddy and Izzy,
my rays of sunshine

I declare before you all that my whole life, whether it be long or short, shall be devoted to your service and the service of our great imperial family to which we all belong.

Princess Elizabeth on her 21st birthday, radio broadcast to the Commonwealth.

Oh, they've sent the hearses.

Queen Elizabeth II on her return from Kenya following the death of her father.

2016

Bognor Regis

I never thought I'd be old. But here I am, sitting on a wee-resistant armchair in the overheated lounge of a residential home on the south coast.

I wasn't supposed to live. I came early, the dead hour of the night, my mother exhausted and on the verge of giving up. A scrawny rat of a thing.

'Three pounds and a bit,' the midwife informed Doctor Parkin, dragged from his warm bed by my father.

Doctor Parkin looked me over, handed me back, a parcel of liver. 'Keep Baby with Mother,' he instructed.

That's all Doctor Parkin had to say: *Keep Baby with Mother.*

I could've been buried in a shoebox that night, but those few words saved my life.

★   ★   ★

They named me Elizabeth, after the brand new princess, born at the exact same time as me, only across the other side of the river, to posher parents, with a swankier address. Elizabeth Sarah Sunshine, to be known as Betsy. The princess was given a string of names that would grow ever

1

longer when she unexpectedly became queen so that in some ways she would always have more than me. In others, we'd be exactly the same. But she didn't get the Sunshine.

Sunshine by name, more cloudy by nature, perfect for undertaking, the family business. Not for the faint-hearted but secure, that's what Mum always said.

Keep Baby with Mother.

Three pounds and a bit and here I am still.

★ ★ ★

Death gets us all in the end and my end is approaching, maybe tonight, maybe next year, or maybe once I've got my telegram off the Queen, if she makes it till then, which I hope she does.

I don't fear Death; we've lived cheek by jowl all my life. When I'm gone, I won't be here no more. I'll be somewhere else. Or nowhere at all. Either way, there's nothing I can do about it.

We don't know how or when. I've seen all the ways he can think of: illness, accidents, birth, old age, murder, war, suicide. The kiddies are the worst. Those little coffins carried in a father's arms. The look in his eye that breaks your heart.

My own funeral is planned down to the last nail in the coffin. Nothing fancy. No doves, no bearded mutes, no ostrich feathers. No horses, no Robbie Williams, no Celine Dion. Just my twenty minutes in the crem with the people I love. And Perry Como, because he reminds me of my Mick, bogtrotter, love of my life.

★ ★ ★

There's one thing I'm afraid of, being buried alive. Goes back to the war. The Anderson shelter. And poor old Janet. More a sister to me than Margie ever was. Margie was always competing, always pinching stuff off of me, from lipstick to boyfriends. Even had to die first, despite being four years younger. But now Margie's gone, I miss her too.

You always want what you can't have. That's what I used to say to Margie. Though she usually got what she wanted, so it didn't apply in her case. I mean, three husbands? Who needs that many? And I don't suppose she wanted that fatal stroke neither.

I never wanted a baby, not really. I didn't long for one, didn't think I was the mothering type. But then, once I'd got wed, it was expected, only it didn't happen, just the monthlies, one after the other after the other. I shrugged it off at first, but then another month went by, and then a year, and it wasn't so easy. And then. My cuckoo. My lucky egg. My nearly-twins.

★ ★ ★

When I lost him, Charlie, I didn't know how to get him back. I didn't know if I deserved to. Or if I even wanted to, which is bad, seeing as I wanted him so much in the first place. And now everyone keeps nagging me.

Tell him. Tell him. Tell him.

The biggest nag of all is my conscience, which

3

I thought I'd buried along with my soul on a sunny day in Kent in 1949.

I have to try, now, still. Before it's too late.

★   ★   ★

The ghosts come back to haunt you, if you let them. The trick is not to let them. But at the grand old age of ninety, it's getting harder. They're everywhere: Mum, Dad, Nana, Bert, Margie, Mab, Janet, my Mick. Some dead. Some alive. Some missing.

And Charlie. He's all around, like a fly on a hot day, pestering, needling. However much I swat, he never leaves me alone.

So here I am, in my wee-resistant chair, staring out the smeary windows at the splendour of Bognor, thinking about Charlie.

Keep Baby with Mother.

I wish.

It's all to do with the training: you can do a lot if you're properly trained.
Queen Elizabeth II

1931

London

I don't like school, not from the first day I have to go. I am the fiftieth child in the class, spend the morning bawling and snivelling on the poor teacher's lap, as if she doesn't have enough to worry about, like forty-nine other children. I want to stay at home with Mum, only Dad's having none of it. 'You need an education,' he says, ahead of his time, though really it's because there'll be no sons, not after what my little sister, Margie, did to Mum two years back. Feet first she came, stamping her way into the world. Doctor Parkin had to dig deep with some barbaric instrument that saved her life but almost saw Mum off in one of Dad's finest boxes. No more kids after that. 'She'll die,' Doctor Parkin said, nice bedside manner.

Our family knows Death, six generations of it. Sunshine & Sons, that's what the business is called. Only, because there are no sons, Dad will let us girls join the business when many a father would shut up shop. Not that Marg will want to join, not one for tradition and duty.

That's where I come in, just like my namesake.

As for school, I soon realise that it's a good place because two-year-old Margie doesn't go and I can get some peace and quiet. In so much as you can get peace and quiet with forty-nine other kiddies.

★ ★ ★

'Your dad works with dead bodies.' Joanie Clark is the class bully. She is hard as a butcher's mallet and evil with it. She's cornered me in the playground with her posse of snot-nosed ragamuffins.

'So?' I square up to her. I'm not afraid. I'm only shivering because I'm not wearing my liberty bodice. 'Someone's got to do it.'

But she won't leave it. She goes on and on, saying it's creepy, disgusting, dirty, when she's the one with the head lice and scabs. She's the one that needs a good going-over with a flannel and some Lifebuoy. On and on she goes, her posse standing behind her.

I've had enough. I'm proud of my mum and dad.

'All right, Joanie Clark. Tell me, when you die do you want to be cut up and put in a coal sack? Or would you rather be chucked in the Thames, your body squirming with maggots? And what about your mum? And your dad? And your little brothers and sister?' I go on and on too. I go on and on until I make her and her posse of snot-nosed ragamuffins cry, the whole lot of them.

I get a clout for that later. Two clouts. One off Miss Kenton, our teacher. And a bigger one off of my mum.

'We're respectable people,' Mum says, her lipstick smudged like she's wiped the back of her hand across her mouth, that way she does when she's tired. She's tired a lot. She has to check on the 'boys' at work, clean up after Dad, and deal with the dead. She has to keep a clean house and run around after her mum, that's my Nana Mabel. And, her most important job, she has to look after me and Marg. I'm not too bad but Marg is a pain in the bum, though Mum thinks the sun shines out of it. So I must try harder to be good because Marg won't ever be and Mum'll realise this one day.

⋆   ⋆   ⋆

Dad reads the paper of an evening. The *Daily Telegraph*. We play this game sometimes. He reads out the death notices and we guess how old the deceased was. I don't know who the people are but I like to guess all the same. Sometimes I win. I wonder if I'm psychic. Mum says I'm just lucky. Lots of things are lucky. Rabbit paws. Four-leafed clovers. Horseshoes. The dead can take lucky things with them. 'To make sure they get to the other side,' Dad says, like they're going on the Woolwich ferry. Mrs Sullivan takes her stuffed parrot, Hercules. 'It's her wishes,' Dad says. 'Wishes are important.'

Wishes are everything.

2016

Bognor Regis

Wishes get more simple as you get old. You wish you could wait longer before needing a wee. Spending a penny is an effort when you have to get from your chair to the lav. You have to plan and think about all the stuff that used to come natural. So there's no point wishing for world peace, not when you've lived through the war and seen that people don't change. You can't wish for the advancement of medical science, not when you've dealt with victims of cancer and strokes and all the rest of it. There's no point wishing for your husband to come back to you. Once he's gone, he's gone.

The best wish I can have is for my children, grandchildren and great-grandchildren. That they will be happy.

I sit in my chair here in Sunnydale and I wonder if I was granted three wishes, what would I choose.

They say be careful what you wish for.

Like all the best families, we have our share of eccentricities, of impetuous and wayward young-sters and of family disagreements.
Queen Elizabeth II

1936

London

The church hall is as comforting as the funeral parlour. Not something most girls would say, but I am not most girls. The church hall, appropriately and conveniently next to the parish church of St Michael the Archangel, is a place I love, not because I am especially religious or holy but because it's where we go for a knees-up, a game of ping-pong and, best of all, Brownies.

Thursday night is Brownie night and I get to wear my uniform, but not Margie because she's too young. Ha, ha. She says she's not bothered, that brown's an evil colour, but I know she is bubbling with jealous rage every time my best friend Janet calls for me and we skip off to the hall.

Brown Owl is lovely. Her real name is Vera Parsons. She's young and glamorous, barely out of the Girl Guides herself. She takes us on nature trails to Dulwich Park, on the bus to Surrey Docks. Swimming at the lido, the pictures at Goose Green. Even when we're mudlarking or pond-dipping, she has a slash of red lipstick on her Bette Davis lips and a squirt of *L'Air du Temps*. She is smashing. She's like a big sister, but not bossy or smug. (Margie says I am bossy and smug, but that's only because she is flighty and dim.)

But it is 1936 and Miss Parsons can't be a 'Miss' forever. The dark day comes. She gets engaged to Arthur Bellingham, a bank clerk down the National Westminster. She is a typist and their eyes meet over a clutch of carbon copies. I don't reckon much to Arthur Bellingham, or his eyes for that matter, especially when Brown Owl tells us she's leaving Brownies once she's married. I vow I will never give up anything I love to make a man his dinner. When I tell Mum this, her initial reaction is a smile, followed quickly by a telling-off. Which is pretty much how things are between me and my mum: half pride, balanced out by a quarter exasperation and a quarter worry.

However, there is a silver lining. Brown Owl walks me home one Thursday evening. 'I've got something to ask your mum,' she says.

'Am I in trouble?'

'You, Betsy? In trouble? You're my little star.'

'Am I really, Brown Owl?'

'You can call me Vera from now on, when we're not at the church hall. And once I've . . . stopped.' I think she might have a tear in her eye, or it could be the wind which is stirring up.

I don't know what to say. Luckily we've reached home. The front door's on the latch, so I pull her inside, tugging her hand with the ring sticking into me like a thistle, down the passage to the back kitchen, where I know they'll be sat around the wireless, Margie hopefully tucked up in bed.

'We've got a visitor,' I announce. 'It's Brown Owl.'

Mum looks up from her knitting and Dad gets to his feet, folding up his paper and knocking out his pipe.

'Evening, Miss Parsons. Everything all right?'

'Oh yes, Mr Sunshine. Everything's fine. I just wanted to ask a question.'

Mum puts down her needles, 'Edgar, honestly, where are your manners? Do sit down, Vera. Here, by the boiler. It's cold out. Can I get you a cup of tea? Cocoa?'

'No, really, that's very kind, Mrs Sunshine.'

'Alice.'

'Thank you, Alice. I must be making tracks, so I'll get to the point.' She glances from Mum to Dad. 'I'd like Betsy to be a bridesmaid.'

There follows three distinct sharp intakes of breath. Brown Owl furrows her pretty brow, unsure why there's this reaction and hastily adds: 'That's if she'd like to of course, and if you have no objections?'

I think I might explode. Mainly with happiness but also with fear, as we Sunshines are used to hiding behind the clouds. Apart from Margie, ever the show-off. And where is Margie now? Hopefully not crouched on the landing, listening through the bannisters, picking up fag ends. More likely asleep, the lazy so-and-so. Her head only has to touch the pillow and she's off to the Land of Nod. Anyway, awake or asleep, she's not here.

But I am. With Brown Owl. Vera. Soon to be Mrs Bellingham. Soon to be walking down the aisle of St Michael the Archangel with me dressed up like a princess, clasping the hem of her train.

I look from one parent to the other; neither has said anything. Maybe they're in shock. Undertakers are considered a bad omen, the poor relations of the Grim Reaper. Who would want the undertakers' daughter to be their bridesmaid? Especially the less pretty daughter.

'How lovely.' Mum breaks the silence, passes the buck to me. 'What do you think, Betsy? Would you like to be a bridesmaid?'

If it was anyone else in the world, I would probably say no, but because it's you, Brown Owl, I would be honoured. That's what I'd like to say but the cat has got my tongue, so I nod like a nitwit, like my head's going to topple off, and they all laugh at me, but I don't care because I am going to be a bridesmaid!

'Have you set a date?' Dad is concerned with logistics.

'June 30th.'

'Where?'

'St Michael's.'

'Splendid. Well, she has our permission, doesn't she, love?' He turns to Mum.

'Course she does. Thank you for asking, Vera.' Mum's in control again. 'How about a glass of sherry while you tell me about your dress and how many bridesmaids. I'd be thrilled if you'd let me help.' She pats Brown Owl's pretty hand with its sparkling ruby ring. 'Edgar?'

Dad gets busy with the sherry bottle and glasses.

'You're a marvel, Mrs Sunshine.'

'Alice.'

'Alice, I hope you didn't think I'd asked Betsy

14

so as you'd help out with the dresses. But I'd love it and I don't expect you to do it for nothing.'

'If you and your mother sort the fabric, I'll be more than happy to make the dresses. How many bridesmaids?'

'Really, Mrs Sunshine?'

'Alice.'

'Yes, Alice, well there's my sister, Cathleen, she'll be maid of honour. Arthur's three-year-old niece, Tilly. And your Betsy.'

Three of us. I'll be the one in the middle. Not the maid of honour. Not the sweet little one. But I don't care because I am going to be a bridesmaid. And I'm sure Brown Owl asks me because I remind her of the other sister who died of influenza after the Great War. Not because my mum is the best seamstress in south London.

'Cheers!'

They clink glasses. I fetch some milk and join in with the toasting and, all this time, Margie is asleep, unknowing, upstairs.

That night I drift off to sleep dreaming about tulle and satin and organ music and frothy posies of lily-of-the-valley. But, looking across at Margie, half in half out of her bedclothes, her thick chestnut hair over her pillow, a smile on her dreaming face, I have to chase away thoughts that I'll never be the bride.

★ ★ ★

On the eve of the wedding, I try on the dress one last time, twirling round and round in front of Margie in our bedroom, and up and down the

15

landing. Margie is livid, her cheeks cochineal, her fists clenched so tight her knuckles are sharp and spiky. I can't help myself; it's hard to always be the good one. I hang up the dress on the back of the door, stare at it for one more moment, taking in the white satin with delicate pink rosebuds sewn all the way down the front.

'Isn't it lovely?' I say to Marg, not expecting an answer, enjoying my reign of superiority, which is soon over when Mum calls us down to dinner.

Once we're sitting at the table, Marg gobbles up the liver and bacon and then asks to be excused before we've even had afters, but then it is rice pud, which isn't her favourite, so Mum says yes, she can leave the table. Quick as a flash, she's disappeared upstairs. Five minutes later, she's back, wearing a queer expression, a concoction of accomplishment and terror — like a cat that has cornered a mouse three times its size. She sits and watches us finish our pudding.

Then it's Dad's turn to excuse himself. He has a call-out. After we've washed up, dried up, and put away, Mum sends Marg and me upstairs. 'You need your beauty sleep,' she says. 'Busy day tomorrow.'

As I lie in bed, waiting for Mum to tuck us in, my tummy is all tickly, I'm that excited. I gaze at my dress for a moment, only then I hear myself scream.

'WHERE ARE THE ROSEBUDS?'

I leap out of bed and stare at the dress, as if the rosebuds might reappear. But they don't. They've been snipped off. One of them lies deadheaded on the floor. Next to the nail scissors.

16

'*MARGIE!*'

I'm screaming her name louder than I thought possible. She has the decency to cower under her blankets briefly but still manages to dodge Mum when she comes running in, all panicked, what's happened, what's happened. Marg thunders down the stairs and Mum is torn between comforting me, examining the dress, and catching Marg. Justice wins and she stomps down the stairs after my horrid little sister.

Mum finds her in the lav, reading the toilet paper.

I don't know what Mum says, neither of them ever tell me, it goes to their graves. But when they return together, to the bedroom, Margie's all contrite, holding out her hand to me. 'Sorry, Betsy,' she says. 'Don't know why I did it. I'll sew them back on.'

'Oh no you will not, you stupid moo.' I ignore the outstretched hand and look to Mum, but she's no help.

'Let her do it, Betsy. Punishment. She's a good seamstress.'

'She's six.' I feel the tears brewing behind my eyes. They'll overflow and never stop if I let them begin. 'I'll have to do it.'

Mum laughs, the worst thing she could do at that moment. A brief laugh, one of them nervous ones, but even so. It's not funny. We all know I can't sew for toffee. My fingers don't do what they're supposed to and my hands get all sweaty. But I'm not letting Marg anywhere near my dress, not on your nelly. I'll never forgive her for this. Never!

I reach for the nail scissors on our dressing table and in a flash I've grabbed Margie's hair and snipped off a lock. More than a lock. You could call it a tress. A ruddy big tress. In my hand it feels how I imagine a fox's brush to feel, glossy and slinky.

Mum and Marg stare at it, hanging limply, trying to make sense of what's just happened. Then the wail starts, quiet at first, but, within seconds, it is full throttle and eardrum-bursting, like the sound of a Moaning Minnie that we'll come to know all too well in a few years' time. She throws her limbs about like a cat in a fight and goes for my face with her jagged, bitten fingernails and I know the scratch across my cheek won't half look angry by morning. Now we're on the floor, Marg on top of me, slapping my face, my head, and pinning me to the bedroom boards like a dead weight.

Then Dad walks in. Mum is standing in the doorway, not saying a word. She's never seen the two of us in full flow like this, but Dad's sides-of-ham hands soon have us separated. I'm sent to the front room while Marg gets sent to bed. I don't know which is worse. I don't trust her with my things.

Marg has left her knitting by the sofa — I can't help it if it unravels as quick as dominoes falling one against the other, all the way till there's no cardigan left, just piles and piles of tangled yarn, which I burn on the fire, bit by bit, so the front room smells like sheep. A burnt offering. So I shove the rest of it under the sofa, to be disposed of later in the boiler or

18

somewhere it'll never be found.

I'll have the last laugh.

I don't realise that at that very moment Margie's in our bedroom, cutting up the dress with nail scissors so that it's no longer ballerina length but what Mum would call trollop length.

★   ★   ★

'White makes a change from black, but I can't say it does much for your complexion, Betsy.'

It's the next morning and Mum's curling my hair. I check in the looking-glass. Have I come down with a fever? And what about that big red welt across my left cheek?

'Are you feeling all right, love?' Mum does her litmus test, placing the back of her hand against my forehead, closing her eyes, channelling the temperature straight through to her brain. She gave up on thermometers after Margie crunched on one when she had the whooping cough as a nipper. Which might explain a thing or two.

'Christenings, weddings, funerals, Betsy. You mark a life with these occasions. They're official. They get written down in documents.'

I must be staring blankly at her because she goes on.

'They're milestones in life — they mean you counted for something. You won't be forgotten. Long after you're gone, it will be recorded somewhere that you were born, christened, wed, dead and buried.'

These are important words. I know that. They get me thinking.

19

'If you were born at any time, any place, and could go to any funeral, Mum, which one would you choose?'

'Well, now. Let me think.' She continues hacking her way through my tangles with a sparse hairbrush, wrinkling her forehead so she looks like my nana for a moment, but I don't tell her that. I'm not stupid. 'Probably Nelson,' she says. 'Admiral Nelson.'

'Why?'

'He was a hero. He died in Battle.'

'Against the Frogs.'

'Betsy Sunshine!' She slaps my arm with the brush. 'Don't call them that.'

'Ow!' I rub my arm, more from a sense of injustice than pain. 'Sorry.'

'After he was killed on board the HMS Victory, instead of burying him at sea, which was the usual way, they decided to bring him home for a hero's send-off.'

'That would've stunk the ship out. Did they embalm him?'

'Not exactly, no, Betsy. They pickled him in a barrel of brandy.'

'Brandy? That's what you drink when you have a shock. I thought sailors drank rum.'

'Well, I expect it was reserved for the officers. Rum was probably for all the crew. Anyway, I thought you wanted to know about this funeral.'

I nod my head as vigorously as I can with a hairbrush tangled in it.

'He had this massive procession up the Thames, laid out in a coffin made from the timber of a French battleship he'd blown up

20

during the Battle of the Nile. All the way from Greenwich to Whitehall and then onto St Paul's. Imagine that, Betsy. Your final resting place being St Paul's.'

'Beats Camberwell.'

'Nothing wrong with Camberwell, Betsy. Don't you forget that.'

'Sorry, Mum.'

★   ★   ★

It's a boiling hot day. Everyone's huffing and puffing in the sweaty heat. The men do nothing, as usual, except for drink, and the women, perspiring in their finery, run around like the Germans are about to invade, which in hindsight isn't so ridiculous a thought.

My dress isn't too bad, from the waist up. The rosebuds have been sewn back on by the elves, who've also done a repair job on the bottom half. I almost feel like a princess and I wonder if my 'twin' — Princess Elizabeth — feels like this all the time? Joanie Clark curtseys whenever she sees me in the playground. She knows my birthday and she knows how much it riles me, but I don't do anything. Sometimes it's best to do nothing. Sometimes you have no choice.

Right now Margie has a foul expression; she has to wear one of my old summer dresses with a strawberry print and Peter Pan collar and she knows she can't do any more damage, though I wouldn't put it past her to come up with something.

'I look like a baby,' she moans.

21

'You are a baby.'

'Betsy Sunshine, be kind to your sister,' Mum orders. 'This is difficult for her.'

'Difficult? As if I care.'

'You should care, Betsy. You should always care about your sister.'

'She doesn't care about me.'

'Don't answer me back. You're the oldest, therefore it's your duty, and that's the end of it.'

There's not much I can say to that. I'm going to enjoy my moment because I don't know when the next one will pop along.

★   ★   ★

Miss Vera Parsons, spinster of the parish (at 22 years old), marries Arthur Bellingham, bachelor of the parish (at the ripe old age of 25), at St Michael's the Archangel on a hot day in June 1937. The bride's father, Reggie Parsons, the ironmonger on Lordship Lane, walks her up the aisle, his daughter a vision in white with a swathe of pink roses and a froth of foliage. Her maid of honour, her sister Cathleen, is a younger version, also in white tulle with a small posy of roses. Then there's Arthur's niece, Tilly, who's not much more than a toddler. Then me, in my beautiful dress with a net-curtain fringe round the bottom to protect my modesty.

Margie sits in disgrace between Bert and Nana Mabel. But she doesn't leave it there. Just as the bride and groom have exchanged their vows, and we're singing 'I Vow to Thee my Country', Marg starts to sway, from side to side like she's on board a ship, the sea rolling under her, till her legs buckle, and she slumps sideways between Bert and Nana. She has chosen her own glorious moment to faint. And I don't care what anyone says.

I know she is a faker.

★ ★ ★

The photograph, when Vera gives it to me, is only of my face. I've remembered to cover up my front teeth with my top lip. But my eyes sparkle with ice. They tell the story of Marg and me, and whenever I feel myself softening, I make myself stare at that picture and I don't give an inch, because whatever I do in life, Margie will no doubt do her utmost to scupper that too.

Years later, when Margie gets married for the third time, I remind her of this day.

'Why did you do it?' I'm genuinely curious.

'Jealousy, Bets. Pure and simple jealousy.'

'Why on earth were you jealous of me? I never got picked out for stuff like that. It was you that was the pretty one — you still are.'

'But that's exactly it. You've always known your role. What about me? If you're the heir, then that makes me the spare.' And then she starts to wail.

Silly moo.

2016

Bognor Regis

One of the staff, the fat one, brings me a letter. Can't remember her name as it's one of them daft made-up ones. She wants to chat but I want to watch the news. People stop watching the news when they get to my age; they say it's too depressing. But I like to keep myself up to date. I like to know what's happening in the big wide world, because Gawd knows I can't get out and about no more.

There's a war on, only they call it a conflict. As far as I'm concerned war is war and it doesn't matter what name you give it. If you're armed with a gun, or a dagger, or a hand grenade and if you shoot, stab, or let rip, then you're taking part in a war, all because you want what someone else has. As if we learned nothing from Hitler and Mr Churchill.

I shouldn't be thinking of Winnie. I should open the letter, but my heart's knocking because I recognise the handwriting.

'Are you cold, Betsy? You're shaking.'

'Cold? In this place? I don't think so. I'm old, that's all.'

The Fat One looks put out at my tone, which I suppose is a little abrupt, so I relent. She likes to feel needed. Who doesn't?

24

'Can you open it for me, love?'

'Course, Betsy. Do you need me to read it for you?'

Flip sake. 'Just pass my glasses, will you. I'm not ga-ga yet. I can still read a ruddy letter.'

She swishes off and leaves me to it, which is what I want, some ruddy peace and quiet.

⋆　⋆　⋆

Janet says she's in England and she wants to visit me, which is odd because the last time we saw each other, whenever that was, we parted on bad terms. I want to see Janet, but the thought of it makes me feel something peculiar, something I can't pin down.

Mick used to say feelings are feelings. They're not right or wrong. But what if you can't name them, these feelings? Then what do you do?

I'm not ga-ga. I'm old.

I cannot lead you into battle. I do not give you laws or administer justice. But I can do something else. I can give my heart and my devotion to these old islands and to all the peoples of our brotherhood of nations.
Queen Elizabeth II

1939

London

During wartime, there's different rules, that's all I can say.

I am thirteen when Hitler goes on the rampage and invades Poland. We all sit round the wireless in the back kitchen, Mum, Dad, Marg and me, and we listen to Mr Chamberlain announce we are at war with Germany. I don't know what this means except that my dad has tears in his eyes and my dad never cries. All those bodies he's taken care of, all those grieving families he's had to deal with — mothers, wives, husbands, sons — and he holds it together, a ray of sunshine in the dark times. I feel my own eyes glisten, my throat fill with phlegm. Mum leans over and pats Dad's hand like he is an old man, like he's her dad. He is older, by twelve years, but not actually old enough to be her dad. He is old enough to have fought in the Great War though and I realise at this moment, sitting round the wireless on that September day, that Dad has been through it all before and doesn't want to go through it all again.

'Will you have to go to war, Dad?'

'We'll all have to go to war,' Mum says and I picture her in a helmet charging across no man's land wielding a bayonet. 'Let's have a nip of

27

something shall we, Edgar?' She hands Dad his pipe and fusses about in the sideboard for a bottle. Brandy.

'It don't seem right, Alice.' Dad shakes his head. 'It don't seem right when we were told the Great War was the end of it.' He grips the glass that Mum offers him, sinks it down in one, which is not like him as he's not much of a drinker as a rule.

Marg has that weepy look, glistening eyes and sticky-out bottom lip, so Mum offers her lap and Marg slides onto it, the crybaby. Then Dad ups and leaves us there, with the wireless quietened. The ticking of the clock on the wall above the boiler, the one that's always set ten minutes ahead so we're never late, it's louder than it should be.

Tickety-tock. Tickety-tock. Tickety-tock.

Mum sets Marg down so she can refill her glass. My sister bursts into tears.

'That's enough, Margie,' Mum says. 'Blow your nose and get ready for bed. We don't want tears now. There's plenty lying on the road ahead of us. A great puddle of them.'

Margie flees from the room and up the stairs. She isn't used to Mum snapping at her, but I can see Mum's not in the mood for hysterics right at this moment.

'I'll make us some hot milk, Betsy, and you can have a nip of this. Help you sleep.' She holds up the brandy bottle like it's the FA cup and a picture of Admiral Nelson pops into my brain, dead, bloated and pickled.

I don't like to say I've got homework. I've got

an essay to write on bananas in the West Indies. I don't want to pass over the chance of my first nip of brandy. I'm not an idiot. So I drink my milk, sipping it very slowly, not a flinch, the warmth of the alcohol easing the phlegm in my throat so I don't cry. I don't cry one drop of tears because I have to be a big girl for my mum. Because she needs me.

★　★　★

The next morning, Dad is back at his usual place, the kitchen table, sleeves hoicked up with elasticated garters, demolishing his bacon and eggs, scraping the blue and white china that's for every day, not the wedding present tea set, displayed in a cabinet in the front room, gold-rimmed and delicate violets, for best.

'Morning, Betsy. Where's that sister of yours?'

'Says she don't feel well, Dad.'

'Don't talk with your mouth full,' Mum says.

She sighs and leaves the room. We listen to her thud up the stairs. We wait. Then we hear it. Margie crying.

'She can raise the dead with her crying,' Dad says. And he's never one for graveyard humour, won't have it at work. Gives the boys a right rollicking if he overhears them being disrespectful, tells them they can shove off and get a job with Old Vickers down the road if that's how they intend to carry on. None of them want that. Old Vickers might let them mess about but he doesn't look after his men like my old dad looks after his boys.

'Respect in life, respect in death. Never you forget that, Betsy Sunshine.'
'No, Dad. I won't forget.'

★　★　★

'The curse,' says Mum. 'That's what this is all about. She's not even eleven years old.' She's back at the table, cradling her cup of tea, her wedding ring tip-tapping on the china.

'We'll have to watch that one, Alice — '

'Shush.' Mum pulls a face at Dad, one of them secret-message faces, then she's out of her chair, making a start on the dishes, swiping Dad's plate while he's still mopping up the gooey egg with his crusts. 'Disgusting habit,' she mutters under her breath and Dad pats her bum.

I leave the room.

★　★　★

'How comes you've started your monthlies and I haven't?'

'Some of us are more mature than others. Mum says I'm a woman now. I'll be in a brassiere soon, before you with your two fried eggs.'

'Shut up, you cow.'

'Mum! Mum! Betsy called me a cow!'

'Elizabeth Sunshine, get down here and go to school now. And don't forget your gas mask.'

Margie pokes her tongue out, not quite a woman yet. I do my best flounce and leave her with her stomach ache. I hope she's in agony.

30

Mum's waiting for me at the foot of the stairs. She's taken off her pinny and is buttoning up her overcoat, her own gas mask swinging from her shoulder, ready to go to work.

'What about her?'

'Your sister's staying here.'

'Is she always going to get a day off school when she has her monthlies? Will I?'

'No,' Mum says, final like.

I don't know what she means 'no' to. So I pick up my satchel and leave. I don't even say goodbye. Which is something I always take care to do. Dad says you never know when someone will take their last breath so it always pays to say goodbye, then you won't have no regrets.

★   ★   ★

I worry all day at school. What if Dad has a heart attack? What if Mum gets run down by a bus? What if Margie bleeds to death? It might not be her monthlies. She's only ten and three quarters after all. It might be haemowotsit like that Russian prince, only I think that's just for boys, but I can't remember. I do remember learning about those poor children shot dead in the snow in the forest. That was in the last war. Will the Germans come and shoot us? Are they on their way right now?

Margie might be the crybaby but I am the worrier. She already thinks the worst has happened. I am forever waiting for it to dump itself on our doorstep. Actually, it usually creeps in the back entrance of the yard behind the shop.

31

Because of course the worst that can happen is Death. Death means you won't never see that person again. All you've got left of them is memories. And a photograph if you're lucky.

★ ★ ★

On the way home from school I pop into our shop on Lordship Lane.

Behind its discreet net curtains and dried flower arrangements, there's Dad's walnut veneered desk with his baize blotter, his pen, his green lamp. He could work in a bank with his dark pinstripe suit, only he works with bodies, not money.

There's a simple wooden cross on the wall behind. No crucifixes because we don't do the Catholic funerals as they give Mum the heebie-jeebies and she doesn't like Father Daniel.

There's much more out the back, behind the scenes. That's where the coffin workshop is, the garage for the Daimler (Dad's pride and joy), the stables for Othello and Desdemona (Bert's pride and joy), and the building yard, as we're still doing a trade in that as well as funeral directing.

We'll soon be pushed for coffins when the Nazis have their way and drop bombs on us. There'll be lots of rebuilding and all because they are going to destroy our homes. They are going to kill us. They might rape us before or after we are dead. That's what Margie's friend Beryl's sister June told her. I said it wouldn't bother me if it's after as I'd know nothing about it. But Margie started up again. Boo hoo. *I don't want to be raped and murdered.*

'Who's going to be raping and murdering you? Your snotty nose would frighten them off.'

'I've got my monthlies. It means I could have a bun in the oven. I'm too young for that.'

'Henry VII's mother was thirteen when she bore the future king of England.'

'Well, then her mother should have stopped her.'

This is how our arguments go. Back and forth, on and on, like an endless game of spiteful ping-pong.

Today, Dad's here, sitting at his desk, filling in his ledger with lines of copybook handwriting, sloped and looped, official and formal with erratic downstrokes. The nib scratches the paper and makes me think that those letters he's forming are coming to life, like they are ants crawling across the page, leaving their little black footprints of the costs of Death.

'You all right, love? You look peaky.'

'I feel sick, Dad. And my tummy hurts.'

He leaps up from his chair; I've never seen him move so fast. 'Get in the back, Betsy, quick as you can. We don't want a mess on the carpet. I've got old man Drummond expected any minute. Your mother should be out there somewhere.'

I just about make it out the back when I can keep it in no longer. I'm sick in a soapy bucket of water that Stan must've used to wash the Daimler. Stan is my friend from Sunday School. He drives me up the pole, but is loyal as a dog,

33

always at my heels, gazing up at me with his big brown eyes. Stan should've poured the dirty water away, but that's Stan for you. Bits of my breakfast float on the scummy surface and that makes me chuck up again. Then there's this squeezing feeling in my tummy and I think here it comes again, but instead of spewing something else happens. A trickle down my legs. For a second I wonder if I've peed myself, but when I have a look down, there's a bloody stripe running down my calf into my socks.

I've caught Margie up!

I'm not really sure what to do though. There's no sign of Mum, or anyone else for that matter. (It's like a morgue in here!) I search around for some sort of cloth or rag but have to make do with a chamois and sort myself out as best I can before one of the boys gets back. There's no way I'll make it home. I'm feeling faint, need a lie-down.

Mrs Drummond's coffin is almost finished, only the handles to go on. It looks so cosy, resting there, on the trestles, so before I can decide if this is a good idea, I am up the steps and lying myself down in the coffin. It's clean and snug and the smell of sawdust and wax is comforting and familiar. I'll have a quick rest while I get my breath back.

Mum gives me what for later and says it was almost a double funeral. How was I to know old man Drummond would ask to see his dead wife's coffin?

2016

Bognor

I should answer Janet's letter, it's good manners and good manners are important, but my hands hurt too much. Arthritis is ruddy painful and my fingers are gnarled like I'm an old tree woman. When I think of all the work they've done over the years, most of which I don't like to tell people about because most people don't have the guts for it, it's not surprising. But the work was all right. On the whole, it was comforting, knowing you did the last job for someone in the best way possible, with dignity and compassion. But sometimes it was downright grim and there was no getting around it. You had to do your job. It was your duty.

I know I should answer the ruddy letter, but it must've got chucked out with the recycling, so I don't have Janet's address. They recycle everything here, it's like being back in the war, never wasting a scrap. Make do and mend when sometimes you yearn to go to Marks and Sparks and splash out on something brand spanking new.

It's not my fault if I can't find the letter.

Cowards falter, but danger is often overcome by those who nobly dare.
Queen Elizabeth II

1940

London

I am fourteen when I touch my first dead body.

It happens when Mum sends me on an errand to Mrs Dart round the corner to say her dress is done. Mum makes dresses for the living as well as gowns and coffin linings for the dead. She makes me and Margie little dresses for our dolls out of the scraps. My doll, Wednesday, is at the back of the wardrobe somewhere. I was supposed to give her to Maureen Cavanagh who smells of fish and looks like she's only half-done. But I never give Wednesday to Maureen Cavanagh because I know she'll leave her on a wall somewhere. Or drop her down the privy. Me and Margie used to play funerals with our dolls. We'd shroud them in Mum's remnants, put them in a shoebox for a coffin. Perform the last rites. Bury them under our beds.

We share a room. Me on the left by the window. Margie on the right by the door. She won't sleep by the window because she reckons the bogeyman might get in. She doesn't care if the bogeyman gets me, just as long as it means she can escape. So although Margie's all into our funeral game, she gets scared at night, the doll bodies buried under our beds, as if they'll come alive and haunt her. Silly moo.

My first proper dead body is Miss Bowles. On my way back from Mrs Dart's, my errand done, I get stopped by an anxious-looking Stan. He's always anxious, Stan. He has that hunted face on him, like he's in trouble, which he often is, because it seems to follow Stan around like a bad smell, even when he's minding his own business. He doesn't help himself, mind. At Sunday School he was always asking awkward questions. None of the old dears were sure how to answer and it wasn't unknown for Reverend Peters to cuff him round the lughole. (*What is God? How big is God? What does God eat?*)

I reckon Dad must've took pity on Stan when he asked him if he'd wash the hearse, pocket money as his mum's always left short by her bloke who spends his wages on stout down the Crystal Palace Tavern. I don't know why Dad trusts Stan with his pride and joy; he won't let me or Marg anywhere near it. It's hardly used these days anyway, what with petrol on the ration and the lack of tyres. I prefer the horses, Desdemona and Othello, they're warm and fuzzy and smell like a summer's day even in the darkest of winter with the wind blowing and puddles all around.

Today, Stan's been out on an errand himself, dropping something off to Miss Bowles. When I come across him, he's standing there on her doorstep like a window licker, the front door ajar. He's holding a brown paper package and I wonder fleetingly what it is. I can hear the rustling of the paper because Stan's hands — the ones Dad trusts with the Daimler — they're shaking.

'Whatever's the matter, Stan?'

'Come with me, Betsy,' he says. 'Something's wrong.'

I have a bad feeling about this, Stan's more anxious than normal, and I know I'll have to take charge. I'm two weeks older than him, but it's more like two years. Boys are so daft.

'Come on, then. Follow me.' The trick is to sound in control even if you aren't entirely sure that you are.

I push the door open, slowly, slowly, Stan holding onto my jumper. In we creep, like there might be a burglar waiting to bash our brains out, my heart hammering because I know. I know there's no burglar. I know Miss Bowles has been suffering from a 'woman's complaint' that will see the end of her. And there she is when we step inside the front door and into the murky hallway with its brown skirting and pastry-coloured Anaglypta, lying on the stairs as if she is sprinting up them, only she isn't going nowhere. She is flat and still on the threadbare carpet runner, but the position of her arms and legs make it look like she's competing in the race of her life, her face twisted to one side to catch a last breath.

'Blimey, Betsy. Poor old Miss Bowles. She's dead.'

For once, Stan speaks it as it is. Miss Bowles is indeed dead. You can see that whoever Miss Bowles was — spinster, fiance killed in the Boer War, dancer — that person has now gone. This is her body. Her dead body. I go over to her and I reach out my hand, slowly, slowly, to touch her face. The skin is soft and smooth. She's put on her rouge as she always does. Her white hair's in curlers. She looks like she's still alive, but she's dead, so I do what I know I must do: those dazzling baby-blue eyes, the last reminder that she was once young and beautiful, I close them.

Stan is hovering in the hallway.

'Don't worry, Stan. Go and fetch my dad. I'll wait here with Miss Bowles. And shut the door and the curtains in the front room on your way out.'

I'm a natural at this.

Only then one of Miss Bowles' baby blue eyes pops open and I scream. Stan legs it and I almost follow him, but I stop myself and I remember that I am a Sunshine and must remain dignified at all times around the dead.

They say that boys are the brave ones, only I'm not so sure.

★   ★   ★

There aren't any bombs yet. People are calling it the Phoney War. Most of the kiddies who were evacuated straight off have come back. We're all waiting, holding our breaths, listening out, watching every stranger who walks down our street in case they're a spy. But nothing. Life is much the same. Dad is still here, excused from signing up because he's needed on the home front and when those bombs eventually drop out of the London sky, killing people left, right and centre, he'll be needed even more. He's too old anyway and he's done his time in the last war, a scar on his arm that you can catch a glimpse of when he's shaving at the kitchen sink, dressed in his pyjama bottoms and string vest.

We soon get used to what changes there are, the blackout every night and air-raid practices at school, and carrying our stinky gas masks wherever we go. (Not that a gas mask would help you if a bomb dropped on your head.) There are sandbags and soldiers everywhere, tape on the windows, bacon, butter and sugar on the ration. But no bombs. No war deaths down our way, apart from Mr Collins who tripped over one of those sandbags a couple of weeks back, stumbling in the pitch-dark on his way home, two sheets to the wind, from the Crystal Palace Tavern. Pneumonia, boom, gone.

But something momentous has changed. Me. I am older now. I have done my first death. Miss Bowles. Mum says I can come in to work, out the back, see how it's done. Mum lets me give her a hand with the cosmetics. I don't touch the dead — I still can't get over poor Miss Bowles' baby-blue eye. But I enjoy the time I spend with Mum. It's hushed and reverent, like being in church or school assembly, and there's always a slim chance she might let something slip, stuff she'd never say at home where Margie's ears are always flapping.

Today is Saturday and Margie is at home with the measles. I've already had them so I'm allowed to go with Mum while Dad stays at home doing his accounting.

Mrs Clark is laid out. Poor Mrs Clark. And poor Joanie Clark, her daughter, my nemesis. I wouldn't wish losing a mother on anyone, even Joanie. Mrs Clark had a nasty accident. Mum tells me her poor face was in a bad way, so she's been putting it right, using Plaster of Paris. Now it's time to apply the make-up and I'm allowed to observe.

'What's going to happen when we get short of make-up?'

'We'll have to be resourceful.'

'Make do and mend?'

'Exactly.' Mum sighs. 'Mrs Clark deserves to be done up nice and proper.'

'For Mr Clark?'

'Him? No! Not for that wretch of a husband. He's the one what drove her to an early death. That's why she's here now, on this cold slab, with Plaster of Paris on her tired, worn-out face.'

Mr Clark, Joanie's father, is a nasty piece of work. Her mum's a drunk. The kiddies are wild. It's no wonder Joanie's a cow.

'Did he kill her?'

Mum avoids my question, but I can sense that whatever happened it's going to be hushed up and kept behind closed doors. 'Don't let your father hear you say that.'

'What do you mean?'

'We can't get involved. That's for the coroner.'

'The coroner?'

'Sssh, Betsy. Keep your voice down.' There's only Mum, me and Mrs Clark, so I don't know who she thinks is eavesdropping, though we are told to keep things hush-hush as walls have ears. Still, marriage is a mystery to me. 'You've no idea what that Plaster of Paris is covering up,'

42

Mum whispers and a shiver takes hold of me.

'Did you tell the police?'

'They've already got him. Well, the military police at any rate. He'd gone AWOL.' She purses her lips. Then she sighs and adds: 'Poor Joanie.'

'Yes, poor Joanie.' Now that I have such pity for her, she doesn't seem like my enemy no more.

★　★　★

That evening, me and Margie are in the front room with a treat of a fire, doing homework in the quiet so Mum and Dad can listen to the wireless in the back kitchen and keep tabs on Hitler. I keep thinking about poor Mrs Clark. It doesn't matter that she liked the booze, she shouldn't be dead with her head stoved in. I hope he rots in jail or, better still, gets shot or hung, which maybe he will, and good riddance. I don't say this to Mum because somehow I don't think it will go down too well.

I watch Marg, leaning over her exercise book, her neat sums, doing long division. Margie will find a nice bloke, good-looking and a decent job, once this war is over. I'm not so sure I want to get married at all.

Suddenly there's an almighty smash.

'What the ruddy hell was that?' Margie asks.

'Language, Marg,' I manage to say, but she's taken the words right out of my mouth. What the ruddy hell *was* that?

We look at each other, on the same side for once, fearful of whatever it is that's occurring in the back kitchen. No raised voices so we don't know what the crash was all about. An accident? A disgruntled customer? We creep out the front room, down the passage, and that image of poor Miss Bowles flies to mind yet again, running up those stairs with one blue eye open, and I wonder briefly what happened to that brown paper package Stan had for her.

But this is now and here Mum is, standing still like she's playing a game of musical statues, hands clenched, face red, eyes livid. And there is Dad, picking up the pieces of her favourite tureen, a wedding present from Auntie Ida, pea soup all over the scullery floor.

'I'm sorry, love,' he says to Mum, unaware he has an audience. 'These things happen.'

I'm not sure if he's talking about Auntie Ida's soup tureen or something else entirely.

Then he spots us, caught out like when Margie has her hand in the biscuit tin. 'Oh,' he says. 'Girls.' As if he's forgotten we even exist, but not in time to stop Mum saying, 'Elsie Canning? Tell me Edgar, why Elsie Canning?'

⋆　⋆　⋆

Later, when we are in our room, Margie and I, sitting in our beds in our flannelette nighties, trying to get warm under our sheets and blankets, my sister looks more like a little girl than a woman who has started her monthlies. And now I've got mine too, I wish I could be little again, so I didn't have to think about the confusing world that grown-ups belong to. And

44

we wouldn't have to put our doodahs in the boiler so that everyone in the house knows what you're doing and you feel Mum's eyes watching your every move, keeping count, checking up.

It's always a worry having girls, I hear her tell clients and neighbours, anyone who'll listen.

If you ask me, it's always a worry having parents. And what's Mrs Canning got to do with it?

★   ★   ★

From now on, Mum starts watching herself too, more specifically her figure. She eats less and less until her portions are child-sized, which is just as well, what with the rationing and Dad's appetite being what it is. Her slacks hang loose and her cardigans swamp her, like a child dressed up in her mother's clothes. She starts wearing more make-do-and-mend makeup too. Skilfully done of course, so most people wouldn't know. But I can tell.

★   ★   ★

The bombs come one night in September, a year since we listened to Mr Chamberlain on the wireless, and we know we aren't practising any more. This is real. Dad gets busy. Ever so busy. Bodies are parked up in the warehouse like they are queuing at the fishmonger's. The Great War was different. The bodies never came back. They're all over there in Flanders Fields, rows after rows of them young men, lost forever

45

except in the mind's eye of their loved ones. But now the war comes to us, our island, over the Channel in the form of the Luftwaffe.

7th September 1940 they start. On and on until the following May. But by now we have our very own anti-war machine: our new Prime Minister, Mr Churchill.

I love Mr Churchill. He is clever and brave and says what he thinks. He tells us it is going to be hard and we'll have to dig deep. And I want to do it for him and for London and for Great Britain. I have a picture of Mr Churchill, cut out carefully from the *Picture Post*. I keep it in my Children's Bible, on the page of Shadrach, Meshach and Abednego in the fiery furnace. Margie is frightened of that page, so I can't show her and she won't dare pinch my picture. Not that she covets it, having her very own Jimmy Stewart on the wall by her bed. She likes a man in uniform.

★　★　★

We are prepared. We have not been idly waiting. Dad has put his skills to good use and built an Anderson shelter in our back garden. Mum furnishes it out, does her best to make it homely, as she seems to think we'll be spending a lot of time in there, and she's right of course.

It's not too awful. We have bunks with blankets. Hot-water bottles, if there's time to make them. 'Like camping,' Dad says. We've never been camping. We've never been away for holidays as Dad won't leave the business. We've had day trips to Margate. A day is enough. When I'm grown up and married with kiddies, if it comes to that, we're staying in Bognor.

Dad's usually out fire-spotting, so it's nearly always just us girls. Mum knits or mends. I hate knitting and mending. The wool ends up in a damp, tangled mess and I prick myself countless times with the needle. Margie has the knack and can knit and purl with her eyes shut, which is just as well as it's ever so gloomy, only the oil lamp on a small table to see by. I read a bit, but it's a strain on my eyes and I don't want to wear glasses because Marg will never let me hear the end of it.

After a few nights in the shelter, once the novelty wears off, it's squashed and uncomfortable. Margie gets a chesty cough that Mum blames on the damp. Ours is a good shelter because Dad constructed it properly with a pump and everything to keep the water out, but, being underground, it still gets damp. Like being in a cave. Or buried in a coffin six feet under. I tell Marg to pretend we're a family of foxes in a den or a nest of squirrels, because she likes reading Beatrix Potter and *The Wind in the Willows*.

But the noise breaks through the pretence. The droning of planes, the dropping of bombs, the ack-ack of anti-aircraft guns. You know it's safer than being inside, you hope it is, but the bombs sound ever so near.

Mum is always calm and poised, like the Queen, who has stayed put in Buckingham Palace with the King.

'The Germans are after the docks, Margie. Don't fret.'

'That's our guns, Margie. Don't moan.'

Mum has this endless patience with Margie. But I long for my sister to shut up so I can concentrate on my *Picture Post*. So I can daydream. So I can salivate over thoughts of food. So I can sleep.

★   ★   ★

In October 1940, we listen to a special broadcast from the BBC, the four of us sitting round the boiler, waiting for the air-raid sirens to go off.

It's Princess Elizabeth's first wireless broadcast.

Thousands of you in this country have had to leave your homes and be separated from your fathers and mothers. My sister, Margaret Rose, and I feel so much for you, as we know from experience what it means to be away from those we love most of all. To you, living in new surroundings, we send a message of true sympathy; and at the same time we would like to thank the kind people who have welcomed you to their homes in the country.

The princess is fourteen, same as me. How can she be so like her mother? So calm and poised? I wish I could be like my mother, but I get nervous if I have to stand up in class and recite a poem.

But at least I'm more calm and poised than

Marg. She might be a show-off, she might be able to recite a whole canon of poems, but she's a crybaby Bunting.

'Will we get sent away, Mum?' she moans, lower lip wobbling, slime bubbling from a nostril.

'Not on your nelly. I'm never sending you away.' Mum is adamant. She doesn't even confer with Dad and Dad simply shrugs when I look at him. I sort of take a fancy to the idea of living in the country and falling in love with a farm boy, who must be nicer than all the scabby ones down our way. I could learn how to milk a goat and drive a tractor. I could have lots to eat, cheese and butter and eggs and bacon, and never go hungry. But, when all's said and done, I'd rather be here at home with Marg than stuck with her in the middle of nowhere and she'd be so pretty done up as a milkmaid and all the farmhands would ignore me.

'We'll take our chances,' Mum says. 'If a bomb has our name on it then it'll seek us out wherever we are.'

Margie is too stunned to cry. She sits in silence, her shoulders drooping. Mum gets up from the table and cracks on with the dishes. Dad fetches the tea towel from the clothes horse.

'Come on, Margie.' I force a smile at my sister. 'I'll test you on your spellings.'

She follows me into the front room and I stoke the fire. We sit on the couch and she hands me her spelling book and to look at the pair of us you'd think we were as thick as thieves.

'Incendiary,' I say in my best Princess

Elizabeth voice, the first spelling on Marg's list.

Well, this starts her off again and I get the blame for that as if I started the ruddy war myself when I was only trying to help.

★   ★   ★

I was always trying to help, but the only thing I've ever been able to do without a hitch is help with the bodies. You can tell them all your troubles. And they don't talk back at you. And they certainly don't give you a clip round the lughole.

2016

Bognor Regis

From my armchair, I can see the arrivals and departures, the inmates and visitors, through the big double doors, all glass, leading off the residents' lounge to the entrance hall and the porch. The front door's always locked and there's a buzzer so you can't get in or out, all Nazified.

It must have been some posh family home back in Victorian times, a seaside retreat. There would have been maids and butlers, cooks and gardeners, and what would they reckon to these old dears in their ensuites?

I can see when the postman comes. He has to ring the buzzer because there's always packages and parcels and junk. I don't want him to bring me any more letters. It's bad enough having this one that I don't know what to do with.

It didn't go in the recycling after all. It turned up on my bedside cabinet next to the glass of Steradent and my specs, which give me a headache, so I can't be reading it now. And I can't ask the Fat One because I've upset her.

I don't mean to upset people. I've spent my life biting my lip, holding back my emotions. The curse of the undertaker. Me and the Queen have that much in common.

But once you hit ninety, you can't help your-self.

When life seems hard, the courageous do not lie down and accept defeat; instead, they are all the more determined to struggle for a better future.
Queen Elizabeth II

1941

London

Janet is my very best friend. Janet and I walk to school together as we live in the same street. Janet is acceptable to Mum because she isn't common, common being something Mum doesn't approve of when it comes to us girls, even though we don't judge, we never judge. Janet's father used to work as an accountant for Marks and Sparks before joining up in the RAF. Janet's mother is busy with three younger children as well as Janet. Their names all began with a 'J' — John, Jean and Jeffrey. I reckon it's sweet but Mum says it's twee, which is quite something coming from the woman who knits covers for the lavatory seat.

One afternoon, Janet comes out of school crying.

'What's wrong, Janet?' I hand her my hanky from up my sleeve and she wipes at her face, making it go even more red and blotchy.

I don't need to ask; I know what's wrong because I was in the maths class with her. Janet can't do arithmetic. Her mind goes blank and she panics when faced with a blackboard of numbers. They float around and do silly dances, according to Janet. When she tells the teacher this — Major Carter, a veteran of the Great War — he shouts at her, 'YOU SILLY, IMBECILIC

GIRL!' His booming voice batters her, his face turning puce like a fat tomato and I want to rip it off and stamp on it. But we all just sit there, some of us gawping, some of us picking at our desktops, all of us relieved it's not us in trouble.

Then, right when we think it might blow over, he thwacks her about the head with his maths book. Poor Janet is deaf in one ear from when she caught measles as a baby. Major Carter chooses her good ear to clout, either by luck or misfortune, depending on which way you look at it. Now poor Janet can't hear anything and I don't half feel sorry for her, which is something I become accustomed to over the coming years.

'Come round the shelter tonight,' I shout. 'I'll give you a hand with your homework.' I do a little mime and she smiles, so she must understand somehow.

Mum says it's fine for Janet to stay over this once; Dad will be out fire-spotting so there'll be space enough in the shelter if it comes to it, which it most probably will because the bombs have been coming night after night. She tells Janet to ask her mum for permission and Janet skips away, sloughing off her woes as she goes, in that sweet forgiving way she has that makes me love and hate her all at once, but mainly love because there's not a bad bone in her body.

While Janet's gone, I snitch on Major Carter and tell Mum exactly what happened at school and her mouth goes tight and her shoulders stiffen. Later, she gives us tea in the kitchen with Margie. Cabbage and faggots and boiled spuds. It's yummy. And it doesn't pass me by that Janet gets an extra faggot, which she wolfs down.

Then the siren starts up its wail and we trundle down the garden to the shelter, a bright moon so we're conveniently lit up for Jerry. Mum holds the rear, ushering us three girls, armed with a flask of cocoa and biscuits. We settle in and it feels more like camping with Janet here and it's actually quite nice. I help her with her homework and now she is calm, she understands the numbers much better. They stop jigging about and stand to attention so she can multiply and divide them and even make them into fractions.

But the bombing is bad that night. Thud after thud, getting closer and closer. Mum starts a sing-song — the times tables, never one to miss an educational opportunity and because she can see that Margie's gearing up for one of her fits of hysteria. Janet is happy enough, being with me and because she can't hear half of what we can with those ears of hers. But bombs are far more than noise.

As Janet finishes her last equation, there is a bomb so near we can feel it through the earth, so violent it plunges us into a darkness only the underworld can know. The bomb crashes into our heads, expands, takes up all the space, barely leaving enough room for thoughts. Soil and grit cascade and spill, pelting us like hail, and the world trembles all around us so I think we are done for. I can taste dirt in my mouth, and blood, I can taste blood. I can smell burning, smoke, fire, gas, that smell you get on bonfire night. But I can't see a thing. I wonder if we are all dead or if it's just me. Then there's a glimmer of light. Mum has managed to strike a match from the box she always keeps in the pocket of her apron. It illuminates the mess of our shelter for a split second before snuffing out and plunging us back into blackness. But Mum knows where we are now. She shuffles onto the bottom bunk with me and Janet, pulling a mute Margie with her. Either that or I am gone deaf like Janet because Marg is never mute.

And then I wonder with a giddy jump: Where's Dad?

After the longest time, it goes quiet, except for the ringing in my head. When we get the all-clear, Mum tells us calmly to stay put while she goes and investigates. She fumbles for the lamp and gets it going and, I have to say, I've never been so grateful for its beautiful light. Trouble is, now I can see that Mum is covered in filth and dust, but, worse than that, I can see that she is trying hard to be brave for us but she's fiddling with her wedding ring. She clambers up the ladder, tries to open the shelter door, but struggles, bashes and bashes it with her bare hands but it won't budge, it won't open and I have to remember to breathe because I don't want to be entombed in here forever, not with Margie, not without my dad, and so I jump up to help her, scattering soil and muck as I go.

'Pass me that plank of wood, Betsy.'

I hand it over.

'And Dad's motorcycle helmet.'

I hand that over too, wondering what on earth she is doing. She puts on the helmet. 'Stand back, love.'

I stand back, clamber onto the bunk and squash up with a shaking Marg and a shocked Janet, both of them looking like they've been doused in talcum powder for a production of the Mikado. We watch her, my small, petite mum, as she batters away at the door, shrapnel bouncing off the helmet. Just as she seems to flag, she gives it an almighty ram like she's knocked back a tin of Popeye's spinach and the door opens with a whoosh and tumble of earth. Mum is silhouetted for a moment against the bright, welcoming moon, then she's up and out, closing us away, leaving us in the gloom.

While she's gone, we recite our times tables. Ten minutes turn into thirty. We've gone all the way up from 2 x 2 to 12 x 12 and back again. Marg is nodding off and Janet's snoring gently by the time Mum eventually returns, covered in filth and brick dust, her slacks torn up one leg. She says the house is still standing but the doors have blown off and the windows have shattered.

'What about Daddy?' Marg wails and I want to join in, but there's something on Mum's face that tells me to hold it together.

'Don't panic,' she says. 'Daddy's all right.' She squeezes onto the bunk between me and Marg, wraps an arm around each of us. Janet is still out for the count, curled up the other end like a cat in a box.

'I saw Stan,' Mum tells us. 'And he says that Dad is putting out fires.' She pulls us closer to her, so tight I can hardly breathe, but I don't care; the relief is like nothing I've ever felt in my whole life. Only then she goes quiet as if she wants to say something but isn't sure if she should. Mum turns to look at Janet, lets go of me briefly to touch her hand, ever so soft like, and in that gesture I know that something terrible has happened.

'I'm afraid it's bad news, Betsy, Margie.'

'What, Mummy?' Marg has stopped crying. Her eyes are big and dark and I feel like I've swallowed a pebble.

'Janet's shelter took a direct hit. They're gone, all of them. There's only Janet left. And her poor dad stationed overseas.' She starts to cry, silent tears and judders, and I hug her. Even Marg lets up and hugs her from the other side. Mum gives into it for a little while but then takes a deep breath. 'Now, Betsy, be a love and go and fetch your dad. We're going to need his skills.'

By this, she not only means that Dad will be burying Janet's family but that he will be able to break the news to her in a way no one else can. Mum is as much a part of the business as Dad, but he has this knack with the bereaved, he knows the right words and the right way to behave and he somehow smooths the sharpest edges of their grief, enough so they can say a proper goodbye to their loved one.

But this will be the worst. How do you tell a fourteen-year-old that her mother, her little sisters and her baby brother are gone? How do you do this, knowing that her dad is far, far away and that she is completely on her own?

Back in the outside world, this strange other-world, on the street that looks nothing like my street, I'm all out of kilter. I can't hear anything except this screaming in my head and I have to cough to dislodge the grit and dust, but it hurts to try. And the smell, it stinks something horrid, like drains and lavs. And everywhere there's fires, like the picture in my Bible of the fiery furnace, Shadrach, Meshach and Abednego, it's all my fourteen years' worth of November the fifths wrapped up together and doubled, with none of the fun and all of the fear, though we can't have Guy Fawkes during the war — *poke him in the eye, shove him up the chimney pot and there let him die, die, die*. And I try to make sense of this landscape, try to match it to the place where Janet and I used to skip along the pavement to the Infants and Brownies, where we strolled along arm-in-arm only this morning, where Billy Tyler and Margie play marbles in the gutter when Mum is too busy to notice. Where Margie once showed her knickers to the son of the rag-and-bone man and I walloped her one.

The grown-ups are busy rushing round, doing jobs; they don't see me stumble along the road where Othello and Desdemona pull the hearse, dropping their mess where the kids run out to shovel it up for their gardens. There are big gaps where houses once stood. They have simply gone. All that brick and mortar, wood and glass, fabric and metal and ceramics is now in a filthy mountain of mess. Familiar stuff — a chair leg, a shoe, a cricket ball — all jumbled up like a jigsaw puzzle chucked up in the air and dropped from a great height all over the floor so it can't never be put back together.

But I have to find Dad.

I make my way to Janet's house, easier said than done, as I've no idea which direction I'm headed or where I'm putting my feet. The pillar box is still where it should be and so I know this is it, Janet's house, which actually looks all right, almost normal, just the windows blown out and rubble piled up, which will get on Janet's mum's nerves because she's a stickler for tidiness. Only she's dead, isn't she. Dead with her younger three children dead beside her, like baby birds dead in a nest. Dead. But from the front, it looks like maybe Mum made a mistake. Maybe Mrs M is fine and her three Js.

Round the back is a different story. The vegetable patch that replaced the neat lawn where we used to play French cricket with Janet's dad before the war, it's gone. The apple tree that we climb to pick apples for Mrs M's crumbles is blasted and stripped of bark, every single last leaf shed. Smoke, gas, sap sting my eyes so it feels like I've been crying. I am crying. I can't stop crying.

I find Dad there, in the ransacked garden, picking through the rubble with other men, women, uniforms, civvies, working together, bare hands, desperate to find anyone. But it's no good. It's hopeless. Who could survive that?

Dad starts when he sees me, scrambles down off the heap of mess and bricks and timber and chaos and God knows what else and steers me back out onto the street that used to be our street.

'You can't stay here, love,' he says. 'It's dangerous.' Stating the bleeding obvious. Dad's job as a fire-watcher is bad enough, let alone his job as an undertaker, removing bodies from collapsing buildings, dodging flames, falling rafters, poisonous gases. No pay, just rolling up his sleeves and doing his duty, same as everyone else in this country, except for Major Carter who should have stayed in retirement, but then if he had done that, Janet would've had a different teacher today and she most probably wouldn't have stayed in our shelter and she'd be in that pile of rubble with the others.

'This is no place for a girl,' Dad says.

I want to say all sorts to this, but neither my mind nor my mouth can connect my thoughts to any handy words. I manage to say, 'Mum needs you. It's Janet.'

'Janet?'

'She's asleep in our shelter.'

'She is?'

I watch his expression change from one of relief to one of despair as he realises the task ahead of him. We look at each other in the early morning light, dust swirling around us like fog, an orange and red sky above us, rubble beneath our feet. Dad doesn't say it, he doesn't have to, I know he's thinking the exact same thing as me, that maybe it would've been better if Janet had been with her family. But then what about her dad? He has to live for someone. We all have to live for someone.

'I wouldn't want to live without you, Betsy Sunshine,' he says. And he kisses my cheek, knocking my forehead with his air-raid helmet. There'll be a big bruise by morning.

⋆ ⋆ ⋆

Now we have an extra guest. Janet will stay with us for the duration. Mum makes her up a bed on the floor between Margie and me so she won't feel too lonely at night, so she won't be all alone in the world. Though most nights we are in the shelter, squished up on the bunk like sardines. At least Janet becomes proficient at arithmetic, but we no longer play the death-notice game. Papers aren't printing them now anyway as they're bad for morale and morale is what's getting us through the dark days and long nights.

Morale and Mr Churchill.

2016

Bognor

Here at Sunnydale they like to keep us entertained, which is why the telly is as big as a cinema screen. It's always on. Some antiques programme. Stuff we were given as newly-weds going for a fortune. Tat, my nana would've called it.

We have this old girl, older than half the residents here, she comes along on a Wednesday afternoon, right in the middle of *Escape to the Country*, and warbles these songs. Vera Lynn and Gracie Fields. I long for some Perry Como.

This lot don't seem to care much what's on the telly, but they like this old girl with her Vera Lynn's. Takes us back to the war. Always the war, when you didn't know from one day to the next if it was your last day on earth. It made you all too familiar with Death.

We're disconnected from Death now. No one stops for the hearses. No one bows their head. You have to queue up for your slot in the crem. Everyone deserves a good send-off. Every life has some kind of depth, sadness, and moments of extraordinary wonder that should be marked and noted. Don't define an old person by their last few years. They weren't always infirm, incontinent or incapacitated. They've had a whole lifetime before then. They were once a baby, a child, a teen, a sweetheart, a wife, a husband, a driver of ambulances in the war. Life and Death, they're connected.

You have to listen if you're an undertaker. You have to use your ears. That seemingly trivial piece of information a bereaved daughter lets slip in the last moment as she's seeing you out of the door, listen, because it is a story that needs to be told.

We've all of us stories that Vera Lynn could only dream about singing. But I still hanker after Perry Como.

It has been women who have breathed gentleness and care into the hard progress of humankind.
Queen Elizabeth II

1943

London

We have another house guest, swelling our home full to bursting. Nana Mabel moves in when soldiers are billeted in her house two streets down. She keeps an eye on them but doesn't like to stay there at night. She's proper, is Nana. Doesn't like effing and blinding, and soldiers can't help themselves in that department, Dad says, and he should know.

Dad gets on with Nana Mabel, his mother-in-law. His actual mum's no longer with us. She died of diphtheria when he was a nipper and he's lucky to be here. His father passed away when Dad was a newly-wed, so at least he got to see his son married to my mum. And Dad became Mr Sunshine Senior, the sixth generation. And Mum's dad, Bill, never came back from the Front, so that just leaves her mum, Nana Mabel, my favourite person in the world after Mr Churchill, though he doesn't make cakes out of fresh air the way she can, even with rationing, though fresh air's a rare thing in London, especially war-torn London.

Stan helps Nana move her stuff, pushing her suitcase and carpet bag on some trolley that Bert's lent him. She has the box room, no complaining because Nana is the kindest lady you could ever hope to meet. She saw Princess Elizabeth's gran once, waited out on the Mall, waited forever in a big crowd for the Royal carriage to pass by, desperate for a glimpse of the old king and that bat, Queen Mary. Nana was with her husband, Bill, Mum's dad, back before he was killed in the Somme. They had a flag each that they were waving and they were cheering as loud as they could, so proud of their monarchs and the Empire. The carriage drew closer up the Mall. They were so near to it. They could hear the horse hooves clopping like Desdemona and Othello's. They were that close they could almost reach out and touch the rigid garments of the Queen. But the old sourpuss had this look on her face. And my grandmother, my dear nana, she heard her pronounce these words to her husband: 'What a mob.'

Nana Mabel threw her flag on the floor and burst into tears. Granddad Bill had heard it too and he gave her a hug and retrieved the flag from the floor, but it was covered in horse poo, so he chucked it over his shoulder and said, 'Come on Mabel, I'll buy you a cup of tea at Lyon's'.

Nana cries a lot. Mum says that's where Margie gets it from. I reckon that's why my mum doesn't show much emotion. Apart from anger and annoyance. I love my mum, don't get me wrong, but she can't half be a sourpuss herself. But then she has a lot on her plate, including Dad, who can be too much to handle at times, especially where Mrs Canning, the grocer's wife, is involved.

* * *

Rumours aren't good for business, but the war has its uses. People are too busy to take much notice of an undertaker acquiring extra tins of beans. You get what you can in times like these.

To make matters more confusing, my mum gets a bun in the oven. Me and Marg are both scared witless that she will die this time, especially as there is more to it than meets the eye.

We're in bed when we hear the argument. Margie puts her head under the pillow, but I want to know what's going on.

'I'd like to know who got you in this state.'

'Wouldn't you just. What's sauce for the gander.'

'I'm a man, you stupid woman. It's how we're made. We have to have the comfort of a helper.'

'Who do you think helps you every day? Who cuts out and stitches the coffin garments? Who puts the poor souls' faces back together? Who darns your socks, washes your smalls, cooks your tea? I help you in every way except this one, because the doctor told me I might die.'

'What's going on, Betsy?' Margie sounds muffled under the pillow, like she's very far away.

'Nothing for you to worry about, Margie.' I reach across the divide, over a sleeping, partially deaf Janet, and I pat my sister on the back, which is all sweaty and clammy.

It goes quiet for a moment, gives me the chance to think. What has my mother done? Has she really been with another man? And if so, who?

Margie must be having the same thoughts. She pops out from under her pillow. 'Do you think

Mum has done it with Bert?'

'Bert? He's at least seventy. And he pongs. Honestly, Marg, sometimes I wonder if you've got half a brain in that ditsy head of yours.'

'Push off, Betsy.'

'Sorry. I'm in shock, that's all.'

'Me too,' she says. 'Maybe it's Mr Canning? They could have done swapsies.'

She giggles then. And I can't help myself, I giggle too, but not for long because I know that times are going to be ever so tough. There'll be another mouth to feed, though Mum will get extra rations for the bun and milk when it's born. That's if Mum stays alive. That's if Dad doesn't kick her out, which he has every right to do. What was our mother thinking?

Mr Canning?

★   ★   ★

The baby starts to show. Of course, by this time, Mum and Dad are passing it off as their own. Any scandal will rock the business, Mum reckons. The dead will still need burying, Dad says. But anyway they make do and mend their marriage, and when her time approaches, he even shows some tenderness towards her.

'Who knows, love?' he says one day as she's doing the washing-up, he the drying. 'You might have a boy in there.' He rubs her football of a stomach and Mum leans back against him. He stretches his arms around her bump and nuzzles her neck.

'I suppose we've got nothing to lose now,' she

70

says, and leads him by the hand up the stairs.

They think I don't see any of this. They forget I am the daughter of an undertaker. I know how to melt into the background, to take everything in, not to pass judgement. Life is a difficult road to travel and it takes you one way. It's hard to double back on yourself. Sometimes you've got no choice but to go on. That baby's coming out one way or another. Probably soon if Dad jigs her around too much.

★   ★   ★

It starts one night. I hear a scream and a thump as my dad jumps out of bed.

'Betsy, fetch the midwife! The baby's coming!'

Margie starts to cry. Then the air-raid siren kicks in.

'Stay with your mother, girls. I'll fetch the midwife myself.' He appears in our doorway in the early morning light, hoicking up his braces and getting tangled in his cardigan.

Then he's gone, tumbling down the stairs, putting on his shoes and metal hat and grabbing a coat as it's the middle of winter.

Miss Gallop comes with her bag, shouting at the Luftwaffe and telling Herr Hitler to shove his bombs where the sun don't shine. She's delivered a thousand babies, so Mum is in good hands. She asks me to stay and help and sends Margie and Dad to the shelter. Thuds are all around us, but someone is watching over us this night. Out pops my little sister, calm as you like, all five pounds of her with a shock of red hair.

71

Mr Canning is bald, but once upon a time he had red hair. But so did my Granddad Bill who died in the Somme and took my Nana Mabel to tea at Lyon's.

So that's what we call her. Mabel. Only it gets shortened to Mab because we've already got a Mabel in the house, my lovely Nana Mabel who's as pleased as anything to have a mini Mabel to cuddle, with red hair like her long-lost husband.

That's something Princess Elizabeth doesn't have that I do. Two sisters. Lucky thing. Not forgetting poor old Janet.

But still no Sunshine sons, which is fine by me.

★   ★   ★

After baby Mabel's miraculously safe arrival, Mum and Dad get into a different way of being with each other. They are a little kinder. A little more considerate. Dad walks Mabel up and down the landing to lull her to sleep because she has evening colic. She'll settle on his shoulder in a way she won't settle anywhere else. He's as much her dad as he is Margie's or mine. Her new little life somehow helps balance out the death that has been dancing for too long up and down our streets. Mabel is our very own little Winston. And so when she's christened, she is called Mabel Winston Sunshine. The vicar doesn't bat an eyelid. Or the registrar. War has brought them all sorts of surprises. Normal life is on hold. We're all wondering if it will ever come back.

2016

Bognor Regis

I write to her, Janet, at some hotel in London. Used to be a dive, but everything's been poshed up so knowing Janet it'll be a five-star palace now. I keep it short, polite. Can't write much with my hands.

She writes back. Says she'll come down to see me on the train, one day next week. She'll get a cab from the station, stay for a cup of tea and a chinwag.

A chinwag.

I was never a great one for a chinwag. I could talk to Mick about most things. Janet too. There was a time we shared everything. Only then I took something of hers. She wanted me to. She asked me to. But then she changed her mind, but my mind was made up and I saw it through. Call it duty. Call it whatever you like. What's done is done, so I don't know why she wants to see me now.

★   ★   ★

There's a noise this afternoon, something we don't hear too often here at Sunnydale. One of the visitors has brought a baby of all things. It's nice to see a baby, makes a change, but the noise

73

is grating on my nerves. It's a young baby, a few months or so. She's waving her hands about and sucking on a dummy like there's no tomorrow. They used to dip them in brandy or honey. You do that now and you get told off by the busybodies when all you're doing is trying to get through the day and the night.

You do what you can.

Babies.

You can't escape them. Except when you're trying to catch one. Then they can be right little elusive beggars.

Families, friends and communities often find a source of courage rising up from within. Indeed, sadly, it seems that it is tragedy that often draws out the most and the best from the human spirit.
Queen Elizabeth II

1944

London

Our house is full of sisters. Me, Marg, Mab and Janet, who's still with us. She has nowhere else to go. Her daddy is a prisoner of war out in the east and we don't know if or when he will come back.

I don't get blasé about the war as such, just immune to the inevitability. If you are in the wrong place at the wrong time, there's nothing you can do about it. So I stop worrying about what might happen and get on with it. Margaret, however, still dwells on things, continues to be a crybaby, though her outbursts are fewer, more moderated.

Margie has perfected the dewy-eyed look that boys are suckers for. *Let me walk you home, Margie. Hold my arm, Margie. Three bags full, Margie*. At fourteen, she already knows how to pout and preen, with the Yanks all over her.

One yank and they're down, says Joanie Clark, who I don't hate any more, even though she's still common as muck.

But Joanie's got nothing on Margie who, although much younger, has this habit of sticking out her bum one way and her thrupenny bits the other. She's out on the town whenever she gets the chance with the best-looking fellas she can find. She has her pick of them and she only gets away with it because Mum's up to her eyeballs in baby stuff and dead bodies.

As for me, I don't exactly have the pick of them, but I do meet Peter, a Canadian from Kingston, Ontario. Not the best-looking fella, but funny and kind. He calls me beautiful and one afternoon he produces a sprig of violets, which he deftly slips in my buttonhole.

'My dad did a funeral today with these. Gorgeous, aren't they.'

'Like you, Betsy Sunshine.'

These are big claims indeed. I do have an all-right smile if I remember to keep my crossed-over teeth covered with my top lip. Lipstick helps, though I have to share it with Margie, so I hardly get a look-in.

But soon Margie's shenanigans get found out. She's grassed up by Joanie Clark; some people never change. She's given a curfew and a heap of chores. Meanwhile, Peter gets stationed up north before he even gets a chance to kiss me. I've chosen the shyest soldier ever, but at least I finally know what it is to be love-struck.

After I've moped around for a few days, a sulking Marg not helping matters, Dad picks up on my love troubles. He feels sorry for me, I suppose, and that's why he tells me that evening, after supper, me washing up, him drying. Mum's helping Margie do her hair, Janet and Nana are knitting in the front room, and baby Mab is in her crib. Just the two of us and I want to ask whatever possessed him and Mum to go with those awful Cannings, but it's not my place and bygones seem to be bygones, two wrongs made into a right little Mab.

'Betsy, I'm relying on you to come into the business with me.' Dad passes me a sudsy teacup. 'Your sister would be useless. She'd be in tears all the time and there's enough tears around Death as it is. What we need is someone like you who likes the details.'

I do like the details. I like my shoes polished. A bunch of daffs on the dresser. The front step swept and blackened. Margie doesn't have to worry about stuff like that. She only has to put a smile on (with or without lipstick) and she lights up the whole of London like Christmas.

'I've got great plans, Betsy. We have to keep up with the times.'

'There's a war on, Dad.'

'Of course, I know that. But after, things will never be the same.'

'Is that what the Association says?'

'We have discussed it, yes.'

Dad's on the wartime committee. He tells me stuff, takes me into his confidence, ignoring all those orders to keep mum but he knows he can trust me with a secret. He tells me there's a coffin-making factory out in Willesden that's all hush-hush because the government don't want to panic people. They have to keep up morale and knowing there's a factory churning out coffins can only mean there's too many bodies.

And there are too many bodies. Undertakers are pushed, same as everyone else. They have to train up new recruits. Old men come out of retirement. And it's not just the amount of bodies; it's the condition of them. Sometimes they're so bad that Dad can't do much with

78

them. He and Mum have to concentrate on rebuilding the head. Everything else has to be hidden. Which is undertaking all over.

Othello and Desdemona, the horses, are used to pulling the hearse now because petrol and tyres are rationed and they're not building any new hearses. Even embalming is rationed, except for the Yanks, who have to be sent home, back across the Atlantic to Ohio, Alabama and Wisconsin. All those exotic-sounding places that we can't imagine except for what we glean from the pictures, though I do of course know there's more to life than films. You have to dig deeper.

'We'll always keep up the traditions, the top hat and tails and all the rest of it,' Dad says. 'But you mark my words, Betsy. Things will be different.'

'Hopefully you won't have to stop a cortege if you're out during a raid.'

'No, love. That's awful when it happens.'

'And we won't have to carry gas masks.'

'Just the old Vicks, eh, love.'

'Yes, Dad. That old trick.'

A smear of Vicks under your nose when dealing with a decomposing body. And a Victory V in your cakehole.

★   ★   ★

Stan is in Belgium now. He was a telegram boy for a while before he got his call-up papers, rode a motorcycle and delivered those dreaded War Office telegrams. At the sound of his little engine, curtains twitched and you could almost

79

hear the prayers being wafted upstairs.

Please, God, don't let it be him.

Poor Stan's mum is beside herself when she waves him off. I kiss him on the cheek and tell him to come home safe. He smiles at me like I'm Vivien Leigh and for a moment I feel like a film star, even though it's just Stan and poor old Stan's never going to be a Clark Gable. More like his namesake, Stan Laurel. He gives me this brown paper package before he goes and tells me to keep it safe till his return.

Only that's the last I ever see of him. Eight months later, another telegram boy comes along and gives his poor old mum the news that Stan has been killed in action. Her only consolation is that he's mentioned in dispatches for his bravery, saving two men and putting his own life before theirs. Probably not much consolation really. She'd have preferred her Stan back in one piece, no medal other than a service one. But we don't always get what we want.

I go round to Stan's a few days later, taking the brown paper package with me. Stan's mum manages to make us tea, weak, no sugar, chipped cups, no saucers, but she thanks me for coming and I wonder how she's even managing to stand up, though she seems to have shrunk since I last saw her.

It's a humble place. She's got old cinema seats instead of a couch in her front room, so I'm half expecting to hear the Pathé news.

'Stan asked me to keep this safe till his return,' I say, once I've had a sip of tea, though my stomach's churned up and I feel quite sick.

I hand it over. I still have no idea what's in there. Just that it was something he was meant to deliver to Miss Bowles, only she was dead with no family so he hung onto it. I can't even remember where he got it or why I haven't opened it, except that I was custodian.

She picks at the knot of the string.

Inside is a pair of shoes. Ballet shoes. Stan's mum holds the delicate shoes in her washer-woman's hands, turns them over like they are gold. Then she passes them to me.

They are soft as a baby's.

'Pig skin,' she says. 'That's what they use for ballet shoes.'

'Why would Miss Bowles have ballet shoes?'

'She used to be on the stage.'

'I didn't know she was that kind of dancer. I mean, a proper dancer.'

'She was all sorts of things you could never imagine. She was like a mother to me. She'd given me those shoes to clean. She said she wanted one last dance. I think she must've known her time was up.'

That's something Mum says of the old folks. They often know. They're ready. Maybe Miss Bowles was ready. After all, she'd put on her make-up. Maybe she was going upstairs to take out her curlers.

But what about Stan? Did he know?

★   ★   ★

Poor old Janet has a terrible chesty cough. She's left school with her certificates and has a good

81

job at the telephone exchange, but she's not been in the last few days as she's had a fever and a cough that sounds like she's been overdoing the Senior Service. Mum calls out old Doctor Parkin, who is there as quick as his dodgy legs will bring him through the cold, smoggy late afternoon, laden with his bag, his hat, his stethoscope and his gruff bedside manner.

Janet has a bed made up on the sofa in the front room, one of Mum's knitted blankets and a slippery eiderdown pulled up to her chin, and the fire lit. She's like the subject of a Victorian painting with her fair ringlets and face pale as ash. Doctor Parkin looks grimmer than ever as he listens to her chest. Mum hasn't told me to buzz off so I stay, lurking in the background. Once Doctor Parkin has finished his examination, he ushers Mum out of the room. I sit down beside Janet and hold her clammy hand and I can't help but think of the bodies lying in the cold store down the road at work.

'Can I use your telephone, Mrs Sunshine?' I hear him ask and I don't like it. I don't like it one bit.

★ ★ ★

Janet has tuberculosis. She's very poorly. We can't look after her anymore. Two days later, early in the morning, she is bundled into an ambulance and taken away, leaving too much space in our bedroom, though Margie does her best to fill it with her mess. Not that we have much these days: everything is tatty and falling apart. We've made done and mended, but there's only so much you can do without basic materials. I should coco.

Everything seems darker somehow with Janet gone. Inside the house, there's less laughter and kindness and we all miss her sweet smile. As for outside, the blackout continues. You have to feel your way through the streets, trying not to trip or fall in a hole. There are no street names to help you out if you get lost. Old landmarks have been blown away by the bombs. You brush past strangers, and they will brush you wherever they fancy, the dirty wotsits. But most of all you have to feel your way past that old bastard, Death. For Death loves War. They're best pals. Partners in crime.

But in the midst of war and its unspeakable acts, there are moments of friendship and kindness. I'm not talking about the Blitz Spirit, the Piano-tinkling-roll-out-the-barrel Chirpy Cockney Spirit. I'm talking about the sheer bloody-mindedness of the everyday people. A bloody-mindedness that won't let you ignore a neighbour without a house, a child without a family, a pauper without the means to pay for a proper funeral. A bloody-mindedness that won't let TB get one over you. It makes you struggle on through the dirt, dust and smoke. It gets you through the endless waiting. Waiting for the bombs, the telegram boy, the news on the wireless. Waiting for Hitler and his silly, puffed-up Mussolini sidekick. Waiting for the shops to stock the stuff you need, or think you need — stockings, lipsticks, sweets. Waiting and then waiting some more.

The stress we suffer on the home front is not to be underestimated. There are black armbands everywhere you look, a constant reminder of grief, as if we don't have enough of it at work. Though at least Death keeps my family busy, and being busy beats the boredom of waiting.

But the mess. The washbasin in our little downstairs bathroom is cracked, the window frames are splintered and the paint peeling, non-existent in places. When the raids start, the floorboards shudder so you feel you're all at sea. Soot blows out the chimney. We're all tired and cold and grumpy. A horrid last winter — we don't know it will be the last one of war, but we hope. We hope and pray.

We're lucky. Don't ask me how or why, it's just one of those things. While the Luftwaffe are causing havoc all over south London, we're never bombed out of our home or business. And me, I'm lucky too, helping out in the shop, learning a trade so I don't have to worry about making a man his dinner. I start at the bottom, like my dad before me and his dad before that. I run errands. I clean and I polish. I do anything and everything except handle the dead bodies, which I know will come in time, but I don't feel ready yet. Miss Bowles' baby-blue eye keeps popping open.

We're beginning to believe we might be all right, we might live to see the end of this war, when the bombs start up again, only now they're far worse. Doodlebugs, Buzz Bombs, Bob Hopes (bob down and hope for the best), we give them all sorts of names as if by making fun of them, we can keep them at bay. But whatever we call them, they are the same deadly stalker. They don't even need aircrew. The V-1s are a force to be reckoned with, no chance of fighting them off, even with those hopeless barrage balloons bobbing about. We dread them. We dread the noise, but most of all we dread the silence and the holding in of breaths as we pray for it to fall anywhere but on top of us and then feel guilty because we know it's most likely fallen on top of some other poor blighter.

The V-1s all come in the last year. One of the casualties is Brown Owl, Vera, who's not long had a baby. The baby dies too. Her poor husband won't have a home or a family to come back to when he returns from France, if he ever does. This upsets Dad so much that he insists us girls go to his sister, Auntie Ida, out in Herefordshire. But Mum is adamant. 'We're not giving in now,' she says. 'We'll die together if that's what it comes to.' Some might say she's morbid, but I find her words comforting. She makes us feel like warriors, which we are, all of us; even Margie with her weeping and wailing pokes her tongue out at the Luftwaffe and calls them names she's not supposed to know — for my ears only. And I don't even dob her in because I'm actually quite proud of her.

★   ★   ★

We visit Janet in the sanatorium when we can, but it's harder now she's been evacuated to Wokingham. She's still being stalked by her own

85

deadly killer. It's been months, but she's not given in yet. She's weighed every week to see if she's gained or lost. She's over the moon when she's up, distraught when she's down. The place is miserable. There's a stainless-steel sputum mug by her bed and it makes me ill just to look at it. The enormous windows are open all day, all year round, whatever the weather. I hate leaving her there, but then again I'm glad it's not me. And that is what war is like; it makes you feel stuff and then piles on the guilt.

★　★　★

The V-1s stop but there's even worse to come, something you don't even know about till it's all over and done with. No warning. No Moaning Minnie. No silence. The mother of all bombs. Well, let's say 'father' because, after all, it's always the men who go to war, leaving behind wives, mothers, sisters and daughters to pick up the pieces. Bombs are worse than hand-to-hand combat because you can't look your enemy in the eye. Because you can take out those wives, mothers, sisters and daughters and never have to hear their screams. Bombs are for cowards. Look me in the eye if you want to kill me. Don't creep up from behind, Death, you old bastard.

On the first of November 1944, twenty-four poor souls are killed on Etherow Street by a V-2. We're flat out at work, even Nana and Marg help out, while little Mab is taken care of by Stan's mum, which at least is a distraction from her grief. Mab, our golden angel, is also getting tetchy. We're all getting tetchy, but Death has met its match and we will rise to the occasion.

Only it's not easy. Yet again we make do and mend. Due to the shortage of mortuary space, we have to use the public baths. Drained of water, the bodies are lined up in the pool area on tin trays. Dad needs extra Vicks round the nostrils because the stench in there is unbearable. You can smell it from the street and Mum has to peg Dad's suit on the line to air it when he gets home. Death clings something awful.

Mum and I don't do the removals; we're too small of frame to lug dead bodies, for which I am quietly grateful. But Mum has the job of reconstruction, which is sometimes nigh on impossible. Some of the corpses have been unclaimed for days and they're in a terrible condition, decomposing, with flies and maggots. Awful. She gives them what dignity she can muster. Dad gives his time freely to be a mortuary attendant, to remove and store the bodies, helped by his boys, each body labelled with a Bakelite disc and serial number. And they have to be photographed, which isn't so nice, in case people get mixed up.

In case identities get switched.

Everyone does stuff they don't want to do in wartime. Duty, that's what it's called. Only I feel bad for not getting stuck in. I wish Mum and Dad would tell me it's time, but I know they are waiting for me to be ready. Meanwhile, I clean, I polish, I run errands, I pay attention to the details. But it won't be long. I know it won't be long.

Christmas is on its sorry way, a small glow of light in this bleak midwinter, all set to get even more bleak. A few days ago, Glenn Miller's aeroplane went missing over the English Channel, on his way to entertain the Yanks in France. There'll be no more of him and his big band. I'm still numb from Stan's death. This is just another one, but so sad as we love his music. How much longer can this go on?

We visit Janet — me, Mum and Marg. Mum makes us wear our best, which is our school uniform — a Black Watch kilt and a hateful bottle-green jumper that is nearly three quarters darned. And I'm not even at school anymore. There's a Father Christmas who comes to the ward, with a nicotine-stained beard and without the paunch, as not many paunches are left at this stage.

Janet is too old for Father Christmas, but she takes her gift from him nonetheless. A tin of lavender talcum powder which she sniffs deeply and smiles with bliss.

'Beats Izal,' she says. She clutches the talc in her hand as if she's won a medal, which I suppose she has really, for bravery and sheer gutsy bloody-mindedness. She has put on a stone in weight and the doctors are very pleased with her. Mum gives her a pair of knitted striped socks. Marg gives her the most beautiful crocheted shawl, delicate as a spider's web. I can't make stuff so I give her a brooch of a little kitten that used to belong to the grandmother I never met. Dad's mum who died of diphtheria. Janet doesn't own a thing from her past life, there was so little that could be salvaged from her home, so my ancestors are her ancestors, we are connected through war. We're connected through Death's handiwork.

Janet smiles bravely and thanks us and I feel so bad that we are all she's got and that we'll be leaving her behind again in a few minutes because visiting time is nearly up. Janet never moans. She never grumbles. But she can look like the end of the world is lurking round the corner, which sometimes it is. We just never know until we've turned it.

★　★　★

I was right to do what I did. Janet would never have coped. Not with the rotten lungs, deaf ear and feeble constitution. Despite my small frame, I've always been built of far sterner stuff.

2016

Bognor Regis

Young Tom turns up during *Pointless*.

He's a student at Brighton, a train ride away. He's good as gold, likes to sit with his great-grandma. Today he's clutching a bunch of wilting flowers. He means well, but at least they aren't lilies.

'I've got something to tell you, Nana Betsy.'

'What's that then, Tom? You broken that eye-wotsit?'

'No, Nana. The iPad's fine, thank you. It was really nice of you to give me the money for it.'

'Was it enough?'

'Yep, Nana, plenty.'

'And it's what you wanted?'

'Just what I wanted.' He looks at me awkward like, reminds me of his grandma, my Barbara, when she was little. Cut her fringe off once and hid it in the wastepaper basket. Swore blind it wasn't hers when I asked her.

'So if it's not the eye-wotsit, what is it?'

'What's what?'

'Something's going on. Have you got a girl in trouble?'

'In trouble?' He looks confused.

'A bun in the oven.'

'No, Nana.' He looks horrified. 'Nothing's

broken. No one's pregnant.'

'So what then?'

'I'm gay.'

'Oh, well, congratulations. You had me worried for a second.'

'Oh.' He looks deflated.

'Everyone's gay now, even that nice Clare Balding. You can get married, have children and look fabulous. Not like in my day when you'd be called a fairy. Or a faggot. Or a poof. Or a shirt-lifter.'

'Right, Nana. Luckily the world's moved on.'

'This is exactly what Mr Churchill fought for.'

'Gay rights?'

'Freedom. Hitler didn't like the gays.'

'So you're not disappointed.'

'Why would I be disappointed? Don't make a blind bit of difference to me, so long as you're happy. I mean, back in my day they'd have had you locked up and doing hard labour. Just don't go gadding about like that George Michael and you'll be fine.'

He shoves a custard cream in his mouth and slurps his tea, slumped in the chair beside me, like a parrot with his plume of blue hair.

'Have you got someone . . . special?'

'Um, yeah, I think so.'

'You think so?'

'He's called Jerome.'

'Jerome? What sort of a name is Jerome? Is he American?'

'No, Nana. He's not American. He's Jamaican. Well, he's British but his gran came over from Jamaica on the *Windrush*.'

91

'Some of the best funerals, Jamaicans. The men fill in the grave after the burial and they even put the flowers on top. It's very respectful. We've done them all — Buddhist, West Indian, Chapel. Not the RCs though. Is he a Catholic?'

'I think his mum's a Baptist.'

'One of them happy-clappy ones, waving her arms and jumping about?'

'I'm not sure, Nana.'

'I don't know what they reckon to the gays. Are they still bigoted that way?'

'She's fine with it, Nana. I've met her loads. Gone round for tea and everything.'

I've made absolutely sure not to bat an eyelid even though he's batting for the other side. With a West Indian. Who cares, as long as he's happy and not on drugs.

'You're not on drugs, are you?'

'No, Nana.'

'Or in debt?'

'Just the usual. You know, student loans and that.'

'Well, that's good then. Only make sure you use a condom. We did enough of those funerals in the past.'

'Nana, please.'

'If you'd had to tend to those poor young men's corpses you would know. So promise me.'

'I promise.'

'And babies too. Nothing worse than a father carrying his baby's coffin in his arms up the aisle of a church or crem. Nothing worse.'

'No, Nana. Don't worry about me. I'm sensible.'

'Good boy. Now fetch me another biscuit. And get yourself a haircut or does Jerome not mind you looking like a girl?'

What were once only hopes for the future have now come to pass . . .
Queen Elizabeth II

1945

London

When it finally comes, that day we've been waiting for, yearning for, the end of the war, London goes stark raving bonkers. Mum and Dad carry on as normal, as people still keep dying, that's what people do, and the dead won't bury themselves, which is just as well, as they'd be out of a job and so would I, seeing as I work there full-time now.

It's June 1945. Victory in Europe has been declared and Margie has been let out of school early. She falls through the shop door, breathless, bright red with excitement, words tumbling out of her mouth. Thankfully there are no customers or she'd get a scolding off Mum, although maybe today of all days we could be forgiven anything. Margie knows this, which is why she begs, 'Please, Mum, can I go up to Trafalgar Square with everyone, please, Mum, please, to join in the celebrations?'

'What do you mean, 'join in'?' Mum's suspicious as ever.

'To see the crowds,' Margie says.

I sense my chance here too.

'It's an historic day,' I add.

Marg looks at me. She hadn't counted on my support and she doesn't seem all that impressed by it. She obviously wants to go with her friends, but there's no way Mum or Dad will let her go with that rabble. Her only chance is if I offer to be her chaperone and, to be honest, I ruddy well want to go too.

Mum says yes, eventually, after much persuasion and many promises. It's hard to ignore the cheers going on outside, the wireless, the outbreaks of singing. People are coming out of doors to speak to their neighbours, shouting across the street to whoever's passing, anyone who'll listen, and everyone wants to listen.

So, after we've finished work and had supper, me and Marg get the tram up Dog Kennel Hill and onto the Walworth Road. People are everywhere, leaning out of windows, waving flags, jumping up and down like they've got ants in their pants, but it's sheer joy. We're jostled and bustled by all the uniforms you can think of — khaki, grey, blue, women, men, Brits, Yanks, Poles, Indians. It's smoky and airless and there's so much noise, laughing and cheering and screeching and shouting, it's almost as loud as the bombs. And so much kissing, right in front of your eyes, no one's bothered, except me, as I'm not sure where to look. When the bus has got as far as it can go, the crush of people making it impossible to move any further, we jump off, following a group of other youngsters heading for Trafalgar Square.

I've promised Mum I'll stay close to Marg because we both know that Margie won't think to stay close to me, so it's just as well I know how to follow instructions because before you can say Yankee Doodle Dandy, there's one of them, a G.I., tall and muscly and all-over-big so you can tell he's not been on the National Loaf with only one ruddy egg a week. It's just as well, because the Yank, he only goes and grabs Margie, giving her a kiss like he's Rhett Butler and she's Scarlett O'Hara. She's not putting up much of a fight so I yank her arm and pull her along with me. (One yank and they're down.)

'Not here, Margie!'

'Killjoy! I've waited ages for this. Everyone has.'

'That's what I'm worried about.'

That's clearly what Mum's worried about too. All those men. All that pent-up emotion. It's pouring out and I don't know if Marg will be able to stop it. I don't reckon she'll even want to stop it. And Mum'll kill me if Marg gets a bun in the oven. It'll be my fault for not looking after her properly.

'Margie, come here!' I grab her arm a little tighter and she swings round furiously as her soldier gets lost to another woman in the crowd.

'It's the end of the war!'

At least I think that's what she says, but I can't be entirely sure as she's stormed off, quick as you like, without a backwards glance, weaving her way through the crowds. I hurry after, but there's so many people I lose sight of her, which is quite some feat seeing as she's wearing an orange dress that Janet ran up for her using a pair of Nana Mabel's old curtains. Marg can wear anything and look a hundred dollars, as those Yanks would put it. But now I can't find

97

her. I'm searching, searching, here, there and everywhere, but I can barely see beyond the person in front of me, everyone's so tall, all these soldiers and sailors, Americans, Cockneys, Scots, I don't know who to ask and no one takes any notice of me anyway and I don't know which way to go and I don't even know where I am. It's only when I feel the gentle pressure of someone's hand on my arm that I realise I'm crying. Thankfully the hand belongs to a woman. She's asking if I'm all right.

'I've lost my sister.'

'What does she look like? I'll help you find her.'

The young woman has her cap pulled down low over her face. She seems out of place somehow, even though she's kitted up in ATS uniform, maybe the cut-glass accent of hers. But then she's not the only one out of place. Margie, for example, in her orange curtains.

'She's wearing orange curtains.'

'Excuse me?'

'I mean, she has this bright orange dress made out of my nan's curtains.'

'How enterprising. Now, which way do you think she was headed?'

'That way.' I point into the throng. 'Knowing Margie, she'll be in the midst of it.'

'Attention-seeker, is she? I have a younger sister like that. Come on, let's hunt down those orange curtains. I'm dying to see them.' She smiles this dazzling smile and I wonder at the pearly whiteness of her teeth.

We dip in and out of the swarm, pushing and

apologising, my heart thudding because I'm supposed to be in charge and I have no idea where flighty Margie has got to.

'Hang on a tick.' The young woman gets herself up on a plinth, a statue of some soldier or other, smartly hitching up the skirt of her uniform. She's taller now, towering above me so all I can see is her legs and wonder where she got her nylons because we haven't seen a pair of them around our way in an awful long time, not unless you know someone who knows someone, and us Sunshine girls aren't allowed to know people like that, despite Dad's extra cans from the Cannings.

The lady scans the crowds, her cap still pulled low over her eyes so I can't see her face properly.

'Is that your sister, over there?' She points somewhere to her left, so I hoick myself up next to her, squeezing onto the plinth and gripping her arm, catching a whiff of something, I'm not sure what, but it's lovely.

'Yes! That's her!' The relief is so overwhelming I start to laugh like an idiot. Then anger comes. 'Margie!' I scream like a fishwife, but she can't hear me so I jump down, almost squashing an airman, who gives my bum a squeeze. I shove him off but that only makes him more determined and he grabs hold of both my arms with his enormous hands and I know I don't have the strength to fight him off, but my guardian angel comes to the rescue when she slaps him across the face. I think she might be as shocked as I am, I can't really tell, but no time for that, we plough on, in and out, through the crowds, dodging and weaving, pushing and shoving, until eventually there she is, my sister, standing in front of us, with a monkey on her shoulder, like a pirate with a parrot.

'There you are, Betsy! Look, isn't he a dear? He's called Reggie.'

I'm not entirely sure if she is referring to the monkey or the sailor to whom I presume the monkey belongs. The sailor who has his arms around my sister's waist.

'Margie, I couldn't find you. You gave me a fright. I was so worried.'

'Oh don't be silly. I'm fine. I've asked Ken back for tea. This is Ken.' Ken salutes me. 'The monkey's Reggie. Reggie's coming too.' Reggie bares his teeth.

'I'm not sure Mum will be too happy about that.' I take a step back because I don't much like the look of those teeth. 'And, Margie, do thank this lady who helped me find you. I really don't know what I'd have done without her.' I turn round to thank my saviour, but she's already moved away, disappearing into the heady throng. A quick wave and she's gone.

War is like that. You meet someone, your paths cross in a brief encounter, and then you never see them again. Sometimes you wonder what they might be up to now, but most times you forget all about them until something sparks a memory. A whiff of talcum powder or Darjeeling. Poor old Glenn Miller's 'Chattanooga Choo Choo'. The flash of an orange curtain. And then it all comes rushing back, knocking the wind right out of you.

★ ★ ★

After the war, once the soldiers have been demobbed and gone home, if they've still got a home to go to, we move into Nana Mabel's house, two streets away. Mum and Dad rent our place out to Bert. (You're never more than three yards from a rat in London, so they say. More in the war. Well, you're never more than three yards from an undertaker around these parts. We're everywhere, like Death himself.)

Gran's house is much bigger. Us girls get a bedroom each. Mine looks over the back garden, Mab's in the box room next to Mum and Dad, and Marg is in the attic, not afraid of being alone anymore, too busy preening in her looking-glass, dreaming of boys, smoking out the window without Mum catching on.

Only it doesn't last long. No sooner have we moved in when Janet returns from the sanatorium, her chest much better, some weight back on her bones, though she's still frail and we have to take care of her and so she bunks up with me. She has no one else. Her dad isn't back yet. He's out in the east somewhere, a Japanese POW camp, poor bloke. Janet is family.

It's much nicer sharing a room with Janet than with Margie. She doesn't annoy me all that much, and the cough's not her fault. She likes dressmaking, a dab hand at the needle, and Mum has all the patience in the world with her. She says you can't help but want to support Janet. Mum says she can help out in the undertaker's, making gowns, and because Janet's also good with letters and stuff, she's an extra pair of hands in the office when we're hard-pushed. She even helps Bert with the horses even though they make her sneeze. Bert adores her almost as much as he adores his horses. Mum says it's just as well Janet is adaptable and hard-working because she will have to make her own way through life unless she meets a man prepared to take on an invalid for a wife.

The end of the war doesn't bring us everything we were hoping for, not after that initial buzz of happiness. Things are still grim. We're still hungry. More so than ever. While Margie lies in bed of a night swooning over her film stars, I lay awake dreaming of liver and bacon. You never see a fat person. Even Dad has lost his pre-war heaviness. Mum has to wear her wedding ring on a chain round her neck because it keeps slipping off her finger and she daren't lose it.

The war was relentless but it was at least exciting, all those uniforms and the live-for-the-moment mentality. What comes after is dull and dreary and at times downright depressing. Rationing goes on and on. We've won the war but we've lost an empire. We've lost our standing in the world. We are a little country who will have to fight for scraps from now on, that's what Winnie says. I don't know about all that, but I do know that lives have been altered forever. Dead airmen are lost in cold seas. Fathers have never returned. Young lives and old lives have been snuffed out by bombs. Streets have changed.

Houses have gone. Shops are empty. At home, the light bulbs are dim. Fires are meagre. Rugs are frayed. Everywhere you look, things are dirty, damaged, grubby, unpainted.

But we have baby Mabel, our little bright star. Mab is eighteen months old now and as cute as a button, ginger fuzz like a fiery halo. She toddles around, droopy nappy, arms out like a marionette, only no one's working her strings; she has a mind of her own, like Margie. Her first word is 'me' and I know that Marg has a competition on her hands. She might look like an angel, but that's as far as it goes. Only she's just a toddler and you can sort her tantrums out dead easy. You ignore them. She can't bear being ignored and comes running to you for a cuddle. 'Pick you up, pick you up,' she says. 'Oh, all right then, little Miss Droopy Drawers.' And you can't help but pick her up and sniff in her baby smell. Ammonia and Johnson's and a waft of sour milk. The trouble with Margie, when she has a tantrum, the last thing either of us wants is to give each other a cuddle. I'd sooner throw my hairbrush against her thick skull, but I'm the oldest and have to set the example.

★ ★ ★

I've been asked to the dance at the church hall by a medical student called Malcolm. He lives down Therapia Road in one of them massive houses and his dad is friends with my dad, through the Rotary, which Mum doesn't like because they won't have women, which is

103

probably why Dad is so keen. So Mum has to make do with the WI, same as Malcolm's mother, which means there's no escaping this dance invitation.

Janet's gone to stay with a friend for the night, so I have to do my own hair. I don't make too bad a job of it and Janet has done something to an old dress that makes it look quite respectable. But my nerves are somewhat frazzled by the time Malcolm turns up, ten minutes late. Margie is swinging off the bannisters in that way of hers, trying to catch his eye, which, I notice now, is slightly lazy. I hurry him out of there, saying my goodbyes quickly to Mum, and off we go.

The hall is like a woodland scene from a *Midsummer Night's Dream*, all whimsical and folksy. At first glance you'd think someone had gone to a lot of trouble, but actually it's the scenery from a pre-war production of *Babes and the Wood*. Even so, I feel a sense of excitement, like something good will happen but I don't know what.

The band is already in full swing — a four-piece jazz band. One of them, the trumpet player, is a friend of Malcolm's, a fellow medical student, only he's not from the Home Counties. He's from the West Indies. I remember the school book and the homework on bananas I never finished because of the outbreak of war. I can't help but stare at him. He looks magnificent. Like a prince. He catches my eye and smiles and the heat off of my face is enough to light a bonfire. I wish I was brave enough to talk to him, especially as Malcolm isn't what you'd call attentive. Not since Marg has turned up with her friends Vi and Win, not once he's seen Marg in action, dancing a quickstep with Robert Vickers Jnr. Once he's headed off to the gents, and Marg is at the 'bar' having a glass of squash, Malcolm grabs his chance, leaves me for dead, and asks Marg to dance. She says yes, flashing me a look that speaks volumes. If sisterly rivalry were a sport, Marg would be in the Olympic team and on her way to winning gold.

Bob Vickers Jnr is a year older than me, thinks he's the bee's knees, even though we are a better class of family and run a far superior business. Vickers & Sons are rivals, though they've come to the business late — only three generations, compared to our six. They work down the road in Peckham. We are closer to Dulwich. Dad says we are all born of woman and die and return to the ground, ashes to ashes, dust to dust. It might be God that said that first, I'm not too good on my Old Testament, other than Psalm 23. While Stan was asking all those awkward questions in Sunday School, I was more interested in the gravestones and memorials.

Anyway, none of us are better than anyone else, but Mum says Vickers & Sons are brash and ostentatious. 'They'd still do bearded mutes holding trays of ostrich feathers if people could afford them,' she reckons. 'Honouring the dead, not the living, like those ruddy Victorians.'

Mum don't think much of the ruddy Victorians with their mourning and weeping, bombazine black and widow's weeds. All those requiems and ritual. All that grief. The dead are gone and buried (or cremated, except in the war when it's not allowed). Those that are left behind shouldn't dwell on their death, but on the life they lived.

And in this life Marg has just waltzed off with Malcolm, while Bob Vickers, back from the gents, — I hope he's washed his hands — sidles up to me. I try to escape but it's too late, he has me in his grip and whisks me off, holding me a little too close, a little too tight. I feel like a consolation prize because I know his eyes are on Marg, who's busy flirting with Malcolm.

Like I said, the smell of Death clings. It certainly clings to old Bert, follows him around like a storm cloud, but that's because he's not particularly concerned with the ladies or with his old tin bath. You'd think that Bob Vickers Jnr would try a bit harder. There's a definite odour about him, that all too familiar smell I've grown up with. As the number ends, and the band take a break, I duck like a boxer and slither away from him, somehow ending up out the side door, where the trumpet player is having a smoke.

He gives me a smile to die for and my face burns yet again. 'You want one? You look like you could use it.'

'Go on then, ta.' I don't mean to say this because I don't actually smoke, though I know how to do it thanks to Marg's tutorial in a rare moment of sisterly closeness.

He leans forward and lights it for me and he smells a whole lot nicer than Bob Vickers. I try hard to stop my hand from trembling and it's not even that cold, just a bit chilly.

We chat for a while. I tell him I've always wanted to play an instrument, that I really envy him that. He says his life isn't that enviable, but I don't believe it, imagine playing trumpet in an actual jazz band! It's years later before I appreciate what he must've been through, living over here at that time, far from his home in Jamaica.

He's funny. He makes me laugh, but the laughter stops short when he's called back in for the next number. He bows like a gent as he takes his leave and I watch him disappear into the smoky hall, catch a glimpse of Marg with Malcolm in her clutches, and though I don't care one jot about Malcolm, I do care that Marg always gets what she wants. And I really care when I see her pout at the trumpet player even though I don't even know his name. Just his smell and his laughter, that's all I have to go on. But sometimes that's enough.

★　★　★

As I walk myself home, with each step I feel my anger building up so that by the time I reach the front door it has risen to such a crescendo that I slam the door behind me. That ruddy Marg! I hate her!

I stand still in the hallway for a while, try to calm myself, count to ten. All's quiet in the house, but I can hear the band in my head, the toot of the trumpet, Margie's whiny voice. I can see Malcolm's lazy eye fixed on my sister's breasts. I can feel Bob Vickers' greasy palm on the skin of my back and I know exactly where that hand's been rummaging around, because we're in the same business, more's the pity.

If I shut my eyes I can smell the trumpet player, which is a far nicer smell, and I know that he'd be like putty in Marg's hands because she's got that way that I'll never have.

I have to force myself back to the moment, to the peeling wallpaper, the chipped skirting, the ragged runner. Still quiet. Dad must be out on a job, Mab asleep upstairs in the box room, curled up like a plump red squirrel. Where's Mum?

I yank off my heels and throw my coat on the hatstand, go down the passage and put my head round the back kitchen door because there's a light on. There she is, Mum, sitting in her Lloyd Loom by her beloved stove-enamelled boiler, knitting some yellow jacket for Mab who grows out of clothes almost before Mum's cast off her stitches.

'You back then?'

'Yes, Mum. I'm going straight up to bed. I'm tired.'

'Are you sure you closed that door properly? Or is it hanging off its hinges?'

'Sorry, Mum.' I give her a weak smile and reverse out the room. I reckon I've got away with it, no questions asked, but no.

'Where's your sister?'

'She's being walked home.' I do my best to sound casual, like it's no big deal.

'Stop hiding behind that door and come in here.'

I stop hiding behind the door and shuffle in.

'Who's your sister with?'

'Malcolm.'

'The doctor?'

'The medical student.'

'The one you set your cap at?'

'The very same.'

'Oh.' She puts her needles down, bites her lip. 'Come here, love.'

I don't want to go there. I want to go up to bed and cry on my own where no one can see and no one can hear and no one can ask questions and I don't have to think about answers.

Mum puts her knitting aside and stands up. I'm taller than her, even in my stockings. This is what I think when she takes hold of me and gives me a hug, which I don't reckon I've had off of her since the bombs were falling and even then it was usually Margie that got the hugs because it was always Margie that was whining.

'I'll be having words with her, don't you worry.'

'Mum, there's nothing you can say that she'll listen to. Besides, I've gone right off Malcolm. I want to be loved by a man first and last over Margie. And I'll wait till I'm an old woman if I have to.'

Mum sighs. Maybe because she thinks she'll never get rid of me. 'I'll make us some cocoa. You sit here, warm up; you look half-frozen.' She sets the milk to boil and clanks around. I pick up Mab's half-made little jacket and wish I was small enough to wear it, wonder if I'll ever have a baby of my own, not that I particularly want one,

109

not yet, not for a long time.

Dad must smell the cocoa because there goes the front door.

'Keep an eye on that milk,' says Mum, slipping out the room to intercept Dad, no doubt informing him of my disastrous evening, but not putting the blame entirely on Margie. No doubt I share some of the blame for being difficult and awkward when I am only being myself.

★　★　★

We sip our cocoa, the three of us squished around the boiler that heats up the water and warms this back kitchen, and it's quite nice, no Margie. No ruddy Margaret.

'If Malcolm can leave you in the lurch, then Malcolm is most definitely not the man for you.'

'I know, Dad. But Marg can have anyone. Why would she go for Malcolm?'

'Because he's not bad-looking and he's a doctor,' Mum says.

'He's got spots and he's a medical student and I never want to set eyes on him again. Or Marg for that matter.'

'Now, now, love, don't go upsetting yourself,' Dad says. 'You've had a close escape. And if he doesn't bring back that sister of yours soon, he'll have to answer to me.' Dad sighs, reaches for his tobacco and fills his pipe.

'Difficult night, love?' Mum asks, ears pricked up at her husband's sighs.

'A tricky one.'

'Who was it, Dad?'

'Young Gloria Bannister from Pellatt Road. She passed away earlier this evening.'

'Poor Gloria. We was at Infants together. I haven't seen her in ages.'

'She faded away to almost nothing. They couldn't do anything except try to keep the pain at bay, but it was hard on them all. It's almost a relief that she's at peace now. But no one ever gets over the death of their child.'

'No chance of me killing Margie then?'

'Really, Betsy,' Mum chides. 'That's not respectful.'

'They're in bits over there,' Dad goes on, unaware of my distasteful comment. 'I said I'd ask you to come and lay her out, Alice.'

'Now?'

'Would you, love?'

'Course.' The knitting gets put aside again and Mum heaves herself out of the chair. She fetches her coat and scarf and her special bag which contains her tricks of the trade and it's as she's about to go out the back door that I stop her.

'Can I come with you, Mum?'

She turns to me, surprised and maybe a little relieved. 'You sure?'

'I'd like to.'

'Come on, then. Look sharpish.'

★ ★ ★

So Mum takes me round to Gloria's house and I get to lay out my first body. The Bannisters don't have much money. Two-up, two-down, outside lav, no kitchen, no bathroom, a copper to heat

111

up the water. It makes me grateful for our boiler and our downstairs bathroom.

Gloria's dad lets us in. 'The kids are all asleep upstairs. The wife's in here with her.'

Mrs Bannister is in the front room, the best room, sitting in a quiet only the recently bereaved can manage. Shock. Or maybe wondering if they are in a dream, or watching a film. It's a moment anyway before I realise that Gloria is there too, on a made-up bed in front of a pitiful fire.

'I'm so sorry for your loss,' Mum says, cracking the silence.

Mrs Bannister, Agnes, looks up briefly from her trance and then drifts back into it, a better place to be than the desolate Land of Grief. Mr Bannister lurks in the doorway, not sure whether to cross the threshold or not.

Mum takes control. 'Could you put the water on, Mr Bannister? So we can get your Gloria comfortable.' Then Mum asks if Mrs Banister wants to help, but she shakes her head, says she'll leave us for a while to get on with it.

The three of us are left together, me, Mum and Gloria.

'What did she die of, Mum?' I whisper.

'Some sort of cancer.'

'Couldn't they have done nothing to save her? Is it because they, you know, couldn't pay for doctors?'

'We've got the National Health Service now, Betsy, thanks to the Labour government. But some illnesses you can't fix. It was her time.'

If it's your time, it's your time. If that bomb

has your name on it, that bomb will seek you out. If it's Cancer has got his eye on you, you're done for.

And now, when I should be thinking of Gloria, Margie pops into my head, the missile who won't stop till she's got what she wants, if she even knows what that is. If Margie sets her cap at someone, then what can you do?

Sod, ruddy Margie. And sod, ruddy Malcolm, the spotty medical student with the greasy hair and lazy eye. Right now, I've far more issues to deal with. Death. Mortality. Grief. Making Gloria comfortable on her journey to the next world.

As for the ruddy Labour Government, turning over Mr Churchill, well, I could swing for them, but Mum and Dad say they'll put this country back together, only I don't see how anyone can ever do that, the state it's in.

But I mustn't grumble. I've got my health while poor Gloria's dead.

Gloria's dad brings in the water, flannels, towels, and steps back outside to leave us be. We wash her gently, do all the necessary, treat her like she's one of our own, look after her the way we'd want a loved one to be looked after. Talk to her like she's still alive. And I don't know why Miss Bowles' baby-blue eye has put me off for so long because there's nothing to it, it's a body and we've all got one.

'Ask Agnes what she wants Gloria to be dressed in, will you, love?'

So I seek out Mrs Bannister, which doesn't take long as there's nowhere for her to go except the back room. And there she is, with Mr Bannister, sitting at the clothless table as if she's waiting for someone to bring her supper, though I doubt if anyone's done that for her in a very long time. She looks up when I come in, a brief glimpse of hope on her face that I might be her Gloria. But it is me, Betsy Sunshine, harbinger of doom.

'Mum says to ask what you'd like your Gloria to be dressed in?'

She stares at me as if I'm half-mad.

'I mean, does she have a special dress? A Sunday best?'

Mrs Bannister starts to weep, quietly and contained, and I feel like I'm making things ten times worse.

'Do you want me to help you choose?'

'She's not got much to choose from, love,' Mr Bannister chimes in, trying to help me out of this hole I'm digging.

Then Mrs Bannister gets up and disappears upstairs. I stand there like a lemon while she's gone, not sure what to do or say. So I stay put, in the shadows, while Mr Bannister sits at the table, head in his hands, quiet as a ghost. All we can hear is the hiss of the gas lamps.

Silence is fine, Betsy, Mum tells me later. *You'll get better at this.*

Finally we hear faint footsteps. Mrs B has fetched Gloria's summer frock, pale blue with sprigs of delicate yellow daisies.

'Will this do?'

'Of course, Mrs Bannister. Gloria will look beautiful in that.'

Her mother's unsure and I know what she's thinking: Gloria looks like a corpse, not like her lovely daughter. But I'm determined to do my duty.

Mum and I set to work. We dress her gently. We brush her hair carefully. We put on a hint of rouge, keep down her lids, sew up her mouth. Fold her hands, so she looks like an angel. We let the fire die down; we have to keep Gloria cold, which shouldn't be a problem because before long there will be ice on the inside of the windows and the gravediggers will need to hack with picks on the frozen ground.

'Why don't we embalm Gloria, Mum?'

'It's so cold, love. She'll keep and Dad will fit her in as soon as possible. This poor family have been waiting a long time for this. We won't let them wait a moment longer than they have to, despite how pushed we are.'

'Poor Gloria. She was such a lark at school. Used to tear around the boys' playground playing football with them until she got caught out.'

'Maybe she'll get to play football where she's going.'

'Maybe she should have been allowed to play football in this life.'

Mum says nothing to this. I think she's fed up of me nattering. We finish our job and I follow Mum's quiet instructions. Try to copy her calm and poise. I'm proud of her, but I don't know how to tell her.

'So how do you feel about your first body?'

'I've seen one before, Mum. Remember Miss Bowles?'

'How could I forget Miss Bowles? I mean, how do you feel about your first laying out.'

'It's fine.'

'You don't feel squeamish?'

'Why would I feel squeamish?'

'No reason.' She smiles at me and squeezes my arm. 'That's my girl.'

I have to bite down hard on my lip to keep it from trembling, to stop myself from crying.

Keep Baby with Mother.

2016

St Richard's Hospital, Chichester

I've had a ruddy fall. Yesterday morning, I was sitting on a stool in the shower, which I hate because you can't have a proper soak, barely more than a lick and a promise, when I dropped the soap. Instead of pulling the bell cord to get some help, I reached down for it, silly moo, forgetting I'm old and less bendy these days, not the girl who could shimmy up the ropes in the school gymnasium. So it was a surprise, finding myself lying at an awkward angle at the bottom of the shower tray with my head throbbing and my bones all shook up. And I couldn't reach the blooming cord from down there. Eventually little Miss Eva Braun storm-trooped in and scolded me, when all I wanted was a towel and my dignity. Next thing I know, I'm waking up in a hospital bed, which is at least warm and dry and far away from Fraulein Braun.

There's an old dear in the bed next to me. She's about to slip through Death's door, I can tell. It's that time of night, when Death catches you unawares like a thief, which of course he is — a thief stealing your life. I've got superstitious as I've got older, I even scare myself sometimes and I was never the scaredy-cat. That was our Marg, but she left me long ago. She's most

117

probably still rubbing her hands together in glee to have beaten me to the other side.

I could call someone to help the old girl, but what's the point? You can't stop the death rattle. Why try and pull her back from the brink? And for what? When it's our time, it's our time, eh, Mum? Only it's sad to be on your own. I used to have people all around, but they're leaving me one by one, dropping like skittles. It's times like this I think of my Mick.

And I think about Charlie and wonder if I was right.

Tell him. Tell him. Tell him.

There are long periods when life seems a small, dull round, a petty business with no point, and then suddenly we are caught up in some great event which gives us a glimpse of the solid and durable foundations of our existence.
Queen Elizabeth II

1947

London

We get three surprises this year.

On a late afternoon in the spring, a stranger turns up on our doorstep. It's just us girls at home, in the back kitchen, an ordinary Friday. I'm done for the week, in as far as you can be when you're a funeral director on call, so I'm sitting in Mum's Lloyd Loom, reading the *Picture Post*. Nana is dozing by the boiler. Margie, hair in curlers, is filing her nails, getting ready to go out with a fella this evening, poor beggar. Janet is baking a cake. Mab is 'helping' with the mixing, sticking in one of her stumpy fingers when she thinks no one's looking. The wireless is on. Still a while till *Dick Barton*, but anticipation is often as good as the thing itself, if not better.

A loud knock on the door disturbs this unusually peaceful domestic tableau.

'I'll get it, shall I?'

I don't expect Janet to go as she's got her hands covered in lard. And Margie won't show herself like that. So yes, of course, it's down to me. With a weary sigh, I make my way down the passage. There's another knock before I get there.

'All right, all right, I'm coming.' My heart

sinks. Must be a bereaved. Death doesn't care about weekends. But when I open the door it's a man who's familiar but not right.

'Is that Betsy?'

'Um, yes. Sorry, do I know you?'

'You certainly used to, love, but it's been a while.'

They say when an undertaker looks at you, he or she is measuring you up for a coffin. Which is true. Mum and Dad can both guess your height and shoulder width and get it to the nearest quarter of an inch. I'm not so bad myself, only this time I'm not so sure. There's something about the way he stands, something about his voice that rings bells, but it can't be.

'It isn't . . . is it?'

'I've aged, I know. Lost a lot of weight. A lot of hair and all.' He smiles, rubs his bald head, shuffles from one foot to the other. 'My home's not there anymore, Betsy. I wondered if you could tell me where my family is?'

In front of me stands a ghost. And behind me, Janet. She practically pushes me out the way and flings herself into her daddy's arms and weeps and weeps and weeps.

'It's all right, love,' he says, breathless. 'I'm back.'

But I don't think this is the only reason for Janet's tears.

'Where's your mum?' he asks, looking in his daughter's eyes, checking behind me as if she might appear from the shadows, their children in her wake. Those little angels.

★ ★ ★

I'm nearly twenty-one years old and never been kissed, apart from a chaste one off the shy Canadian soldier, unless you count Bert, which I don't, and at any rate he's only ever kissed me on the hand, pretending he's a gent, which I suppose he is in some ways, but not in others. At seventeen, Margie has been kissed lots and lots. Even when she's kissing a boy, she has her eyes open, peering over his shoulder in case there's a better-looking lad she's missing out on. So when I meet Mick that first time on the top deck of the Number 12, I know I shall have to keep him far away from her, for as long as possible. (I haven't forgotten, and I never will forget, the whole Malcolm sorry saga.)

He gets on at Barry Road and sways along the top deck towards me, like a drunk, but it's the driver turning left onto Peckham Rye too sharp. I think he's putting it on though, stumbling over his shoes and falling into the empty seat next to me when there are plenty of others going spare.

The conductor follows hot on his trail, standing tall over us. 'Tickets.' His eyes bore into Mick, who's making a show of emptying his pockets.

'Would you believe it? I've no change on me. Must've fallen out when I picked up that old lady's groceries over there, her weekly shop all over the pavement.'

The clippie and I both check to see where he's pointing and there is indeed an old lady trudging along with a full shopping bag, but who can tell if her groceries were all over the pavement a moment ago.

'Not a soul but me would help. Just like my granny back home, God rest her.'

He's making no inroads with the clippie and I'm squirming in my seat.

'Cough up, or get off.'

'Now, that's not very Christian of you, sir, I'm sure. You'll be making me late for work and I'll lose my job. It's my first day.'

'It'll be your last if you don't pay your fare. Rules is rules, but then you Paddies make 'em up as you go along.'

'I reckon that's uncalled for. Your country needs us over here. We have skills that's required.'

'There ain't nothing you can do that an Englishman can't do better.'

I feel the tension in the Irishman's leg, so close to mine, the hotness coming off it, bouncing up and down like it might drop on the floor and roll under the seat and all the way along the top deck like a bowling pin knocked sideways. I'm not having this so I dig into my handbag and open my purse.

'Keep your money, love,' the conductor says. 'He's no gentlemen.'

'He's more a gentleman than you. Take the money.'

The conductor takes the money, makes a point of handing the ticket to me — which I make a show of giving to Mick — before shaking his head and retreating back downstairs.

Mick turns in his seat, turns right round so

he's staring me full in the face, and he gives me this massive smile. 'You saved my life, miss. Or is it missus?'

'It's miss, not that it's any of your beeswax, and don't go trying it on with me. I helped you out because I don't like the way that horrible man talked down at you. We're all equal. We come into the world with nothing and we leave with nothing and what we have in between is only borrowed us.'

He considers this a moment, most probably didn't expect anything so philosophical at this time of the morning.

'If you give me your address, I'll pay you back as soon as I have it.'

'No need. Consider it a good deed for the day.'

'I think you must be an angel.' His smile is heartening, warm and open like a boy's, like little Stan's used to be.

'I think you must be soft.'

He laughs. 'You sound like my sister, Ita. She says the exact same thing to me.'

'She sounds like she has her head screwed on.'

'She does indeed. Not like the rest of them.'

'The rest of them?'

'The other six sisters. Not a brother to be seen.'

Well, I start to feel sorry for him now. Seven sisters and I only have the two, Marg and Mab. And Janet, I suppose, which makes three, but that's nothing like seven.

'I know there wasn't an old lady,' I say to him, direct, there's no other way in this world.

'There was an old lady. You saw her yourself.'

124

'But did she really drop her shopping?'

'All over the pavement. She had oranges and everything.'

'Oranges? Really?'

'On my mammy's life.'

He has startling green eyes and a look of Perry Como. A scar on his cheek and a slightly wonky nose.

'But is there a job?'

'I'm off to town to see about one. Those Nazis might've created a lot of jobs in the building trade, but once the bosses hear my voice they're not always so keen. I'd put on a cockney accent but it's no good, Donegal always gets through.'

We go quiet a minute, thinking about the war that's only just behind us, that'll always be chasing our tails.

Then he says: 'If you meet me for tea tomorrow I'll pay you back.'

I take another moment, think of Margie's face when I tell her. Maybe I won't tell her. Not yet. 'You can meet me for tea, but there's no need to pay me back. I can pay my way. I have a job.'

'What is it you do?'

'Family business.'

'Which is?'

'Serving the community.'

He waits for me to expand on this, but I say no more. He'll know in good time.

'This is my stop.'

He gets up and moves out to let me pass with a chivalrous wave of his hand and a slight bow of his head so that I get a whiff of Brylcreem. I give him a smile and I feel his eyes on my back all the way down the top deck. And when I'm off the bus, I turn around and he's there beside me on the pavement as the bus pulls away, chugging out fumes, the clippie hanging off the rail, giving us the evil eye.

'What about your job?'

'Don't worry,' he says. 'I'll walk.' He takes my hand. He actually reaches out and touches my hand. If only he knew what I do with those hands. 'I couldn't let you go,' he says. 'We never arranged where to meet.'

So I tell him, a café on Lordship Lane. He says he knows it. Tomorrow. 4.30. He'll be there.

'What's your name? Can you tell me that, miss?'

'My name's Betsy Sunshine.'

'Well, Betsy Sunshine, I'm Mícheál Delaney.' He says it like 'Me haul'. I must look confused because he puts me right.

'Michael,' he says. 'My friends call me Mick.'

'I'll see you tomorrow. Mr Delaney.'

★ ★ ★

Mícheál Delaney is fresh off the boat from Dublin, you can still smell the Liffey off him, an accent so thick you could drown in it, green eyes with lashes I could only dream of having myself. He's on time, early, waiting outside the café in a demob suit, though I'm not sure how an Irishman would get hold of one of them.

Inside, the windows are running with condensation and there's a smog of breath and steam coming off of woollen coats and suits. Our

126

money stretches to a pot of tea and a sticky bun between us.

'Why are you here, Mr Delaney?'

'Mick.'

'Why are you here . . . Mick?'

'I'm having tea with a beautiful girl.'

He smiles, carries on smiling as I cut the bun in half and hand over his share. Despite myself, I can feel the crawl of a blush all over my face.

'As I said, I'm after a job. I thought I had one there, but, as I feared, it turns out they don't like Irishmen.'

'Is there no work in Ireland?'

'I'm not welcome there anymore.'

'Oh?' I wait for him to expand on this but he doesn't. He slurps his tea, cradles his cup in his brawny hand. 'What kind of job are you after?'

'I'm a carpenter by trade.' He swirls the remains of his tea around his cup and I wonder if he is going to read my fortune. 'Like our Lord.'

'A carpenter.' An idea lodges itself in my brain. 'I'll ask my dad. He's after a chippie to help out in the workshop.'

'What trade does the workshop do?'

This is it, I think. This is where he'll show himself to be nothing but a young boy and go right off me in two ticks. Or, he'll show himself to be the man I hope he might be. I'm going to tell him. I'm going to tell him what my family does. I'm going to tell him that as soon as you say the name Sunshine around here, people know what you are talking about. Corpses. Coffins. Cemeteries. Mick doesn't know, he's not been over here long enough to learn the local family names. He's a foreigner, an immigrant.

'So?' He's waiting expectantly, the Irish sea throwing itself against me, the tide pulling me in.

'We're undertakers,' I tell him. 'Only we call ourselves funeral directors now.'

He's quiet. The quiet is big and almost overwhelming.

'Are you saying what I think you're saying? You mean, I'd be making the coffins?'

'Would you have a problem with that?'

'No, no. Not at all. We all need somewhere to rest at the end of the day.'

'Yes, Mick. Yes, we do.'

We sip our tea and tuck into the bun.

'Are you a Roman Catholic?'

'I am.'

'Don't mention that to Dad. Mum don't like the Papists. They give her the heebie-jeebies. And what Mum says usually goes.'

'I won't utter a Hail Mary or show off my rosary. You have my word.' And he reaches across the table, takes my hand in his and kisses it. My hand that takes care of the dead. And I know that he may be a foreigner, an immigrant, but he is a gentleman.

'Are you not afraid of the dead, Betsy?'

'I'm not afraid of anything.' Which isn't entirely true, but he doesn't need to know that.

★ ★ ★

'What did you do in the war?' Dad gets stuck straight in, interrogating Mick in the office out the back. 'Your lot stayed out of it.'

128

This is a question I've been wanting to ask all afternoon but haven't dared because I'm afraid of the answers and how it will make me feel about Mick.

'I was a private in the Royal Artillery.'

'That would explain your demob suit,' Dad says, impressed.

'I'm not welcome back home anymore so I thought I'd try my luck here.'

'Not welcome back home anymore? You in trouble with the law?'

'No, sir, not the law. Not as such. I mean, I haven't done anything criminal, not in my eyes and not, I don't believe, in God's eyes either. It's just that I could be imprisoned for desertion.'

'Desertion? So that means you were in the Irish army?'

Mick nods. 'The Irish Defence Forces,' he says. 'But I couldn't stand by. I couldn't serve a country that wouldn't fight Hitler. So I jumped ship, as it were. My daddy won't speak to me and my mammy has no say in the matter, so here I am.'

'Have you been back?'

'I went home briefly with a mate soon after. To see my mammy. I managed to spend a couple of precious hours with her and my little sisters while Daddy was at work and the older ones at school. But word was out and my mammy told me I'd have to hide somewhere or the Garda would get me. So I hid for a while and made it to Dublin. It was hard to get any work, but I eventually saved enough for my passage. But I was lucky. They arrested my friend right in front of his wife and children, so I heard. He went to prison.'

'Anyone that fought the Nazis is a hero in my eyes,' Dad says. 'A hero.'

Mick has tears in his own eyes. 'I wish my daddy saw it like that.'

(I never meet Daddy, back home in the West, in his damp two-up two-down, widowed and unable to boil an egg or lay a peat fire. But he will have his part to play.)

'Well, Mickey. Your luck's about to turn. You can work with Bert and you can lodge with him and all.'

So Mickey ends up in my old bedroom. The photo of Mr Churchill that used to be in my Bible tucked between the pages of Shadrach, Meshach and Abednego in the fiery furnace, it's still there on the wall where it got promoted to after D-Day. Only Mickey replaces it with a photograph of Our Lady, as he calls her. Don't ask me how I know that. All in good time. He might have done his bit for the war effort, but, whatever he says, however much he protests, cut him and the soft Irish rain trickles out of his veins.

★   ★   ★

My dad's a big man. Frying-pan hands, long legs, broad shoulders, used to bearing the weight of a coffin. Mick's short for a bloke, a couple of inches taller than me. But he's strong. Used to be a prize fighter. A flyweight boxer. Since lodging with Bert and working for Dad, he has put on weight, filled out, become more of a man.

One windy day in March he takes me out for a walk in the park, only it's not much like a park, all churned up with missing railings. Events take an unexpected turn when he drops onto one knee.

'What are you doing, Mick? You'll get mud on your nice new suit.'

'Will you marry me, Elizabeth?'

'You're getting filthy.'

'I don't care. I'm in love and I want us to get married. What do you say?'

'Get up, Mick.'

'Not till you give me an answer.'

'All right, Mick.'

'All right what?'

'All right, I'll marry you.'

'You will?'

'On one condition.' Where there's love, there's always conditions.

'Anything, Betsy. Name it.' He's up on his feet now, holding my hands, staring deep, deep into my eyes.

'Promise me you'll take care of my heart. Don't go playing silly beggars with it.'

'I'll cherish it, Betsy. I'll cherish you.'

And then at the moment he kisses me, there in the wet, soggy, windy park with its gap-toothed railings and dug-over grass, I don't feel the magic I hoped I'd one day feel in the arms of a man. But I do feel safe. So that is good enough for me and I say, yes, Mick, yes.

And that's the second surprise.

131

★ ★ ★

I am twenty-one when I meet Mick. Mum and Dad are giving up hope of either of us girls getting married, but they don't want us ending up with any old husband. But Mick passes the test — not only is he a war hero but he's also a first-rate carpenter. Even so, he still has to ask Dad for permission.

'You'd better ask the wife,' Dad says.

'He's a foreigner,' the wife says.

'He's a Catholic,' the wife says.

'He's got no money,' the wife says.

And this from the family who don't judge other people. Except when they ask to marry one of the daughters.

Finally, when Mum knows I'm old enough to go ahead and marry him anyway, and when she realises they're not exactly queuing up to wed an undertaker's daughter, or even a funeral director's daughter, she relents.

'But remember this, Betsy Sunshine.'

'What, Mum?'

'Husbands are for life.' She sounds like she's a judge handing out a sentence.

★ ★ ★

I always thought Margie would be first to get wed. But, ha ha, it's me, Betsy Sunshine, who beats her to it, though not by far, and that's the third surprise.

Ours is a spring wedding, less Death, more time. Desdemona and Othello will pull an open carriage for me to sit on with Dad. They will wear their shiny leather harnesses and full collars. White ostrich feathers instead of the usual black. Mum makes my dress, sewing on tiny beads and buttons all the way down the back. Janet makes a nightie, sheer and light as a parachute (because it is in fact made out of a parachute).

'Really, Betsy, your bosoms have become quite uncontrollable.' Mum tuts as if I've been growing them on purpose, just to annoy her. 'You need a better brassiere than that. In fact, you need a corset.' I wish I had my fried eggs back, though Mick likes them as they are. I blush when I think of him and hope to goodness Mum doesn't see.

★ ★ ★

The wedding day arrives and Margie is grumpy; she doesn't like it in the shadows. She puts on too much make-up, spends an age curling her hair. She's supposed to be my bridesmaid, my helper, but she leaves all that to Janet.

Janet has become more bold since getting her lungs back. She no longer speaks in a whisper and, when she's of a mind, lets her feelings be known to all and sundry. Especially Margie.

'Make us a cuppa, Marg. Betsy's hair is taking longer than expected.'

I have difficult hair. It's very thick and unyielding. I want to look like Lauren Bacall, but Gracie Fields is the best Janet can come up with. And that's at a push.

Margie flounces out the room in her petticoat,

133

fag in hand, hair in rollers. We listen to her thunder down the stairs and the mouthful she gets off Mum for parading around half-naked like a hussy.

'Put your dressing gown on.'

'I don't have a dressing gown.'

'Then put my dressing gown on.'

We don't hear Marg after that because Janet has shut the door and it's just her and me, sitting on the bed in our girdles and slips.

'Thank goodness it's summer,' I say. 'Or Mum would have us both in those liberty bodices she used to make us wear.'

'I loved my liberty bodice. I felt like a bunny rabbit when I had it on.' She looks wistful. 'Your mum's been good to me.'

'It's not all been one way, you know, Janet. You've brought nothing but goodness to our family.'

She smiles that Janet smile of hers, the one that tugs at your heart and makes you want to tear her hair out all at the same time. 'I got you a present, Betsy,' she says. 'For being my sister when my other family got taken. I'll never forget you.'

'You sound like you're going away.'

'I'll never leave you, Betsy. Even when we're both married, we'll still be sisters.'

'You'd better get your Christopher to hurry up and propose then. Or maybe you should ask him.'

'You are funny, Betsy. I can't ask him. Anyway, he's not the one.' She blushes the colour of a prawn.

'Janet, what aren't you telling me?'

134

'There's this man at work.'

Janet works at the town hall now, typing, shorthand, filing. It would drive me to death by boredom but she loves the petty intrigues of office life.

'Who is it? Have you fallen for someone else?'

'I have, Betsy. He's lovely. Only there's one rather big problem.'

'Oh?'

'He's married.'

'Married? Janet, no.'

'But he says he loves me.'

'*Says*, Janet. *Says*. Words don't mean nothing in this life. It's actions that count.'

At this point, she shuts up and slips her hand under the pillow. She pulls out a small box with a ribbon tied around it.

'Open it,' she says.

So I open it. Inside the box is a delicate gold bracelet.

'Something new,' she says.

'Oh, Janet. That's so kind. It's beautiful.'

'It's only Woolworths'.'

In slumps the bridesmaid of doom, teacups rattling on a tray, sporting Mum's candlewick dressing gown. 'We're out of sugar so you'll have to make do and bloody mend. And I've got a flaming ladder in my stocking.'

'I'll get my nail polish,' Janet says, giving me a wink.

And that's the end of the talk about married men. For now. We have to get a move on so that I can have my very own married man before the day is out.

135

It is hot in a menacing, thundery way. Purply-grey plump clouds hover overhead, like those blasted doodlebugs, waiting to shed their load. I'm not one for omens so I don't hold much store when the lightning beams like a searchlight across the front room's carpet and the thunder booms a few seconds later.

Margie screams. Dad shouts at her and Mum huffs about while Janet tries to keep my hair under control, grips clenched between her teeth.

'Get that red lipstick off, Margie,' Janet says. 'You need peach to match the roses.'

Another flash of lightning comes along, brightening up the room so we're all lit up in our finery and I feel like a princess, for a moment. Then another boom. Then the rain, piddling it down hard. Make of that what you will.

Ten minutes later, in a fuss of brollies and raincoats and perfume, they've all gone, Mum, Marg, Janet and little Mab who looks like a cherub with hair as red as a sunset, plump squirrel cheeks, a posy of peach rosebuds that she's been carrying round the house all morning. There's only me and Dad left, in front of the fireplace. I avoid the mirror, don't want to surprise myself with awkward tears.

'Can you hook me up, Dad? I think the top one's undone.'

He fiddles with the tiny hook with the sausage fingers of his frying-pan hands. 'I remember when you was a newborn,' he says. 'Three pounds and a bit. Your mother was that tired, but she knew you'd make it. She knew in her bones and she kept telling me over and over that night that you'd be all right. And you were. You are. My lovely Betsy ray of sunshine.'

'Thanks, Dad.'

'I've tried to make you feel special. Your mum, well, she's always favoured Margie. That one's such a lost soul that your mother can't help it. It doesn't mean she loves you any less. She loves you both the same. Me too. But you, Betsy, you know where to go, what to look out for. You have your head and your heart in the right place. I'm not sure we can safely say that about Margie.'

We share a wry smile, and then he goes on in what I hope won't be as long as a eulogy because my nerves won't hold out and I need to spend a penny before we go.

'You slept like a dream, curled up small as a kitten in the dressing table drawer. Margie was always kicking off her bedclothes and balling up her fists. A mini Sugar Ray Robinson.

'I'm proud of you, girl.' He reaches into his trouser pocket and pulls out a crisp white handkerchief, boiled, starched and mono-grammed by Mum. He blows his nose and I know I should be touched that he's moved to tears, but it's all I can do not to think of poor Mum's hard work undone in a nose-blow. Is this what married life has in store?

'Don't go leaving your old dad,' he says.

'We're going to Broadstairs. We're back Tuesday.'

'I mean don't go leaving me here.' He pats his heart, beating away inside that burly chest of his.

'Oh, Dad. Stop getting all soppy on me. You'll start me off and Janet will kill me if I ruin my face.'

'You have a beautiful face and that Mick had better look after it. And the rest of you.'

I don't reckon much to the image of body parts but he means well and it's not often he gets sentimental.

'Don't worry, Dad, I'll make sure he does.'

'I'm sure you will.'

★ ★ ★

Desdemona and Othello walk gently, as if they're little ponies. Bert is smart and clean in his funeral gear, top-notch and top drawer, tip-top, clip, clop. Neighbours line the streets and I think this is my moment. This is as good as it will get. My time in the sunshine, even though Dad's having to hold a brolly over me, the rain bouncing off it.

As we pull up outside St Michael the Archangel, Dad smiles and says, 'Makes a change to go to a wedding.'

'It does, doesn't it.'

And the two of us laugh, but soon it gets serious. Bert helps me out, wipes the horse muck off my new shoe with a dubious-looking cloth, sneaks a peck on my cheek and presses a five-pound note into my hand that I have to hide away in my bouquet of roses and greenery.

'This is it, then, love.'

'Yes, Dad.'

'If you don't want to go through with it, say

the word and I'll whisk you away to St Tropez.'
   'That's in France.'
   'I know.'
   'You hate the Frogs.'
   'I know that too. But I love you and I'll do anything to keep you happy.'
   'Mick makes me happy.'
   'Really?'
   'Really.'
   'All right then, Betsy Sunshine.'
   Father Taylor, or the pie and liquor as Bert refers to him, is waiting, hovering on the steps in his robes, and Dad gives him the nod. The bridesmaids appear and get into position, the Wedding March cranks up and we're off.

★　★　★

We go straight to bed, Mickey and me, on our wedding night, which is spent at home, Mum and Dad's house, twin beds pushed together in the back bedroom. Not a lot happens, mainly because Mab gets in with us as she's had one of her nightmares. Mickey says we'd better get used to this — he and his band of siblings (seven sisters!) were always lined up in his mammy's bed because it was the warmest place to be.
   'There'll be plenty of time for romance, Betsy,' he whispers into my ear.
   'I'll hold you to that.'
   'Plenty of time for holding. We've got the rest of our lives.' Which is just about the most romantic thing Mickey ever says to me, and the most terrifying.

That's a ruddy long time. That's what I think, but I don't say it. A ruddy long time. Unless Death has other ideas: a dislodged roof tile, a bad piece of chicken, a fish bone, a bus. You have to try hard to keep these thoughts of mortality at bay when you're an undertaker. You have to try hard to be thankful for every moment.

And this is all the excuse for doing what I did. Like in the Blitz. You take what you can. You take these moments of happiness as you never know how many more there will be.

* * *

I shouldn't have used that excuse; the war was over. And this wasn't going to be a 'moment'. This was going to be a lifetime and beyond. But I did what I thought was best, hand on my heart, for all of us.

* * *

There's another reason the wedding night wasn't quite so special. Forget Mab and the twin beds pushed together and my dad snoring down the landing. Mick and I had already got things underway — though with greater care than Janet and her married man. The silly moo.

Mick was my first, and I his, the blind leading the blind down a dark, unexplored path. We had a few test runs up in my old bedroom. Bert, deaf as the dead thanks to the big guns in the Great War, always had the wireless on far too loudly to hear our footsteps creep up the stairs or the

140

bedsprings being sprung.

The first time was under the premise that Mick would give me back my picture of Winston Churchill. It was a flimsy premise. We both knew that was not the reason for me to go upstairs with him, unchaperoned. That was the sort of thing you'd expect of Margie.

I stood there in my old bedroom, which was tidier that I'd ever seen it. Margie was a slut and Janet not much better, so I'd given up trying to keep it nice in there. But Mick, having been in the army, kept it all shipshape or whatever the army equivalent is. Everything in its place. Not that he had much. But he had me.

I must have been smiling or doing something different with my face, because he looked at me and said, 'You're a beauty, Betsy Sunshine.' And because we were already engaged by this point, I didn't push him away when he kissed me deeper than he had kissed me before. I didn't push him away when he pulled me onto the bed, my old bed by the window, his bed now, his bed that smelt of Brylcreem and Wright's coal tar and Mick, and I didn't push him away when he slipped his hand up my dress and pinged my suspender. I didn't push him away at all. I pulled and pulled him into me until I thought I might gobble him up whole, like one of those man-killing spiders. It was only afterwards that I worried he might've put a baby in me. Only I needn't have worried. Not really. That would come later.

★　★　★

The honeymoon's not much to write home about, but I do send a few postcards: one to Mum and Dad, one to Janet and one to Mab. I relent and send one to Margie as well or else I'll never hear the end of it. I send her one of the donkeys on the beach, a statement in my mind. Not that she'd have a clue, subtlety never her thing.

But something historic does happen. The Princess gets engaged. She will be married in November. I have beaten her up the aisle! She is to marry Philip, after a journey littered with obstacles, mainly contrived on the part of her mother (mothers are all the same!). They might both be great-greatgrandchildren of Queen Victoria, but Philip is foreign. The Queen, his mother-in-law to be, calls him 'the Hun', which is a bit rich considering the Royal family have only recently changed their name to be less German. I suppose it doesn't make sense to marry someone more German just when we've spent six long years fighting them, but Philip is now British, C of E, can play cricket, and wear a kilt, so, after years of frustration, they can finally tie the knot.

★   ★   ★

When the wedding — my wedding, our wedding — is all done and dusted, you'd think Mum and Dad would be pleased to have no more expense for a while. But they have an eye to the future. A glint of hope that the clouds of austerity will clear to reveal a blue sky of growth and enterprise.

They build a chapel of rest. People are dying in hospitals these days, rather than in their own homes, so it makes sense to remove them from the mortuary, straight to our premises, where we look after them till the funeral.

Nana Mabel has these savings which she hands over to Mum and Dad, who've always watched the pennies, so they've enough to buy a second Daimler.

'What about Desdemona and Othello?'

'They can be put out to pasture,' Mum says. 'They've done us proud, but times are changing.'

I start bawling when I hear this. I don't know why, but I get quite hysterical. So hysterical that Mum shouts at me: 'They're only horses, Betsy.'

I bawl some more. Then Margie joins in. And so too of course does Mab. Even Janet gets weepy.

'For crying out loud, you soppy girls. We'll find a nice farm somewhere. I'm sure Bert's sister-in-law will take them on. We're not turning them into glue.'

The thought of horse glue sets us off on a whole new trail of hysteria.

★   ★   ★

It's a sad day when our faithful horses leave the yard. Bert has the task of taking them down to his sister-in-law's farm in Kent. He has tears in his eyes as he leads them into the horsebox. He wipes his nose on his shirtsleeve then takes a letter from his trouser pocket, hands it to Dad.

'I reckon it's time for me to be put out to

143

pasture and all,' he says.

Bert's as old as Methuselah, it should come as no surprise that he wants to retire, but even so, it hits us all hard. I wonder if Dad is regretting his decision to go all modern. But Bert's mind can't be changed, which works out for me and Mick, because with Bert gone, we get to start our married life back in the old house. I have to leave Mum, Dad, Nana, Margie, Janet and Mab behind. But I've got my Mick. Mum says we'll have to scrub the house from top to bottom to remove all trace of Bert's odour. 'Start your married life as you mean to go on. With clean sheets.' Which is good advice if you ask me.

★ ★ ★

It's a tricky time to put on a royal wedding; the country's still on its knees, for goodness' sake. We've suffered hardship for so long we can't remember what it's like not to worry. Rationing's worse than ever. There's a housing crisis. Strikes. Power cuts. Should our taxes be spent on a fancy show? The Government weighs up the options and decides, yes, it's a good idea. 'A flash of colour on the hard road we have to travel,' Mr Churchill says, so if it's good enough for Winnie, it's good enough for us Sunshines. Even Mick, who you'd think would be a republican, says fair play to them. They went through the war too.

We're told the Princess has saved clothing coupons. We're told the Australian Girl Guides have sent ingredients for her wedding cake. We're told she has made sacrifices. But it's not every bride that has Norman Hartnell design her dress. Or has silk made in Britain and white satin shoes. Not every bride gets to be wed in Westminster Abbey. Their sacrifices are very different to ours. Philip might've given up his nationality and his religion but he has a much more cushy life now, after being penniless and living off of his Uncle Dickie. My Mick gave up his religion too because there was no way I was marrying a Roman Catholic. (Not that Mick was all that bothered. He hadn't been to confession since before the war and it's the same God anyway, he said, as if he'd met God down the Crystal Palace Tavern.)

Still, whatever the sacrifices, whatever the doubts, on November 20th 1947 — a cold, grey morning, so she doesn't get everything — we tune into the wireless to listen to Princess Elizabeth Alexandra Mary marry Philip Mountbatten. Her tall handsome husband is now his Royal Highness the Duke of Edinburgh (which is a darn sight better than Philip Schleswig-Holstein-Sonderburg-Glücksburg).

Whatever the differences, we are both of us wives of immigrants. Both of us married to men who have fought the Nazis and who are unwanted by their country of birth.

The Princess won't give up her name, so they double it up with his, eventually, for their descendants. Mountbatten-Windsor. I won't give up mine neither. I couldn't live without the Sunshine.

2016

Chichester

I miss my Mick. Every day. Every night. I know I was lucky to have him. A good marriage. A kind man. But I never expected him to go when he did. I still wake up sometimes and expect him to be there, lying next to me, snoring like a penny whistle.

I liked married life. I felt grown-up and I could have sex without feeling guilty. No need to worry about getting a bun in the oven. And I know I was lucky because Mick and I worked together, for the family, the Sunshines. And my mum and dad loved him. As did Mab. And Margie behaved around him, knew her limits, which was a first.

And now here I am on my ownsome.

I don't want to take my last breath in this place. When I was a girl, people died at home and there they stayed till the funeral, laid out in the front room, usually by the women, often the midwife, sometimes the midwife who'd brought them into the world. Hatched and dispatched by the very same person. Only then the NHS, God love her, meant people popped their clogs in hospital. Straight from there to the funeral parlour. You didn't even have to see the body if you didn't want to.

Janet knows a thing or two about hospitals and now she's here to visit me, after all this time.

'I've got cancer,' Janet tells me, two minutes after she's said hello and sat down in the chair next to my bed, so I'm wondering if I misheard.

'You what?'

'I said I've got cancer.'

'Cancer?'

'Yes, cancer.'

'Oh, well, I'm sorry to hear that, Janet. Is it, you know, serious?'

'Only got a few months to live, so the oncologist says.'

'A few months? But you look all right to me.' And she does look all right to me. Powdered face, set hair, lippy. Nice Jaeger suit and leather court shoes. A bit thin, but then she's always been thin, even with Charlie. We were all thin during the war and for a long time after. Never felt hunger like it. If the Government wants to reduce obesity, then they want to bring back rationing. They want to ban all them burgers and fries and deep-fried everything. Bloody Yanks. Oversized and bringing it over here.

'This is a good day, Betsy. I don't know how many more of these I've got, that's why I had to come and see you.'

We never know how many days we've got, good or otherwise, and I should be grateful that Janet's come to see me when she could be ticking off her bucket list, hiking Kilimanjaro or swimming with those poor imprisoned dolphins.

Why is she here?

I want her to go.

147

My head hurts and I've got a pain in my chest.

She adjusts herself. Her suit's not quite as smart up close. It's shiny round the edges, a patch of foundation or something on her shoulder. She's let herself go since losing Tony. But she can't be short of a few bob, widow of an ambassador.

She's staring at me. I'm supposed to be saying something.

'What cancer?'

'Pardon?'

'What cancer have you got, Janet?'

'A bad one.'

'But where?'

'Does it matter where?'

'Don't suppose it does. And it's bad?'

'The worst.'

First Margie and her stroke, and now Janet. When I go, there'll only be little Mab left. Little Mab who's also a great-grandmother to thirteen. Who's beaten the lot of us.

I look at Janet sitting there, the tables turned, her visiting me in hospital.

'Are you measuring me up, Betsy?'

'What? No! How could you say that? I'm pleased to see you, that's all.'

Five foot four. Sixteen inches across the shoulders.

'I brought you something.'

'Did you?'

She delves into her Margaret Thatcher handbag, rummages around, produces a packet of Victory Vs which makes me want to cry and it's been so long since I last cried, like I've used up my quota of tears, but I must have a reservoir deep within me. I can smell Dad. His pipe, his Vicks. And I even get a waft of Mum's Izal. And the sawdust out the back, on Mick's skin, in his hair. What I would give for one last whiff of him, even when he was drunk and angry with me, which wasn't very often, just one last breath of my Mick.

And the nappies. I can smell them too. See them soaking in a bucket of Milton, flapping on the line on a windy day. And my heart hurts, like a stone's got stuck in my chest, and I find it hard to breathe. Have to count to ten.

'Shall I call the nurse?'

'Me? I'm all right. I've only got a fractured hip and a black eye. You're the one that's got cancer of the bum.'

'Well, that's charming.'

And I know what it is, that feeling. I can name it. It's called guilt. Pure and simple. Guilt.

'We need to talk,' she says.

'It's nice having a chinwag after all this time, but I'm pooped now. And my hip hurts. And you look like you need a lie-down.'

'Not a chinwag, Betsy. A proper talk. About Charlie. There's things need sorting.'

'Like I said, Janet. It's lovely seeing you but I'm that tired now. I need a nap. Can it wait?'

'I've not got long. I've got terminal cancer remember.'

I shut my eyes, turn my face away. I'm exhausted all of a sudden. Hopefully she'll get the message.

These wretched babies don't come until they are ready.
Queen Elizabeth II

1949

London

Mick and I have been married for two and a half years when Janet pays me a visit at work one day in the autumn. This is unusual because she works in Camberwell, a bus ride away. I'm busy with the books, Dad's with a newly-bereaved, and Mum's on a call-out, but as soon as I set eyes on Janet, I know something is amiss. She's twisting her golden locks around her finger in that way of hers she's had ever since I met her the first day in Infants. I picked Janet for my friend from the outset. She was poised and gentle and held my hand at break when I was still crying — probably why Joanie Clark had it in for me, because I got in there first when she'd already had her eye on her. *Thick as thieves, you two*, Janet's mum would say, God rest her soul.

'Fancy a walk, Janet? You look like you could do with some fresh air.'

Of course, Janet can always do with fresh air, what with her lungs and all, but there's not much fresh air to be found on the London streets, but it's better than being stuck in the office with the smog of Death.

We head down Lordship Lane towards Goose Green, past the haberdasher's, the greengrocer's, the ironmonger's, the East Dulwich Tavern, the

151

Odeon, the buses chucking out fumes, the clang of trams and shouts of shop boys.

We find a bench, sit down side by side. There aren't many people about. A headscarved woman pushing a pram with a screaming baby. An old lady shuffling along with a string bag. One of those sad, wretched men in a demob suit shiny with wear, at a loss without a gun or grenade in his hand, his friends gone, drowned at sea, shot down by planes, starved in POW camps.

Leaves swirl around our feet, both of us shod in those clodhopper shoes that make you feel like you're back at school. How I long for a pair of heels like Margie's, but it's not appropriate for someone of my profession to be tottering around. Marg can totter as much as she likes now she's branched off in a different direction altogether with her very own uniform. An air hostess, I ask you.

Janet shivers. Someone's tiptoed over her grave, though her grave's hopefully still a long way off from being dug. She's a cat with nine lives, dodging the bombs and outwitting the disease that tried to snuff out her life. Whatever's going on now, I'm sure she'll be able to deal with it.

'Are you ill, Janet? You look worn out.'

'Thanks.' She attempts a half-baked smile.

I can't respond to it; my face won't move the right way. 'What is it, Janet?' My heart's thumping like a big bass drum but I don't have a clue why.

'I'm late,' she says.

I check my watch. 'It's only ten to. You've got five minutes yet before you have to dash off.'

'No, Betsy.' She gently puts her hand into mine. It's so small and cold.

'Where are your gloves, you silly moo?'

'I left them at home.' Her hand squeezes mine with an electric pulse. 'I'm so scatty right now.'

I don't like to say what I'm thinking: *You've always been scatty, Janet. Have you forgotten those maths classes with Major Carter, the ones that actually saved your life because you ended up in our shelter that night?*

'I'm Late,' she says again, but slower this time, with emphasis. Late with a capital L.

'Late? What for?' But as these words slip from me, I know I am a ninny. That Janet has been a great big ninny. These are the words I always half expected to fall out of Margie's lipsticked pouty mouth. These are words I've been longing to tell my Mick. But Janet? The wind is swiped right out of my own set of perfectly good lungs like I've been whacked in the chest by a hockey stick. 'Your married man?'

She nods, slightly put out at the suggestion she might have another man on the go in addition to the adulterer.

'Does he know?'

'He said he'd leave her. But he hasn't.' She sighs. A sigh as deep as the ocean. 'He's not going to, is he?'

I consider this, keep hold of her slim hand in mine, with its ringless finger. Listen to the cough of the ex-soldier, smoking on the next bench along. The squawking baby that still won't settle,

153

that's making the hair on my arms stand to attention. I have to be honest. 'It's unlikely.'

Janet starts to cry.

'Hush, now, Janet.' I grab the hanky from up my sleeve and ease it into her scrunched-up hand. 'Let's think.'

I shut my eyes, try to gather my thoughts, but I can't get hold of them, they slip through my fingers like ashes. Instead, what I get is a series of images, like the flickering of shadows cast by a gas lamp or when the projector light flashes on and off at the pictures.

'Betsy?'

'Sorry, Janet. How late?'

'Quite a bit.'

'How much?'

She eases up her sobbing, focuses on my question, furrowing her brows, gives me some dates. I do my sums, adding them up, these dates, knowing that this is going to be a tougher test than even the TB. Harder than the iron lung and those floor-to-ceiling windows open all day long. I shiver just to remember, Janet lying there in that awful prison cell of a bed and wonder what kind of bed she has made for herself now, caught out on the wrong side of the blankets. But there's an answer. There must be an answer.

'Have you told your dad?'

'Course I haven't told my dad. It'll break his heart and that's not exactly in the best of strength. I'm all he's got apart from that new woman, who's a cow. I can't do that to him. What would my mum think?'

'All right, don't get your knickers in a twist.

154

We'll sort this out. Let me think.'

'There's something else, Betsy.'

'What is it, Janet? You're scaring me. Is it your lungs?'

'No, not my lungs. I seem to be as healthy as ever. It's just that, well, I've been thinking. I've done nothing else since I found out.'

'Go on.'

'I can't keep the baby. I wish I could but I can't.'

'What are you saying, Janet? You don't mean . . . ?'

'No, not that. I couldn't do that. No, I mean I want someone to take it, adopt it.'

'Oh.'

'Betsy, I want you and Mick to have the baby.'

A baby.

The images flicker again. Knitted booties, fuzzy hair, milky breath. A baby. Janet doesn't know this pain of mine that's been burrowing away inside me for months now, growing like a tumour. She doesn't know that Mickey and I have been trying for a baby for nearly two years but nothing has happened, my visitor turning up uninvited, regular as a full moon every thirty days, each time a stake jammed a little further into my heart. And now here is Janet. With a baby on the way. No ring on her finger. No home of her own. No money to speak of.

A baby.

'Betsy?'

Mab turned out all right. Dad loves her. We all love her, even though she can be a right little pain in the backside. But Mum is her mother,

155

her flesh-and-blood mother. Doesn't that make a difference?

Keep Baby with Mother.

'Janet. I'm not sure about that. I mean, it's a lot to ask Mick to take on another man's baby. Especially after what happened with the Cannings. It'll start all the rumours up again. And well, Mick and I, we've been trying ourselves for a family. It won't be long before I'm expecting myself.'

'Please, Betsy. I can't see any other way out of this.' The tears spill and dribble all down her anaemic cheeks. 'I can't give the baby to any old Tom, Dick or Harry. How will I know they'll give him a nice home? A good life?'

'I don't know.'

'I trust you and Mick. You'd do your very best to bring the baby up as your own.'

'Let me think. I need to think.'

She clutches my hand, briefly, strongly, like a secret handshake. Then she's on her clodhopper feet. 'There's my bus,' she says. 'Shall I see you later?'

I nod. What else can I do?

I stay on the bench, watch her walk to the stop and get on her bus. It feels like I'm floating in a dream, but I know this is real life because my guts are telling me so, the familiar cramps tugging me down. I wave her off, watching the bus for the longest time even after it's disappeared into the smog.

★   ★   ★

156

Eventually I get up off that bench. My bum is frozen, my feet heavy as rocks. I go home for a bit. I should be in the office but I need some time and space to think. I feel a weird mixture of stuff I never expected to feel. Shock and longing. Fear and excitement. And then my stomach cramps up even more, a sharp press across my pelvis, and I know that it's here again. The curse that keeps on giving. And it's almost like an omen. A bloody sign. Like this gives me permission. I'm helping Janet. I'm helping me and Mick. I make up my mind there and then, in the lav, hooking up my sanitary belt.

★　★　★

I find Mick in the workshop, polishing Mr Cartwright's coffin. It's just me and him. I sit him down with a cup of tea, there amongst the sawdust and beeswax, and I tell him what Janet has just told me. I tell him that I think we should do it. To help Janet. To help us. It'll be best all round. His face never gives away much but his arms do. He pulls me to him and sighs and I know that whatever he thinks he'll support me because he's a good man, the best man, and this baby will have the greatest father a baby could have.

★　★　★

Later that evening, I go round to Mum's to see Janet. I'm expecting Mum to be out at her WI meeting, but she's there, in the kitchen, fiddling,

157

so I can't get Janet on her own.

'What are you doing here, love?'

'I want a word with Janet.'

'You two go in the front room. There's a nice fire and I'll bring us all some cocoa.'

Janet and I wait in the front room, side by side on the couch, as if we're waiting for an interview. Mum clatters in with a tray of cups and hands them out. We sit quietly, the crackle of the fire, Mum and me sipping. Janet leaves her cup untouched. She loves her cocoa and Mum doesn't miss a treat.

'You're having a baby,' Mum says.

Janet and I look at each other. There's panic in her eyes, but I nod to her, squeeze her hand.

'Please don't chuck me out, Alice,' she whispers, a sob caught in her throat.

There's a moment, like the intake of a breath, when anything could happen, but then my mum comes good.

'Don't be ridiculous,' she says. 'I took you in when you had no one. I'm not going to chuck you out because of this.'

'Thank you, Alice. Thank you so much. You've been so good to me.'

'You're one of my daughters, Janet. You always will be. I'm not saying this is going to be easy. Unless your man intends to marry you . . . '

'No, Mum, it's out of the question. He won't be marrying Janet.'

'I see. I take it he's already married then?'

Janet nods feebly, shame reddening her face.

'Well, that's his lookout. We'll wipe him out of the equation.'

Equations aren't the best image for Janet, her head confused enough as it is, but we can straighten this out, me and Mum.

'What about Edgar? What about . . . ' Janet looks at the photo of Mab on the mantelpiece.

'I don't know what you mean, Janet.'

'No, well, sorry.'

'Dad doesn't need to know, does he, Mum?'

'I reckon he does.'

And so I tell Mum what Janet asked me earlier and I watch the thoughts ticking over in her brain, working things out, details, plans, what she was brought up to.

'Have you spoken to Mick?'

'I've run the idea past him. He didn't say much, but then that's Mick, a man of few words.' I hold Janet's hand while I say this, the first she's heard of it. For a moment I think she's going to pull her hand away, but it stays there, inside mine. 'I'm not so sure about Dad, mind.'

'No, Betsy. You're right. There's no need to tell your father.' Mum glances briefly at the photo of Mab and I remember Auntie Ida's soup tureen crashing on the scullery floor, the arguments that are so rare in this house, unless one of the Cannings is involved.

Janet sinks back into the couch and her eyelids droop. She looks tired. Worn out. She wouldn't cope with a baby, on her own, all the gossip and hoo-ha. But it's not the sort of thing you can decide in a flash. We agree to mull it over for a few days. We can't take much longer because Janet will be showing soon, Mum says, and so the clock starts ticking.

Over the next few days, I go about my work, doing my duty, but all the time imagining what it would be like to hold a baby in my arms, one that's not my sister, but one that belongs to my sister that's not my sister. Will it feel like mine? Could I love it like mine? Could Mick?

The idea becomes more real.

On the third day, after a long stint at work, Mick and I lie in bed, ready for sleep, but neither of us can quite find it. I know his breathing and I know he is thinking and then he says it, something that's been niggling me but something I've dismissed because it won't happen. I can't see him in the dark, but I know he's looking at me.

'How can we be sure Janet will want to give up the baby? She's lost her family once before. Will she be able to lose her baby too, you know, once she's held it in her arms?'

'She won't exactly be losing the baby. She'll be its auntie.'

'But seeing you with her baby every day . . . ?'

'Plenty of other families do it. Even this family.'

'Little Mab.'

'Exactly. No one's ever who you think they are.'

'What if she changes her mind? How would you cope with that?'

'We'll cross that bridge if need be, but I can't see it happening. She's so relieved not to be going up a back alley or into a mother and baby home.'

160

'They have terrible ones back home. The nuns are like Nazis.'

'Mick! You can't say that about nuns, can you?'

'Oh, believe me,' he says. 'They are. And I can.'

'Well, then, I suppose we're decided.'

'Yes, Betsy. I suppose you are.'

★　★　★

It's all arranged. Mum and I come up with a detailed plan. Janet's so scatty these days, she's not so good with the details, which is my speciality. Janet will go to the farm in Dartford, where Bert lives with his widowed sister-in-law. She'll go there as soon as it can be arranged. The story is — 'the cover' as those detective films would say — the story is her lungs are playing havoc again and she needs some country air, though it's more the tiny pair of lungs curled up inside of her that's the problem.

We don't tell Dad. Nor Marg, because you can't trust her with a secret and she's off with her new life anyway. There's no point involving Janet's dad because life's enough of a struggle for him, even with his new woman. But I've prepared the ground with Bert. He'll do anything for me, but he'll do even more for Janet with that big soft spot he has for her, the daughter he never had. And his sister-in-law, Polly, she's a good sort and lonely since her husband's gone.

A few weeks later, Mum and I wave Janet off

161

at the railway station. She looks so young and forlorn, waving out the window of the train, like an evacuee. As the train pulls away, I want to run alongside it and jump on board but I can't. I have a job to do.

★ ★ ★

He's not as nice-looking as I expected. His hair is a smidge too long, a trifle too greasy, a bit too sparse. His eyes are a startling blue, but they clash with his sallow skin and yellow-brown fingertips, fingertips that are thrumming on his tidy, polished desk, that don't reach out to shake my hand or make me welcome. His suit has a lick of the spiv about it. I've never fully trusted a man in a pinstripe suit since that day.

Janet is a pretty thing, all tame blonde curls and trim curves. His wife is an old bat. She works in the chemist and gossips about the customers and their complaints. Not professional at all. And she's friends with Joanie Clark, so it's not surprising he seeks comfort from a lovely girl like Janet.

'Mr Trigg?'

'Who's asking?'

'Mrs Delaney.' I don't know why I use Mick's name as I don't normally. I suppose I must be hiding behind it, hiding behind my Mick, who doesn't even know I'm here. He's got enough to think about without this.

'The Sunshine girl.' He smiles and shows off a mouthful of crooked, crowded teeth in all their nicotined, gingivitis glory, indicates for me to sit

162

down in the chair, pointing with his foul fingers that have crawled over poor Janet.

'Not so much a girl now. I'm married.'

'Congratulations.'

'Maybe I should be saying that to you.'

'Excuse me?'

'Congratulations on deflowering an innocent young woman. And fathering a child out of wedlock. And cheating on your old boot of a wife.'

The room is so quiet I can hear the shifting of the mechanism in his carriage clock sitting on the desk between us. I can hear the ping of a typewriter in a room beyond. I can't believe I said that, but I did and it's done. A speech Sir Winston would be proud of.

He stares at me, taken aback. 'You leave my wife out of this,' he says slowly, a hint of a threat.

Two can play at that game, mister.

'I don't give a monkey's about your wife. I'm here to talk about Janet. And the baby. Your baby that you put in her.'

'I see.' He gulps.

'Oh you do, do you? Do you see Janet beside herself with misery? Not knowing which way to turn?'

He has the decency to look guilty. Or caught out. 'What do you expect me to do, Mrs Delaney?'

'I expect you to help her out. That baby is coming into this world one way or another but the poor blighter needn't have its life ruined by being a bastard.'

I don't normally use words like that but in this circumstance it is called for. It says what it is.

163

But even so, the word bounces around Mr Trigg's office, ricocheting off his dingy light fitting and skittering along his polished desk, crashing into his precious carriage clock. *Bastard. Bastard. Bastard.*

He blinks in the dingy light.

'I could leave my wife,' he says quietly, half-heartedly, like he already knows it's a lost cause.

'You'll never leave your wife. You don't have the guts.'

He doesn't argue.

'Right, then. Here's what I propose. Write to Janet. Explain that you will never leave your wife. That way, at least she can hate you and not hold out any hopes in that department, which, if you ask me, is a lucky escape.

'You're going to give Janet some money, as much money as you can muster, so that she can go away and have the baby. Give her enough money to help her through the next year, so she's got one less thing to worry about.'

He nods, relief clearly visible in the way he jerks his head up and down, like a boy excused his punishment if he promises to behave from now on.

'And one more thing, Mr Trigg.'

'Yes?'

I could ask for the world and I reckon he'd give it me right now, to save his bacon.

'You're the registrar, aren't you?'

'I am, yes.' He's uncertain, like maybe he's got this wrong, but I know it's right because it says so on his door.

'Well then, this should be easy enough.' And I tell him my plan, one that's been forming in my mind over the last week or so. Something that will make things clearer. Straighter. Formal. Births, marriages, deaths, they are the markers of a life.

He nods his agreement and I get up. He attempts to do the same, but I wave him away. I dismiss him.

'The money, Mr Trigg. Make sure it's a generous amount. You have a fine job here and I'm sure you don't want a scandal to jeopardise that.'

His blue eyes dazzle for a moment, almost long enough for me to catch a glimpse of what Janet saw in him, then the dazzle fades like a dying star and it's clear as day that they are actually a dull battleship-grey.

'And send the letter and the money to the shop, addressed to me. There's no need for you to have Janet's address.'

★   ★   ★

I've become quite the actress, telling people I'm expecting a baby, discreetly, like I'm confiding in them, dressing in baggy clothes, not my usual slacks and blouse. I'm sure people are looking at me differently. I almost feel pregnant. Sometimes I lie in bed at night imagining there's a baby inside me floating around. Sometimes I even think I can feel it kick.

When Janet's time is approaching, I travel down to Kent on the dirty smutty steam train, to stay on the farm. Everyone thinks I'm going to keep Janet company while she's poorly, Mum makes sure of that. They also think I'm going into confinement, some fresh air and rest. Who would question that?

Mick sees me off, tells me to take care. 'Be prepared for the worst,' he says, whispering into my ear, squeezing my arm, so I almost have a wobble, but I don't.

'Janet will be fine,' I tell him. 'She's stronger than she was.'

He looks me in the eye, steadfast and unwavering because that's my Mick, the man who couldn't afford a bus fare. The one who fought for Winston. 'It's not the birth I'm worried about,' he says. 'It's the baby. She might want to keep it.'

'She won't.' I shake my head, flick away that idea. 'She's a clever girl. She knows what's best.'

He thinks about this for a moment, then nods, kisses me on the lips, slips his arms round my waist. 'Hurry back,' he whispers.

★　★　★

I take a suitcase with me, filled with napkins and safety pins, a shawl, and baby clothes made by Mum. Bert collects me from the station. On a tractor. It's so lovely to see him, I don't mind the pong.

Back at the farm, I'm greeted by scruffy dogs and a robust Polly.

'Welcome,' she says. 'Come in and have a cuppa.'

166

I follow her across the yard and into the kitchen, the smell of freshly baked bread wrapping around me, the dogs sniffing at my legs. Janet is in a rocking chair by the window that overlooks the green fields. She's knitting something small, what might be a bootie. The scene is idyllic, her bump enormous, like she's got a barrage balloon stuffed inside her tent of a dress. She smiles up at me and I want to run away, get back on the stinky tractor and onto the smutty steam train and hightail it back to London. But Janet is on her feet, the knitting put aside on her chair, and she has me in her arms, her balloon belly pressing against my own flat one.

★   ★   ★

At four o'clock on the following Sunday morning, the baby pops out far too easily for a woman who has been sick half her life. A scrap of a thing, barely five pounds, but still bigger than I was.

It's a boy.

She calls him John Charles, after her dad. To be known as Charlie. She holds him, tight, like she'll never let him go and I'm worried she'll squash him, you hear such tales from the old women round our way. Tears shine in her eyes. She's tired. She's got a touch of the baby blues. That's what it is. She'll be all right. We can do this. It will all work out for the best.

★   ★   ★

We get into a routine. We share the baby care, Janet, Polly and I. Even Bert will have a cuddle of an evening. The baby doesn't mind his smell. It seems to settle him as he has a tendency to be a bit crotchety.

Charlie sleeps in a drawer by Janet's bed so she can feed him at night. I've heard her singing to him. Lullabies, nursery rhymes, George Formby. She coos over him, talking and whispering and murmuring sweet nothings. She gazes at him like he's the best thing in all the world, the only thing that matters. She doesn't know that I see her. She forgets I am an undertaker.

One morning, after a bad night, she's exhausted, walking around like she's Wee Willie Winkie in a trance. I urge her back to bed, suggest it's time to start weaning him, get him used to the bottle. She nods her head, too tired to argue, thinking of sleep in a way only the sleep-deprived can think.

I make a bottle and he gobbles it down. I wind him and burp him and he nods off, twitching and murmuring, and he's mine for the moment, just mine. When I hold him in my arms, look at his little sleeping face, his closed eyes with the long lashes, his puckered skin, his scaly scalp, when I feel his warmth and weight, I know this is what I want. This is right.

★　★　★

Later that day, after Janet's slept and had a bath, she comes downstairs, brighter and perkier. I reckon we're through the worst of it and it may be time for me to take Charlie home. I tell her I have an errand to do. I get Charlie ready to put him in the pram, but then from nowhere there's the sound of thunder, like on my wedding day. Janet says can it wait, your errand. And I say no it can't, I need to sort something out in town. So she says she'll watch Charlie while I go and do it.

'Don't forget his nap,' I say. 'And his next feed is in an hour. I've made the bottle.'

'Yes, Betsy,' she says, like I'm her mother, but she needs someone to take things in hand.

★   ★   ★

When I get back, the kitchen is empty. I find Janet sitting on her bed, her back to me.

'Janet? Everything all right?'

She turns suddenly, surprised to see me there. We've all got used to creeping around so we don't wake the baby, though I know my mum would have something to say about that. *Don't work around the baby, let the baby work around you.*

Something's wrong.

'Is he all right? Is he ill?'

But it's not worry on her face, it's guilt. When I walk around the bed to check, I am quite startled by what I see. She's holding Charlie, when he should be napping in his drawer. He's at her breast. And I fear the worst, so much so that I feel a tightening in my own breasts.

Keep Baby with Mother.

Charlie has dropped off, let go of Janet's

169

nipple. Her dress has a wet patch.

'I was in pain, Betsy. He was crying and he wouldn't take the bottle, so I gave in. It was easier and the relief was something else.'

'He's confused. He can smell your milk. He'd best come in with me tonight. It's time anyway.'

I pick up the drawer and lug it next door to my room, place it on the floor between the twin beds. Then I go back to see her. She has tears in her eyes.

'Pass him here, Janet. I'll put him down in my room. He's got to get used to this.'

I reach out my arms, but she keeps hold of him.

'I don't think I can do this,' she says.

And I realise I've been waiting for her to say this, so I am ready. 'Course you can. It's the best for him.'

'I could stay here with Bert and Polly,' Janet says, clutching at straws, while my plan builds up all solid around her like a brick wall you could never blow down. 'They love having me around. They love Charlie. They say he's a little angel. A little golden angel.' She drops a kiss on his angelic tufted head and my belly aches.

'They're getting on, Bert and Polly.' I keep my voice gentle and steady, like I'm with a customer, the Sunshine voice. 'They won't be here forever. Chances are they'll sell up before long and then where will that leave you?'

She shakes her head. She doesn't have an answer for this.

'Your life will be a struggle, Janet. It'll be tough on the poor little mite, having no father.

Every boy needs a father.'

And then I go in for the kill.

'You'll never meet a man.'

'Who says I have to have a man?'

'You'll want one sooner or later, a lovely girl like you, just like I've got my Mick. You'll want him on a cold winter's evening. When you're invited to a party. When the bins need taking out. And this man, he won't want another man's child now, will he?'

This is when she starts to cry and I wonder for a moment if I have gone too far, but deep down I know this is right. It's the right thing to do. All over the Empire there are children brought up believing their mother is their sister, their father is not the milkman. Not the rag-and-bone man. Not the unknown G.I. from Ohio, Alabama, or Idaho. It's part of the natural order of things. A cuckoo in the nest. I am doing the best thing for Janet and Charlie. And if I happen to get a family into the bargain, then we are all winners. That's how I see it.

'We're all put on this earth to live our lives as best we can, Janet. To live it for others.'

Her shoulders slump and what little energy she has fizzles out like a sparkler in a bucket of water and she gives me a nod. A small nod. 'So it's done then?' she asks with a shudder once her tears have subsided into a stream rather than a torrent.

'Mick and I will say he's ours. That's the best way. It'll protect you and keep him in the family. I'll stay on here a while longer and then take him back to London. It's a good job he's on the small

171

side so I can say he's younger than he is.'

Janet thinks about this — arithmetic never her strong point, arithmetic being what brought her over to our shelter on that fateful bomb-ridden night.

'Then when you've got your strength back, get a job. You've a good brain and you're a hard worker. You could join the Foreign Office.'

'The Foreign Office? I'm never good enough for the Foreign Office.'

'Course you are. More than good enough. As a secretary.' Janet's not exactly diplomatic material, though she has shown her abilities in this department over the years, particularly between me and Marg in our many stand-offs and skirmishes. 'You're quick with languages and writing and everything. You can do shorthand and typing and organise a works do. And don't you remember geography at school with old Mr Kennilworth? You used to dream about visiting those pink countries splattered across the globe on his desk. Now's your chance. The Foreign Office can take you all over the world. Think of that. You couldn't do that as an unmarried mother.'

'No, I don't suppose I could,' she says. 'But I'd never get in, would I?'

'It's only a test and an interview. They'll snap you up.'

'Will they?'

'Yes. I know they will. You know more than you think you do.'

And I know more than she thinks I do. As does my mother, who pulls some strings with a friend in the WI who is married to a man in the Diplomatic Service.

It's not just me who believes this is the right thing. My mother does too.

★ ★ ★

It's a straightforward transaction. Janet gets a decent cheque from Mr Trigg and a few extra bob I've saved for a rainy day. She'll need to buy fabric to run up a new dress. A new coat and a pair of smart shoes, so she can go for interviews without looking like a scruff, with darned skirts and mismatched blouses. She'll need food and shelter and has been offered a place in a women's hostel in Sloane Square. Janet will get a new wardrobe, a new career, a new life. Mick and I will get a baby boy, John Charles Edgar Sunshine. Fair's fair.

★ ★ ★

When Charlie is four weeks old and fully on the bottle, I've made sure of that, it's time to say goodbye. Janet has run up a pretty dress with polka dots and put on some pink lipstick; a young woman who might not have a care in the world. And as for Charlie, well, he looks smashing in a knitted romper suit of blue and white, courtesy of Polly, who has tears spouting from her eyes every time someone mentions Janet and Charlie leaving.

On the final morning, D-Day, Janet and I leave Polly in the farmhouse kitchen having a last

173

cuddle of the cherub. We head across the farmyard to collect eggs. It's going to be a warm summer's day in the Garden of England, a buttercup sun sloughing off its heat. Othello and Desdemona are grazing out in the paddock, all thoughts of coffins and mourners and ostrich feathers quite gone. Their coats are glossy, their tummies taut and shiny. They'd never pull a hearse these days, lazy things. Eating's all they're good for now. They whinny contentedly when we head towards them, a basket of pretty duck eggs hooked over my arm.

We stop at the gate. Janet plucks a carrot out of thin air, snaps it in half and offers each part to the old faithful servants. The sweet smell of dung takes me back to the war, Dad spreading muck on the vegetable plot that used to be Mum's garden, all those roses and hydrangeas and blousy flowers she favoured, wiped out and replaced with potatoes and onions.

'We can't eat flowers,' Dad reasoned, knowing it was breaking Mum's heart. But she came around. She had to. We all had to make do and mend.

That's exactly what we are doing now.

'Just think, Janet, if you get this posting, which I bet you will, you'll be off on your adventures in no time.'

'Here's hoping,' she says. 'Somewhere far away.'

'It'll work out just fine. You wait and see.'

'There is one thing, Betsy.'

'Oh?' My heart goes doolally because I know what she's going to ask, because I know the

174

question I'd be asking if the tables were turned.

'Will you let me see him?'

'Who?'

'Don't be like that, Betsy. You know who. My son.'

'He's my son now, Janet. It was your idea after all.'

'But what if I've changed my mind?'

'That'll be the baby blues talking, you silly moo. You know it's for the best.'

She looks uncertain, pale in the sunlight, as if her legs might give way. Another of those doleful tears trickles down her gaunt cheek and I have to quash any sentimental feelings. This is for the best. Still, I need to make sure this is done and dusted.

'My name's on his birth certificate, Janet. Mine and Mick's.'

'What?'

'Your married man had some use after all. He wasn't ever going to leave his bat of a wife, but he did do this for his son. Gave him a name and a home.'

'You saw him?'

'Months ago.'

'Is that why he wrote to me? Sent me the money?'

'I put him straight on a few things.'

'But . . . ' Realisation dawns on her face. 'Polly said I still had another couple of weeks to register him.'

'No need to worry,' I tell her briskly. 'It's sorted out.'

'But how?'

'I went to the register office in town last week. It was time for your Mr Trigg to pull in some favours.'

'But he works in London.'

'He's a Mason. He knows the local registrar.'

Janet cries now. A cry so profound, I think I'll give in, give all this up as a bad lot, but I don't listen, I keep going. But I have to offer something back.

'You can see him whenever you want. You're his auntie after all. You're part of this family. You always will be. And one day, in the future, when you're ready, you'll meet someone decent and have a family of your own.'

'I thought I already had that.' She shudders again and wipes her nose with a hanky, then nuzzles Othello's big head, taking courage from the solid old stallion.

I get a pain in my stomach. Must be my monthlies on its way, but none of that matters now. Things are different. 'It's the best way. The best way for us all to be happy.'

'Then why do I feel so wretched, Betsy?'

I sigh, because I feel wretched too, but we've made the decision and there's no going back. 'Like I said, baby blues. You'll soon feel normal again.'

'I can't remember what normal is.'

'I don't think there actually is a normal, Janet. All we can do is get along as best we can.'

'Make do and mend?'

'Make do and mend.'

'It's as if Mum and Dad and my brothers and sisters were never here. I had them taken away and now my little Charlie.'

'But you're my sister, Janet. Never forget that.'

I feel like a rogue as I hold her in my arms, but I have to do this for all of us. It's the only way.

★ ★ ★

'It's done then.' Mick stares at me, head up from his paper at the dining table, stares wide-eyed at Charlie in my arms, swaddled in the woolly shawl crocheted by Bert's sister, Polly, using scraps of yarn so it's multicoloured like a Suttons Seeds catalogue.

'Course. Why wouldn't it be? This was the plan.'

'Things don't always go according to plan.'

'Well this time they did.'

'And how's Janet?'

'Don't you want to hold him?'

His eyes rove in panic over the baby in my arms. Then he pulls himself together, takes a deep breath, tries to steady himself by gripping onto the edge of the table, and pushes himself up and out of his chair, scraping it back on the floor tiles so it makes Charlie twitch in his sleep. He takes a step towards me, us. In his socks he's not much taller than I am, but I feel like one of them tribeswomen we used to marvel over in the geography books of the Empire at school. I feel tall, and strong, and powerful, with a mighty weapon in my hands. Charlie.

'Are you sure about this, Betsy?' he asks.

'We're giving this poor child a good home and the chance of a decent upbringing. He'd never have got it with Janet and no father to speak of.'

I have to swallow the feeling that I have done something not quite right. I'm tired and I realise I've got a way to go with Mick, who looks like he has doubts when there can be no doubts.

'Charlie's ours now. John Charles Edgar Sunshine Delaney. Our names are on the birth certificate.'

'How?'

'Her married man works at the council. He's a registrar.'

I can see his brain working, like he's been woken up in the middle of a dream and is trying to orientate himself. He can't make the questions come out, not the right ones, so he just says, 'What if she wants him back? She might change her mind and then where will you be?'

'She can't. I told you, it's done.'

For some absurd reason, I long to hide in the old Anderson shelter, Charlie and me, Charlie who's flinching in his sleep and I already know that means he's waking up and any minute he'll be squealing for his bottle. But, instead, I bundle Charlie over into Mick's arms, after all he knows how to hold a baby, there was always a baby in his mammy's house, and he'll be all right while I put the milk on. He'll be all right if he can only feel the weight and shape of the baby, smell that newness and hope. It'll all be all right.

But Mick follows me round the kitchen, carrying the baby like a rugby ball, a ticking time bomb.

'For goodness' sake, Mick. It's done. He's our baby. You agreed.'

He gives me this look I've never seen before. It chills me right down to the bone. I take Charlie back off him and settle into the chair by the boiler and give him his bottle. I hold onto Charlie and feel the warmth creep back into me.

When the bottle's gone and Charlie sleeps in my arms, I realise Mick has slipped out the house. It's just me and the baby. My baby. Our baby. Janet will be fine. In a few weeks she'll be off to Germany of all places, on a posting. I don't know how she can go there after what those Nazis did to her family, but she says it's something she needs to do. And who am I to say anything when I've done so much to make this happen?

It is the right thing. The best thing.

★ ★ ★

Mick can never stay upset for long. I know how to make him happy. I know how to stop him even thinking about straying from our bed. I work my magic on him that night, long before the sun rises, and by the time I've brought him breakfast in bed, he is cradling Charlie and singing him a lullaby that speaks of peat bogs and that soft Irish rain.

If truth be told, and let's face it that can be a hard thing to do, I find this much harder than I thought I would. Baby Mab was a doddle, before she found her feet and temper. She was a docile baby, either sleeping or gurgling. If she did cry, Mum knew what to do to stop it — wind, feed, sleep, she could sort it out.

179

Charlie is not a happy baby. He has colic. He cries every evening. For hours. He won't settle. His little face contorts in pain. Janet would never have coped with a difficult baby like this and I won't let myself think that maybe Charlie would've been all right with Janet, that he knows I'm not his birth mother, he remembers the months in her womb, the weeks at her breast.

Keep Baby with Mother.

I won't. The choice is made. I will love him. He will love me back.

★　★　★

One morning after a long haul of a night, Mick brings me a cuppa in bed while Charlie sleeps on in his topsy-turvy circadian rhythm.

'Having a nice lie-in?'

I hear the smash and clatter of china against the wall before I realise the teacup is out of my hand. At least Mickey has the decency to scoop up Charlie on his way out to fetch the dustpan and brush.

I hear him later, whistling along to the wireless. I suppose I should be thankful he's not sleeping with his secretary. Not that he has a secretary and they are all men at work apart from me and Mum. Only, I suppose, if you look at it another way, he is sleeping with the secretary, because that's me: secretary, book-keeper, funeral director. Jill of all trades.

Later still, when I've dragged myself out of bed, had a wash and made myself decent, I shuffle downstairs, guilty and contrite, yet still

180

bristling with annoyance. Mick says, 'You look nice, Betsy.' I've put on some lipstick and some rouge — not too much as I don't want to look like one of the corpses. ('We're morticians, not beauticians,' Mum told Margie when she had a go once, before deciding she'd rather be flying across continents than submerged in death.) 'I've given him breakfast and changed his nappy.'

He's got most of the breakfast over his clean shirt and the nappy is already half off, but Mick's heart is all gold and he'd never upset me knowingly. And Charlie is gurgling contentedly, the way babies are supposed to. They look like father and son.

'I'm sorry about the cup.' And I am. I am sorry. But saying it never comes easy. He has no idea how much it costs. Or that my monthlies are well overdue.

2016

Chichester

'You're going home today,' the nurse says to me. 'The doctor's really pleased with your hip, so you'll be mobile in no time as long as you don't go turning cartwheels.'

I don't think about my hip. I don't think about that patronising tone. But I do think about that word: home. And for a moment I imagine Nana Mabel's house in East Dulwich. I imagine that is where the ambulance will take me. Though of course that's all rot. Home is now Sunnydale in Bognor.

There's nowhere quite like London, not in the whole wide world as far as I can see, not that I've seen much. But London has seen it all. Upheavals, invasions, destruction. Plagues, fires, bombs. Romans, Vikings, Normans. The Luftwaffe, the IRA, American werewolves. Russian Oligarchs, non-doms, Yuppies, fundamentalists. But it's survived them all. The Armada tried it. Napoleon tried it. Hitler gave it a right rollicking go and kept the family business busier than ever. But it was tricky. For a country that was once all forest, we were struggling to get wood. We could have used shrouds but Dad refused — said that was a pauper's burial. Instead we made the coffins thinner, no more than 5/8 of an inch thick, using low-grade timber, even cardboard sometimes, but disguised, using *papier-mâché* and the like.

You do what you have to do. You rethink your ways out of necessity. You make do and bleeding mend.

I said I'd never leave London, but once Mick was gone, I found I was able to consider it. All around me, all my life, I was surrounded by the Dead with a capital D. But by now my own personal dead were piling up. London wasn't the same. Where the terraces had once been, the bomb sites, the concrete estates, they'd been washed away and replaced with clean shiny empty buildings. London was a ghost of its former self and it broke my heart. Which is how I ended up in Sunnydale residential home for gentlefolk in buggering Bognor.

'Cup of tea, Mrs Sunshine?'

'A strong one, please. Splash of milk and two sugars.'

'Two?'

'Two.' Silly moo. I've earned my two sugars, thank you very much. All those years we had to do without.

She bustles off. She's friendly enough, but another fat one. Her legs make a swishing sound when she walks. Everyone's fat now. If you want to know how the nation's diet is, ask an undertaker.

⋆　⋆　⋆

Tom was a big fat thing when he was born, soft and yielding like Mum's bread, a headful of

183

Brylcreem-slick hair and creased skin from being squashed inside his mother too long, two weeks late. Late like his grandmother, my Barbara, never on time for anything, except for her own birth, which took us all by surprise.

'You'll be late for your own funeral,' Dad would tell Barbara. She loved her granddad. He was a better granddad than he was a father. Not that he was a bad father — just distant, busy, arms plunged up to the elbows in Death's doings. 'Someone's got to do it,' he'd say. The family motto.

Tom's baby fat is long gone. He's a beanpole now. A streak of piddle, Mick would've said. Irish tinker, I used to call Mick when he was getting on my nerves. Bogtrotter. But mostly we rubbed along, never went to bed on an argument. Except that one time when I came home with Charlie from the farm. Never seen him so confused — and that was before the surprise we had laying in store, planted inside me like a juicy plum.

They say you wait ages for a bus. That's what happened to me and Mick. We waited and waited and there was no sign of a baby. Then along came Charlie, followed six months later by Barbara, which took some explaining.

And I remember the tears. As I pushed her head and shoulders out of me, I thought of Janet and wept for her, going through all that for nothing. And when I held Barbara in my arms, her misshapen head and bluish skin, I knew I could never let go of her.

Chance would be a fine thing now. She's

184

always checking up on me, hardly giving me a minute's peace, even with the A3 between us.

Mick treated the babies both the same, except for one's a boy and one's a girl and this was long before feminists came along upsetting the apple cart. I don't think I favoured one over the other, but Barbara, although exasperatingly slow, was easier somehow. Charlie was what you'd call high-maintenance. All that colic, teething, measles and mumps at the same time, and then all that other business. The company he kept.

I blame that on his grandfather. Not my dear dad, but the Irish one.

★　★　★

It's not like Janet came out of it with nothing. She had a career. She was thriving. And she had a gentleman friend. Several. She said she had to swat them away like flies. And while I didn't feel a spot of jealousy, I missed her.

I still do.

I want her to come back and see me, but then again I don't.

The true measure of all our actions is how long the good in them lasts . . . everything we do, we do for the young.
Queen Elizabeth II

1950

London

Charlie's closer in age to my little sister, Mab, than I am to her. He thinks she's the bee's knees and his eyes follow her around the room. She comes in to play with him on her way home from school. She is spoilt and has a shocking temper, so it's good for her to be the older child for a change. She's quite different when she's with Charlie, careful and quiet instead of loud and abrasive.

Today I take Charlie round to Mum and Dad's because it is Mab's seventh birthday. She is having a tea party after school and has invited her friends Vi and Win from across the street. I could do with putting my feet up, I'm ready to have this baby any day, but Mab loves her Charlie and so I've spent the early part of the afternoon with Mum making jam sandwiches, sausage rolls and fairy cakes. And there's jelly and ice cream for afters. Mum has even stood on a stool and strung up the banner along the picture rail in the front room. It gets brought out every birthday and Christmas. It says 'God Save the King' in Armistice colours (make do and mend). Parties wouldn't be quite the same without it.

The girls are tucking into their sandwiches,

187

Charlie's gnawing on a crust with his new tooth, and us grown-ups are having a cuppa, when there's a rap at the front door. Mum freezes, as if she knows it's an unwelcome guest, one that Dad won't be too pleased to see and he's due back from work any minute for his dinner.

'Get that will you, Betsy.'

When Mum asks you to do something, you do it. She doesn't have to raise her voice; there's a tone to it you can't ignore, like a siren luring a sailor onto the rocks, though not as romantic or deathly. But I don't want to open the door, not because my legs are killing me and I never knew I'd be this tired with a bun in the oven, but because I have a feeling that whatever, whoever, is behind the front door will be as explosive as a bomb.

Mr Canning, clutching what appears to be a birthday card for Mab. A dolly tucked under his beefy arm. To give him his dues, he looks worried, his cheeks flushed and his teeth clicking. I'm debating what to do, when I hear the back door crash, followed by whoops and cheers.

Dad.

I reach for the card in Mr Canning's freckled hand, a gesture of acceptance rather than hospitality, hoping he'll get my drift and leave. And he does. He hands it over, shoves the doll into my arms, turns to go, head down, shoulders stooped. But before he can take a step, my father, in his best work suit, appears from nowhere, pushing me out of the way so my arm knocks the picture of Princess Elizabeth off the wall with a smash and splinter of glass. Dad lunges at Mr Canning. Mr Canning lies sprawled on the pavement, his dentures lying beside him in a macabre grin. Then Dad executes a perfect kick to the dolly, who flies through the air and lands in the gutter, legs akimbo, and no knickers.

★   ★   ★

Mum is livid. 'You can't go showing yourself up like that.'

'Me? She's my daughter. Mine. She's got nothing to do with that bastard.' He doesn't get the irony in his words. But still. Mab is his daughter. His alone. Nothing to do with Mr Canning. Same way that Charlie has nothing to do with Mr Trigg.

Though, in a long, wakeful, fretful night shift, when I'm wading through nappies and bottles and Milton, I wonder what would happen if I showed up on Mr Trigg's doorstep, with a screaming baby in my arms, demanding that he lend a hand. But men are rubbish with babies. They don't understand what it is to feel your baby's cry in your heart, even when it's not your baby but it is your baby. I'm not saying my Mick doesn't care. I'm not saying he hasn't grown to love Charlie. But Mick can switch off the noise. He can sleep through it. Listen to the wireless through it. Read the paper, do the crossword, smoke a pipe. But for me, if I hear one tiny mewl from Charlie, I'm there, picking him up, winding him, rocking him. All there is in the world in that moment is me and him.

And Janet. There's always Janet, looking over my shoulder.

★ ★ ★

The whole sorry episode is buried as deep as a metaphorical body, though bodies can always be exhumed. But, for now, peace reigns once more: once Mab stops asking questions, once Mum gets over Dad showing her up, once Dad yet again forgives the whole indiscretion of his wife with Mr Canning because he knows that he was lucky not to father a child out of wedlock with Mrs Canning. And anyway, once Barbara finally shows up, she takes over the limelight.

Oh, what a tangled web we weave. The spiders have been busy in our house and up at the grocer's and down at the farm, but hopefully this is an end to it. Dad buys Mab a bicycle and Mick teaches her how to ride it and so she's not bothered about all the kerfuffle, not when she can tear up and down the street with the wind in her red hair like a mini modern Queen Boudicca, terrorising the smaller kids and the boys.

But the main reason that things are set to change for the better is that the Cannings sell up and move to Ramsgate to run a guest house. This is not only good news for the Sunshines, but it is good news for our rivals, the Vickers, who buy the grocer's shop for quite different purposes. They may only have been trading for three generations, as opposed to our six, but they are now trading from East Dulwich as well as

190

Peckham. Dad's lost one rival, but he has gained another.

Mum says, 'You don't need to worry, Edgar. We've got loyal customers and we do a decent funeral.'

Dad says, 'Vickers will do it for less and with more flash.'

Mum says, 'We've faced Hitler, we can face Vickers.'

And you can't argue with that.

★ ★ ★

But, in the way that time does, it tells. Bob Vickers Jnr is put in charge of the new premises, while his younger brother runs the Peckham branch, with Bob Vickers Snr supervising both Peckham and East Dulwich whilst working his way towards semi-retirement. This means that I have to put up with Bob Vickers Jnr loitering around Lordship Lane. He pops up when I least expect him. I might be queuing in the bank and he'll be there with his bags of cash. He'll step out of the Crystal Palace Tavern reeking of smoke just at the moment I'm passing by with my shopping. I don't like to think that he is following me, a married woman, but I do wonder. I have to keep checking behind me as if I am being shadowed, but more often than not, it's my imagination.

By the time 1952 rolls around, Charlie is three years old and Barbara two and a half. Most things are finally off the ration, but not sugar or sweets. It's not so bad for our kiddies as they've never known any different, nor Mab who's now nine years old, spoilt as anything, worse than Margie ever was. I almost miss her now she's gone, Margie, the jetsetter. Once a fortnight a BOAC postcard flutters through the letter box and drifts onto the doormat. Rome, Cairo, Karachi, all these exotic places, each one with her trademark *Wish you were here!* which I doubt very much. And not a Broadstairs donkey to be seen on any of them.

★   ★   ★

At the beginning of February, the King dies. We are a nation in shock and mourning. He was only fifty-six. Poor man was never meant to be king and then he had to take us through a war. That took its toll, plus he had feeble lungs like Janet. Only she's fighting fit now, on a new posting somewhere in the Orient.

Princess Elizabeth is in Kenya when she receives the news that she is now Queen. She is twenty-five years old. Same as me, only I'm stuck in London with the dead bodies, which is how I like it.

2016

Bognor Regis

There's an old bloke lives here, Frank, thinks he's the cat's whiskers, reminds me of Prince Charles, walking around with his hands behind his back like he's been cuffed. I've never thought much of that Prince Charles, always sticking his oar in, with his old-fashioned buildings and organic carrots. The Queen stays out of things, though she can beam her thoughts with the flash of a look. I hope she lives as long as her mother. That way the monarchy might skip a generation and it'll be that lovely William, who has his mother's heart, if not her fine head of hair.

The Queen never expected to be queen. Not until her uncle gave up his throne for the American woman. My mum couldn't stand Mrs Simpson. *What does he see in her, the ruddy beanpole*, she'd say. But then we didn't know war was around the corner and we'd all be ruddy beanpoles. Then we needed the Americans. We needed their food. We needed their troops. We needed their boats and planes. But they took their time. Not like those brave Canadians and Indians and the rest of the pink lands splashed all over the globe, all those loyal subjects who wanted to serve the mother country.

Only then, when the war was over, so was the Empire. Fair's fair.

Throughout all my life and with all my heart I shall strive to be worthy of your trust.
Queen Elizabeth II on the radio broadcast for her Coronation

1953

London

The day of the Coronation is historic in more ways than we could ever imagine. We, the so-called New Elizabethans, spend the day at Nana Mabel's — though dear Nana's no longer with us, having passed away the year previous, same as the king. It's only Mum, Dad and Mab living there now, what with Janet and Margie all over the place.

Mick, myself, Charlie and Barbara go round for the celebrations. It's all planned. Watching the new television and a high tea later on. Mum's doing salmon mousse and melon cocktails as demonstrated by Marguerite Patten on 'About the Home'. The front-room curtains are drawn to keep out the sunlight — not to keep a dead body cool but so we can see the crackling picture as clearly as possible. Dad paid up front for our television set, as he won't get stuff on the 'never never'. The walnut-veneered thing dominates the room, much as a coffin would and has done in the past, with Nana last year for instance.

Mum's done the place up nice for the occasion. We can't use the 'God save the King' banner anymore, so she runs up a new one: 'God save the Queen', with crowns and orbs and sceptres. She's also knitted a coronation jumper each for Mab, Charlie and Barbara, red, white and blue hoops with 'QEII' stitched over their hearts.

The television screen might be small and fuzzy, but it is magical. We take it in turns to have a better view, as there's quite a few of us packed in the room, seeing as some of the neighbours are sharing the joy. *Vivat Regina!*

Along with the many heads of state in all their glory, Mr Churchill is there, Prime Minister again, the only MP to have served under the two latest queens, quite a record, but that's Winston for you.

'Your nana would've loved this,' Mum says. 'She liked the Princesses and she loved the King. It was his parents she couldn't stand. All stiff upper lip and snobbery.'

What a mob.

By the time Queen Elizabeth, in the abbey, radiant in another beautiful Norman Hartnell dress, and weighed down by the burden of a huge crown, has emerged from her tent where the bishops have anointed her with holy oil, the children are pent up with boredom. Barbara is rolling around the rug waving her flag and Charlie is unravelling his coronation jumper. I pretend I haven't seen as it's keeping him quiet.

There's a pall of blue smoke hanging in the air, a mixture of Player's and Senior Service and Dad's pipe. You wouldn't have it these days, not around kiddies. But then there's a lot you wouldn't have these days. Dad used to enter bombed-out buildings, risking his own life to

197

retrieve the bodies. Or what was left of them. So a bit of fag smoke doesn't come into it. He's entering into the joy of the occasion and is on the stout. He's knocked back far more than usual and looks a little worse for wear, flushed from the heat, the booze, the excitement.

'It's not often you get to see a queen crowned,' is what Dad tells Mum when she suggests he slow down. He pauses briefly, empties his glass. 'Anyone know what time Miss Lipstick's back?' Margie's due about now, said she'd pop in for tea and that she has a surprise, some knick-knack or other she's brought back from her travels. He stumbles as he goes to refresh Mick's whisky and Mum eyes him like she's not sure if something's going on.

Something is indeed about to go on. And it's Miss Lipstick herself who's to blame, maybe not completely, but it's going to be a difficult one to live down, an impossible one to forget.

We don't hear the front door, so when Marg appears in the room it's a surprise, as if Dad has summoned his second daughter simply by asking after her whereabouts. She's less poised than usual, hesitant on the threshold as she beckons forth a man.

And what a man.

Now I know she's been seeing a fella called Benjamin, but I don't think this can be him.

Or can it?

Oh, my God, it ruddy well is!

It's him, the trumpet player from years back, the one at the dance, having a smoke outside the church hall, while Marg was hogging Malcolm, the spotty medical student. The trumpet player talking to me like I was someone who mattered.

Benjamin.

What the hell is Marg doing with him, here, in Nana's front room, Mum and Dad's house, with a coy look on her face?

She's done it this time.

It's all gone quiet. Everyone is staring from Marg to Benjamin as if she's dragged in an alien. But Mum pulls it together. It won't be too long before she does her first West Indian funeral — I'm praying it won't be Benjamin's, the way Dad is squaring up to him, his face now more of a bluish colour.

Marg breaks the silence, which is getting ever so big.

'Mum, Dad, this is Mr Benjamin McGuire. Benjamin, this is Edgar and Alice Sunshine.'

Benjamin McGuire holds out his hand and Mum steps forward to shake it. Dad, more hesitantly, shakes it next.

Charlie, Barbara and Mab stare with mouths open and I have to remind all three to find their manners. We Sunshines don't judge, we don't comment. We come into the world as equals, we leave as equals, and in between we should treat each other as equals. The new queen on the box might have a rollicking big crown on her head, but she still does her job, for the country, same as my mum and dad, same as Mick and Benjamin who fought in the war, fair's fair.

And things might've worked out all right, despite everything, the difference, the surprise, the hows and whys, if Marg had only given it a chance. But she doesn't. She flashes her hand, like she's the ruddy queen herself waving to her subjects, and we all see it — even Mab, who scrambles up from the floor and goes to her sister and touches it. A ring. A golden wedding band.

Always one to outshine, is Margie.

'Is that what I think it is?'

'Yes, Dad. It is. We got wed.'

'You got wed? Just like that? You didn't even think to ask me and your mother what we thought about it?'

'I'm twenty-two. I don't need your permission.'

'Please, Mr Sunshine, Mrs Sunshine.' Benjamin's voice is beautiful, smooth, but with a hint of roughness too — all those hours spent in smoky clubs. 'I love your daughter. I'm honoured to have her as my wife. I'll be a good husband, you have my word.'

Dad rubs his arm like he's cold, though it's sweltering in this front room, suffocating, all these bodies and emotions. Mum's mouth's trying to move but it's not going well. I wish Janet were here. Sweet Janet. She'd calm things down, but she's in Buenos Aires of all places, a two-year secondment, secretary for the Ambassador, far away from this family drama.

You've got to hand it to Marg. This beats all her old tricks. A lovely, clever, talented man who happens to be from the West Indies and she's tied the knot with him before anyone can stop her. A done deal. Mum and Dad will have no choice but to accept it, the same way they accepted my Mick, the same way the Queen Mother had to accept the Greek.

Dad fumbles for his armchair, practically falls into it, knocking a teacup on his way down. Mum's telling him to be careful, but he flaps her aside. I'm down on my hands and knees picking up the pieces and I know I should get up and try and help this situation, only it's easier to stay on the floor, like I'm bobbing down and hoping.

'Where are you going to live?' he says. 'How are you going to live?'

'Not now, Edgar. You need to calm down. We'll work it out.'

'No, Mum.' Marg's voice sounds quietly determined. 'Benjamin and I will work it out. He's got a good job.'

'What's that then?' she asks.

'I'm a musician.' Benjamin is the calmest one in the room when he's the one who has every right to feel outnumbered.

'A musician?'

We don't have much call for musicians round here, apart from the organist at St Michael's and the bloke who plays sing-a-longs down the East Dulwich Tavern.

'I play the trumpet in a jazz band.'

'Jazz?' Mum says the word like it's foreign. It booms around the room, a big fat hornet waiting to sting, but it's soon shut up by this great noise bursting from Dad. He clutches his arm and moans and his face has gone quite white and he's gasping for air like one of them goldfish you get at the fair, the ones that die before you've even got them home.

Mick chooses this moment to walk in. He's been down to check on the bodies, not so bothered as the rest of us about the monarchy, and now he's back, loosening Dad's tie and feeling his pulse, while the rest of us stand there, immobile, useless.

'I'll fetch the doctor,' Benjamin says.

I tell Mab to show him where the doctor lives. Thank God Dr Parkin's retired and we've got a new chap who knows his stuff and can get a sprint on if needs be, and yes it needs be.

Dad's stopped breathing.

Mum somehow gets herself going, moves to Dad's side, calmly, quietly, and the three of us, Mum, Mick and I, help Dad lie on the floor, a dead weight but he's not dead, he's not dead. Margie howls. 'For God's sake, Marg, take the kids into the other room, will you. Give Dad some space.' Barbara has already fled — a scaredy-cat like her Auntie Marg — but it's too late for Charlie. He won't move. His little shoes are stuck to the floor. I know he's there, but I can't do nothing because I'm trying to get Dad to stay with us, so poor Charlie watches his beloved grandfather struggle for breath, sees the pain on his face and no one able to help him.

It's too late. There's nothing anyone can do. The King is dead.

Long live the Queen.

★　★　★

Sometimes Dad used to call on us to attend a funeral if there weren't enough people. There's

202

nothing worse than a funeral with no people, no one to witness the passing of an individual life from this great heaving mass of humanity. A life should mean something, but if there's no one there to record it, if there's no one there to say goodbye, then what does it all mean?

I tell Mick I don't want Barbara or Charlie going to Dad's funeral. They are only three and four years old and although they understand a bit about death — how could they not — this is their grandfather. And besides, it's all been traumatic, what with Dad going so suddenly, in front of us, and especially for Charlie, who's taken it very hard. The funeral will be one step too much and it's best he visits his granddad's grave afterwards, when this time of raw grief has eased, so that he can say his goodbyes properly.

I should have let them go. I should have known better. I was in a state, holding everyone together, but I still blame myself.

★ ★ ★

It might not quite be on the scale of the King's last year, or a Wellington or a Nelson, no gun carriages or military salutes, but now it's Dad's turn to go, we pull out all the stops. He doesn't have the Daimler for the final ride, as much as he loved that car; we have something far more special planned. Bert brings up Desdemona and Othello for one last outing. They have black ostrich plumes, black velvet livery and all the gleaming brassy tack. You'd think they'd never been away, apart from their fat bellies. Bert walks out front in his full regalia, top hat, walking cane. It's tasteful, with just enough theatricality to make it one to be remembered. We put Dad's watch in the coffin with him so he'll always keep track of time, a stickler for punctuality.

Everyone says it was a good send-off. There's a crowd comes back to the house, so it's much the same as the day of the coronation and I wish we could rewind the clock so I could make sure Dad didn't drink that stout and that Margie didn't give him such a shock.

'He was a good man,' Bert says to me, standing by the back door having a roll-up. 'The best.'

'Thanks, Bert. And thanks for bringing the horses. Hadn't you better be getting off soon? It's a long day for you all.'

'I was just going to say my goodbyes to your mother. But I wanted to ask you something first.'

'Oh?'

'I was wondering how Janet was.'

We're standing out in the yard now. Charlie's consumed with his marbles, in a world of his own, humming a tuneless song. I try to keep my voice controlled and quiet. 'She's doing very well. She's enjoying Argentina, says her boss is lovely.'

'I know that, Betsy. She writes to us too, but we always wonder, Polly and I, if she's managed to, you know, put her losses behind her.'

This swipes the wind from me; I've never heard Bert say such a long sentence. So I take a breath and gabble, doing my damnedest to keep my feet steady. 'I don't suppose she'll ever get over losing her family, at least she got her dad back, he's enjoying living in Hastings and she goes to see him when she can, though obviously that's not quite so easy from Buenos Aires — '

'Betsy, wait. That's not what I mean.'

Before I can find out what Bert means, though I'm pretty sure I know what Bert means, Charlie has chosen this moment to look up from his game and I wonder if he's been earwigging. 'I want to see the horses,' he says.

'Not now, Charlie. Bert's got to take them home.'

His little blue eyes well up — Mr Trigg's eyes — and Bert says, 'It's all right, champ. You can help me get them ready. If that's all right with Betsy.' He ruffles Charlie's hair, avoids my eyes. 'Your mum.'

I nod, swallowing a scream, and watch them walk hand in hand down the side of the house, wishing it was Dad's hand that Charlie was clutching, Dad's face that he was gazing up at adoringly. But I thank God that Dad never knew what I'd done.

And Janet. Have I ever given her a thought in all this? Is she all right?

Of course she is. Janet's all right. Janet's living the life of Riley.

205

2016

Bognor Regis

'Hello, Mum.'

There's this shadow looming over me and I can't for the life of me make out who it is. Only now I do.

'Barbara? Is that you?'

'Course it's me, Mum. Who did you think it was?'

'I don't know. I was thrown for a minute.' I shiver while someone tiptoes through the tulips and all over my grave. 'I sometimes think I'm going ga-ga. Maybe it's catching, all these old dears.'

We both look surreptitiously around us, Barbara and me. It's residential, not nursing. If they think you need extra care, you're out on your ear. It's easy enough to see the ones who're next to go. I hope to goodness it don't come to that. I'd rather kick the bucket the same way as my mum did, slipping away, no trouble, all marbles in place.

'You start forgetting, Barbara. You get muddled and you can't remember when it is or where you are.'

'You're in Bognor, Mum. It's 2016.'

'Well, I know that. It was only for a moment.'

Barbara's in full Technicolor now, no dress

206

sense, all scarves and voluminous tunics in a futile attempt to cover her ample backside. At least she's not one of them feminists with a boy haircut and checked shirt. I've done one or two of them and all. We never judge.

'You caught me on the hop, that's all. I was having some shut-eye.'

'It's all right, Mum. You are allowed, you know. You've earned the luxury of an afternoon nap. You've worked all your life.'

'I'm not dead yet and did you know your grandson is a gay?'

Barbara's been fussing with the magazines on the coffee table. (*Saga. Woman. The Economist.* Sunnydale caters for all tastes and shades of the spectrum.) But now she's pulled up short and sits herself down on the pouffe by my feet.

'Who told you that?' she asks, snappish, like it's an M15 secret.

'He did.'

'Oh, I see.'

'And did you know?'

'Yes, I knew.'

'And what about his parents? They're all right about it, are they?'

Tina, Barbara's only child, is a social worker, so she'll be delighted, but I'm not so sure about Sean, who I'm pretty sure is a closet Tory. A strange coupling if ever there was one. I never expected their marriage to last but they're nearly at the silver mark, so fair play.

'Barbara?'

'I think they always knew deep down, Mum. I certainly did.'

'You never said anything. I didn't have a clue. Just expected him to grow up, settle down, maybe have one or two kiddies.'

'Does it bother you?'

'Now why should it bother me?'

'Well, it's hard for your generation.'

'I'm not a bigot, Barbara. You can't be a bigot in our line of work. And you're no spring chicken yourself. You're a grandmother for goodness' sake. A ruddy pensioner.'

'Sixty-six soon. Can you believe that?'

'You should put your name down on the waiting list for this place.'

'Ha ha.'

The Fat One waddles in with some tea. She could give Barbara a run for her money — not that either of them could run far with their ankles. This one's at least a twenty-inch shoulder width. Would take a whole oak tree to box her in.

Barbara fusses around, getting us both sorted with teacups and sugar and biscuits, making small talk with the large one, then, when she's wobbled off, my daughter turns to me.

'I had an email,' she says.

'Oh?'

'From Charlie.'

Charlie. That stone scratches my insides so my gut feels all red raw. I don't feel so good. Need a nap.

'Mum?'

'What does he want?'

'Not sure he wants anything, Mum. He's lonely.'

'He made his bed.'

'You always made his bed.'

'Don't be flippant. Besides, he had to make his bed in prison. Fat lot of good that did him.'

'Come on, Mum,' she says, holding onto my leg, as if I'm going to run off, as if I can run anywhere with this hip, though I could probably still beat her and the other one. 'Can't you let bygones be bygones? You know what they say?'

'What do they say, Barbara?'

'Never go to bed on a quarrel.'

'This was more than a quarrel and I'm not dead yet.'

'You're not getting any younger.'

'Nor are you.'

'You're so annoying when you're in a mood like this. Are you in pain? Is your hip troubling you?'

'Nothing I can't bear.'

'You don't have to grin and bear anything, Mum. You can have a painkiller or two.'

'I'm not a pill popper, you know that.'

'The Blitz spirit, eh, Mother, dear?'

'Don't make fun of me, my girl.'

'Sorry, Mum. Your generation were a tough lot.'

'And you Baby Boomers never had it so good.'

'That's what they say. Not so sure Charlie would agree.'

I must doze off soon after because when I wake up, she's gone, a dent in the cushion where she was sitting. She's put on weight, got all matronly. And I've just realised she'll have no great-grandchildren as her only grandchild is a gay one. Although anything's possible these days if you have enough money — you've only got to look at that Elton John. Now, his is a funeral I'd like to do. Can you imagine?

It always falls butter-side down, doesn't it?
Queen Elizabeth II

1959

London

It's Charlie's ninth birthday. I have a little panic that it'll be a repetition of the whole Mr Canning and the doll fiasco, an uninvited guest, a ghost from the past. And even though I know that Janet is far away across the Atlantic, I'm on edge. Jittery. Maybe that's why the day turns out the way it does.

Charlie doesn't want a party, he's quite clear about that. I'm not surprised. He doesn't like being the centre of attention, which will make him perfect for undertaking. He doesn't even want any friends over. He does have friends, a small select group who he plays Cowboys and Indians with on the bomb site. He loves *Bonanza* and *Gunsmoke* and anything with John Wayne in it. And so this is why Mick and I give him a cowboy outfit, including a holster and gun, for his birthday present. I secretly wish Charlie would choose to be an Indian because their outfits are prettier and the bow and arrow seems more skilful somehow. But a gun is what Charlie wants. Don't all boys? He makes guns out of sticks and offcuts from the workshop, so it's not like we're putting ideas in his head. Stan was the same at his age. All the boys in the class were. Most of them, apart from the quiet ones, which

212

are the ones they say you have to worry about.

It's a Saturday, so straight away he dresses up in his new costume. He's a bobby dazzler with his fair hair and pale eyes. I thought he'd be embarrassed to venture out in it, but he wants to go to the pictures to see the new John Wayne. And he wants to go dressed as a cowboy.

I get ready, do my hair and put on some lipstick, but he says he wants Mick to take him. Not me.

'Can't Mummy come to?' Mick nicks his cowboy hat and puts it on his own head, which covers the bald patch that has lately appeared.

'It's a Western,' Charlie says. 'She won't like it.'

'Who's she? The cat's mother?' I try to sound light and breezy, like I'm not bothered, it's all fine, but I feel a pang deep inside. 'You two go ahead. I've got lots to catch up on, including a cake to bake for a certain someone's birthday tea.'

'Can I have chocolate?'

'Don't see why not.'

I wave them off from the window in the front room. They walk down the street hand in hand, though Charlie marches to a different beat than his dad.

★　★　★

Two hours later, they're back. Charlie's eyes are red and his nose is all snotty. He's been crying.

'Whatever's the matter, love?'

'He's in trouble,' says Mick. 'Go to your room

213

while I talk to your mother.'

'Why?' He tries to outstare his father but it doesn't work.

'Because I said so,' says Mick.

Charlie skulks upstairs, quiet as anything, rubbing his eyes and sniffing.

'What's going on, Mick?'

I can smell the cake. It needs taking out the oven.

'He insulted a little Indian boy.'

'But that's the idea, isn't it? Cowboys and Indians? You were watching a Western after all. You know he gets really involved in all that stuff.'

'No, not a Red Indian. A boy from India. The new family that have moved in down Barry Road. I was mortified.'

'What on earth did he say?'

'We were coming out the Odeon and there was this little lad with his father who wears a turban on his head. Charlie pointed to it. And he laughed. Then he saw that the little lad had a bun thing on his head and he laughed at him too.'

By this point there's smoke in the air. The ruddy cake! By the time I grab it out the oven, it's too late. I have to chuck it out the back door. It's ruined.

★   ★   ★

So Charlie doesn't get his chocolate cake. He spends an hour or so in his room, then Mick fetches him down for a talking-to.

He sits at the table, contrite, I think, but silent,

214

so I'm not sure, though his eyes are red and his nostrils crusted. But it's not enough to feel bad. We Sunshines don't judge. We must be calm and poised.

We make him write an apology letter. This takes quite some time as he's not the best writer. But I don't feel his apology is meant. He doesn't seem to know what he's done wrong.

So I put my foot down.

'Right, Charlie. You're going to give that little boy your gun and holster.'

Charlie looks at me, wide-eyed, looks to his dad for help.

'No, Betsy,' Mick says. 'He's been punished enough. He's said he's sorry.'

'Sorry isn't good enough. He's going to give his gun to the little boy.'

So I march him down to Barry Road and we find the door of the Indian family's flat and I bang on it until the father answers. He is rather taken aback as Charlie hands over the gun.

'For your little boy,' I explain. 'To say sorry.'

'Oh, no, no, really,' the father says, shaking his head. 'We cannot take the gun.'

So Charlie gets away with it.

But the funny thing is, he never dresses up in the cowboy outfit again. It hangs in his wardrobe next to his school uniform. And the gun disappears. I have no idea where.

2016

Bognor Regis

Mothers always tell a certain truth. It might not be the actual, actual truth, whatever that is, but it is their truth, handed down from their mothers, and their mothers before them. Years after Mum's gone, I still hear her talk to me. Not in a mad way, more of an echo, like a liturgy in a Papist church. *Don't put your shoes on the table. Turn off the light. Shut the door. Where did you last leave it? Life's not fair. You'll understand when you're older. You don't know where it's been. If you can't say something nice, don't say anything at all. You're the oldest, set a good example. Because I said so. Over my dead body.* (I'm not sure she ever saw the many ironies in that last one.)

Because I said so. I said so to Janet. I told her, didn't give her the choice. And now she's got cancer and Tom's gay and Charlie's God knows where, writing emails. Marg and Mum are gone, along with all the others. I haven't seen my dad since 1953, though it seems like yesterday he was drying up the dishes at the sink.

What would he reckon to all this?

From the nation and the Commonwealth in grateful remembrance.
Elizabeth R

1965

London

I'm on my hands and knees scrubbing sick off the kitchen floor when I hear that Mr Churchill has died. I cry. I weep and wail all on my own on the kitchen floor that's half done. This is my Kennedy moment. Not so long since the President was gunned down, but this, Sir Winston's passing, hits me in the guts like a cannonball on the battlefield. Winnie's been like my second dad and now he's gone and all. And I know I will have to go and pay my respects to him while he's lying in state at Westminster Hall, for the man he was to the country, for the man he was to me. And I know that I will take Charlie and Barbara.

But first things first. I do a display in the shop window of Sunshine & Sons. I find a photo frame for that old picture of him that used to be in my Bible, then on my bedroom wall, watching over my family every night of the war. And we only ever lost the windows of our home, blown out by that bomb that killed Janet's family, so he did his job.

I drape the window with black crepe, Dad's shop window that used to have sandbags all round it, and I festoon it with poppies. And next to Churchill's photograph, I lay a cigar, an old

218

one of Dad's that's been lingering in a drawer for far too long.

★ ★ ★

We wait in line for over three hours, the queue stretching down to the river, a tributary of hats running along the Embankment, and over Westminster Bridge, sometimes barely moving, sometimes shuffling forward a few feet. When we finally get inside the Great Hall, it's silent, hushed, and reverent. A mighty catafalque holds his coffin, which is covered with the Union Jack. On the coffin lays his insignia of the Knight of the Garter. It's a fitting tribute and I can only wonder at the funeral to come.

By the time we get out, it's so cold I can't feel my fingers or my face and we are so thankful for the Bovril given us by the WRVS in Victoria Gardens. When you most need a hot drink, there's a woman with a tea urn. Back in the war, when you were bombed out, there they'd be, those women, making cups of tea, finding clothes, putting straight the chaos. It's always the women who do the stuff that goes unnoticed, even in undertaking. So I change all that. When Dad's gone, I get myself a top hat and walk out front, carrying his cane. It's what I was born to. I wish I could do it for Mr Churchill.

★ ★ ★

We stroll back to the bus stop, the three of us, manage to squeeze on the 63. They're teenagers now because teenagers have been invented. Barbara fifteen, Charlie sixteen. And that sick I was scrubbing this morning was because he tried his first beer last night and woke up feeling like Death himself.

'I want to go to Ireland to meet my granddad,' he says, once we're on the bus. I don't know if it's the cavalier driving that makes me feel nauseous or the thick smoke or squashy throng of people, but I'm worried it's my turn to vomit.

'Mum?'

'You might not be welcome.'

'I know he disapproves of what Dad did, deserting — '

'Your father never deserted. He fought the Nazis.'

Charlie thinks about this for a moment before plunging right in with hateful words. 'Churchill was a warmonger.'

I look at him in disbelief, sitting there on the bus seat with the work trousers I made him wear, an unfathomable expression on his face.

'I beg your pardon, Charlie Sunshine?'

'Churchill committed war crimes.'

'How dare you say that. He was a great man. If it weren't for him, *Sir* Winston, we'd be talking German and eating sauerkraut right now.'

He knows how to wind me up, that boy, thinking he's a man when he's not. I don't speak to him for the rest of the journey. He sulks. Barbara dozes off. Sometimes I wonder if other mothers feel like this.

★ ★ ★

Three days later, I make my second pilgrimage, to see Sir Winston off. Barbara and Mum come with me, Charlie refusing. But I'm not thinking of Charlie today — I've left him with Mick, hoping he'll get to the bottom of this Irish fantasy.

We make our way to the riverbank in the Docklands and wait in the cold and mist, my daughter, my mother and I, wrapped up warm, with a flask of cocoa in case there are no WRVS. There is complete silence. I'm sure I can make out the muffled drum beating the march step across the river as they take him on a gun carriage to St Paul's, that sacred place he protected through all those bombs and fires because he knew how important it was to us Londoners, us Brits.

We're out in force today. Even the Queen goes to St Paul's, waiting on the steps for Winston to arrive, and she doesn't do funerals unless it's family. He was her first prime minister. He was up there on the balcony on VE day when there was an ocean of Union Jacks (or the Butcher's Apron as Charlie has taken to calling it). Today all the flags are at half mast and the crowds are in black armbands, sombre and tearful.

As Mr Churchill leaves the cathedral and is put onto the barge at Tower Pier, for his journey back down the leaden Thames to Waterloo, the pipers' lament curling through the eerie silence, the cold and the mist wrapping itself around us, I think I will burst with all the sadness my heart contains. But as he passes under Tower Bridge with its arms lifted, the mighty cranes of Hay's

221

Wharf dipping in salute, bowing down to him, as he floats past, the Union Jack over his coffin, the soldiers in uniform standing guard, in the bitter wind, as we listen to the nineteen-gun salute and watch the RAF fly-past, sixteen Lightnings, the roar in our ears blocking everything else out but the moment, then my tears fall and fall so I'm a right soggy mess and Barbara and Mum have to prop me up, one on each side, a hanky apiece.

Later, when we're back home, there's a letter — well, more of a note — from Charlie. Mick, who's making a corned beef hash, his signature dish, pretty much his only dish, hands it to me. He's got grease spots on it.

Dear Mum and Dad
I've decided to go to Ireland to stay with Granddad Delarey.
I want to explore my Irish heritage. With a surname like Delarey, what else could I do?
I'll write soon.
Charlie xx

I have to sit down at the table before I fall down. 'It was only a few days ago I was cleaning his sodding sick off the floor and now he's got himself on a ferry to Ireland?'

'Actually, no. Your sister organised a flight for him.'

Ruddy Marg. 'I didn't even know he had a passport.'

'He does. An Irish one.'

'An Irish one?'

'He's entitled.'

'Is he now, Mick? Is he now.'

'He'll be back, Betsy. There's no way the bastard will see him.'

But I know this is it, the moment I've been dreading ever since that sunny day on the Kent farm when I took him away from Janet.

I've lost him. And, what's worse, he was never even mine to lose.

★ ★ ★

But the bastard does see him. Charlie is the prodigal grandson that his unknown grandfather is only too happy to welcome into his damp two-up two-down, to show off down the pub. A pub known for its Republican views, where he's respected and revered for being a guerrilla fighter back in the 20s. Who shunned his own son for fighting the Nazis. And now he has his clutches into his grandson and I don't know if he will ever let him go.

2016

Bognor Regis

I've never eaten so much as I eat in here. Three meals a day, like school dinners, only less grisly, designed with dentures and gums in mind. Shepherd's Pie, meatballs, rice pudding, semolina, custard, jelly, ice cream. Sometimes you wonder if you've gone back to a second childhood, full circle, though we went without in the war. Always hungry. I'd have given all the money in my piggy bank for a bag of sweets. Now I'm swimming in biscuits. Biscuits for elevenses, biscuits for tea — not the best biscuits but bourbons and digestives and ginger nuts, what I always bought my family down the International so I'm not complaining, unlike Frank who likes his Fox's. I need to ask Barbara to shop for an elasticated skirt from Marks. She knows all about elasticated skirts.

When you look out the window of the lounge, you can see these huge trees, they're like the ones you get on those big estates — not the housing estates, the opposite of them, I mean those big country estates like you see in *Downton Abbey*. Cedar trees, oak trees, Scots pine, ash. Mick could name any tree, any piece of wood, he got his carpenter hands on. He'd like it here. I wish he was here. I get really cross sometimes when I think of him, knowing he's not ever coming back. We'll have no more corned beef hash (also good for dentures and gums). No more banter. No more sex. Because even when you're nearly ninety you still think about sex from time to time. Not so much the passion, that's more of a dim memory that sparks up every now and then, but the intimacy. Knowing someone else's body, that's not dead, that's alive and kicking, that loves you, that worships you and thinks you're beautiful, a body with warm skin, a beating heart, lungs that breathe air in and out, arms that wrap around you, knowing it's the only place you want to be. What do you do when that's gone? You miss it. You get angry. You get sad. You feel wretched and you dream of old times and maybe of times to come in the future in the next world, if there is one, whatever it is, you can only imagine.

I miss having a man. One that's not ga-ga. Or dead.

Good memories are our second chance at happiness.
Queen Elizabeth II

1969

Bognor Regis

Finally, we are going on holiday, a week at Butlins holiday camp in Bognor Regis. Me, Mick and Barbara, who's not long turned nineteen. She wanted to stay at home and help look after the business, but we've got it covered. Any major problems, Mick and I can get straight back up to London on the train. Mab's also here with her husband, Dick, and her three-year-old twins, Billy and Bonnie (I ask you). They're in the chalet next door to ours. Dick says it's like being back at Catterick where he did his military service. Mick agrees, says the place is like an internment camp with its low-lying buildings and barbed wire all around. It takes him back to army days, somewhere he doesn't really like to go, hates it from the first moment, but being a trooper does his best not to be grumpy. His Irish skin turns bright pink, then red, then flakes off like a snow shower, so he has to sit out of the sun, which isn't too difficult seeing as there's not much of it. Just as well he likes reading. He becomes pals with a cabinet maker from Prestonpans who is a staunch Jacobite. The Jacobite laughs at the Butlins Redcoats because where he comes from the Redcoats are quite another thing. Every time he sees one he shouts out 'Long Live the King' which confuses everyone, as we all know only too well that we have a queen. (*Vivat Regina!*)

Barbara, not usually a joiner-in — not like me with the Brownies, the WI and the Association — decides that seeing as she's here, she might as well enter into the spirit and hurls herself into the holiday with the force of her burgeoning weight. She chums up with a girl from Cirencester called Pam and they spend much of the daytime on the sunbathing lawns, even though there's a perfectly good beach a stone's throw away. They fully avail themselves of all the food on offer as if we've just come off the rations. They enter the contests and the competitions, but neither really come up trumps, so they become enthusiastic spectators, which I suppose could be a philosophy for life.

And then there's the two American girls, Martha and Darlene, who are spending the summer working in the coffee lounge before they head off around Europe by rail. They are anti-Vietnam and anti-men and once they've clocked off they wear the shortest miniskirts or else denim jeans, and make the most of the social life on offer. Barbara and Pam are mesmerised by these creatures, neither of whom wears a bra, as Mick points out to me and he doesn't usually notice such things as his head's always stuck in a book.

'Don't you even think about getting rid of your bra, Barbara,' he says that night in the refectory hall. 'Bognor won't know what's hit them.'

He's been on the pale ale.

As has Dick. 'Two atomic bombs,' he chips in. Mab has to elbow him in the ribs so that he almost chokes on his pint of Worthington's. She tells him to drink up and packs him off to the putting green with Bill and Ben as penance.

The next day, there is a near miss at the swimming pool when a little lad nearly drowns. He's scooped out of the water by the brawny lifeguard, who has to give him the kiss of life with all of us spectating enthusiastically, urging the little lad to splutter and breathe. But this is one show that Barbara and Pam miss. I look around for them to check they're all right, but there's no sign of them. Thinking they must've headed for an ice cream or a soda, I make my way to the chalet, hoping for some shut-eye. I feel a bit shocked by how events can take such a dramatic turn, and I should know all about that, how delicately life hangs in the balance.

I let myself in quietly, because I notice the curtains are closed. In the half-dark I see two figures on the far bed, side by side, heads together, and it's a moment before I realise that Barbara and Pam are actually kissing. I don't say a word, don't take a breath, let myself back out into the warm afternoon sunshine, feeling the earth shift yet some more.

Later, I sit by the pool with Mab. The twins are off with some older kids in the playground and our husbands are in the Pig and Whistle bar. We enjoy the peace and quiet for a moment, Mab reading an Agatha Christie, while I shut my eyes and lie back on the lounger, trying to work out what Barbara and Pam could possibly have been doing. Practising their kissing technique? Sharing bubblegum? Who knew?

Soon it's time for Miss Lovely Legs and all the young girls are lining up in their swimming costumes alongside the pool's edge and all the men are ogling them freely, their wives not in the slightest bit interested, taking the opportunity to read a magazine or suck on an ice lolly, knowing the kids are being taken care of.

Dick returns as if he has a sixth sense for lovely legs and says, 'What, no Barbara? She's got lovely legs.'

'More like thunder thighs,' says her father, holding up the rear, with a hat like a gypsy king and a paper tucked under his arm, and not for the first time that day I decide that my Mick is not so good on the booze when there's Dick and sunshine involved.

'There's more to a woman than a pair of legs,' I say and I'm perfectly aware I sound like one of the braless American girls.

'I agree,' says Dick. 'There's also a pair of — '

Mab elbows her husband in the ribs.

'I was going to say 'knobbly knees',' he protests.

★ ★ ★

Mick takes me for a spin around the ballroom. He knows how to dance. His sisters taught him before the war and he went to plenty of dances during it. He's nothing like spotty Malcolm or sweaty Bob Vickers Jnr. He's in command of me, leading me this way and that, through the waltz and the quickstep and the jive, pulling me along the wave of Bing Crosby and Glenn Miller and ol' Blue Eyes. I watch the couples spinning around us and smile when I wonder at what they would think if they knew what us Sunshines do when we're not having a really wonderful time at Butlins by the sea. And I forgive Mick his vulgar comments earlier and am thankful that Mab is the one married to dirty Dick.

★　★　★

The last day of the holiday is here. Barbara and Pam take a final trip round the boating lake. Pam is at the helm, while Barbara gazes adoringly at her so that I know that kiss was definitely a kiss.

On the train journey home, Barbara makes an announcement.

'I've got something to tell you,' she says.

My heart stops beating for a few seconds. It actually stops beating and I hold my breath so I'm all dizzy.

'I want to be a Redcoat,' she says.

After a while, I realise that everyone in our carriage is looking at me, while I cannot find a way to stop laughing, not just because of the incongruity of our Barbara entertaining the troops, not just because she's born to undertaking, but because sometimes you laugh when you're relieved about something and sometimes you laugh because otherwise you would cry.

★　★　★

Once back at home we are able to gather together as a family to watch the moon landings on our television (an updated version from the one on which we watched the Queen crowned). I feel Janet and Margie's absences keenly when I think of them both living and breathing on that ball floating in space which looks so small but is so vast, it's like I could just reach out and touch them, but nothing in life is ever that simple.

★   ★   ★

Moon landings aside, it's a busy year in terms of world events, but then isn't it always. Concorde, the Beatles, Woodstock, the Kray twins, Prince Charles, Yasser Arafat, Colonel Gaddafi. Homosexual riots. Student protests. Young people pushing, the establishment resisting. The world is changing. My world even more so, but I don't know that just yet.

For now, by September, Charlie is back briefly. It has taken him four years to escape his grandfather and now he has been through all the girls and pubs in that small Irish town in Donegal, he gets away. He goes travelling for a time, sees the world, then he joins the business on his twenty-first birthday. The Sunshine undertakers has a son again. Maybe it will all come good.

2016

Bognor Regis

Frank's taken a shine to me, dirty sod. He's got at least ten months on me and not a chance in hell. There's been no one but Mick all my life and I'm not going to change that for some randy old git, though he might have been all-right-looking once upon a time. He's easy-going, unlike some of them in here, grumpy so-and-so's. Nice enough to talk to. Sometimes he sings. A deep voice. Deep and full of the weight of years. Puts me in mind of Perry Como.

Maybe the old boy's all right. We have this joke. He says, 'Can I be Frank with you?' And I say, 'If I can be Betsy.' It's not all that funny really but it makes me giggle like a young girl. It's ages since I've giggled like a young girl. I don't think I even did it when I was actually a young girl. That was Margie's forte. She knew how to get a man. And she got plenty of them. Three husbands, I ask you. One's more than enough. Except when he goes and dies, leaving you all on your Jack Jones.

Today Frank sits next to me in the lounge. We listen to Vera Lynn, who's tottered in to see us again with her keyboard. She finishes off with a rendition of 'Jerusalem'. Maybe she was a member of the WI. Maybe she still is. There's no age limit.

You always have to delve deeper, that much I know as an undertaker. Like with the song 'Jerusalem'. It's not all about xenophobic English rugby fans. It's actually a rebel song, sung by the suffragettes and taken on by the WI, some of whom had been suffragettes themselves, even been on hunger strike and all the rest of it. It's not just jam. Dig deep and you never know what you might find. Dig for Victory as our Winnie would've told us. So we did. We dug. Only sometimes you have to cover it up again. Backfill the hole with soil. Grass it over. Stick a headstone on it. And an epigraph. *I told you I was ill.*

Maybe Frank's all right. He fought in the war, emptied the German tanks when Berlin fell, made sure them Nazis were dead. Said he snuck a Swastika flag back home and burnt it on a bonfire in his back garden at Cheam along with the weeds that had took over in his absence, watched the smoke curl up into the sky and disappear. I didn't tell him at that point that I was an undertaker, that I'd watched many a corpse go up in smoke — the connection of crematoria seemed insensitive in the light of what we found out after the war. All those poor people massacred.

But he knows now. He asks me to help plan his funeral.

'Is there something you want to tell me, Frank?'

'I'm afraid of dying alone.'

234

'We're all afraid of that, Frank. But you're never alone, not with your memories. Do you have good memories?'

'I do, Betsy. The best.'

'Then tell me about them.'

'I can't remember half of them.'

'Then tell me the half that you can.'

Work is the rent you pay for the room you occupy on earth.
Queen Elizabeth II

1974

London

The 1970s are not all Angel Delight and Morecambe and Wise. There's all sorts of drama and crises that pave the way for that Thatcher woman. The three-day week. The Winter of Discontent. Rubbish on the streets. Inflation. Power cuts. On the news, there's footage of gravediggers on strike up north, pictures of coffins that have to be stored in a warehouse, like the metal trays laid out in the public baths after the V-2, that smell Mum could never get rid of from Dad's suit. Then there's the Black and White Minstrels on the box. Kiddie-fiddlers on the loose. And bombs. Because, oh yes, the bombs are back again. Letter bombs. Car bombs. Boat bombs. Not the Nazis this time, but bombs are bombs whoever's setting them off. As if we never learn.

Today's an average day. I'm back from work, at the kitchen sink, hands plunged in dishwater, spuds bobbing on the hob, veg peeled, three chops ready and waiting under the grill. The radio's on. The pips. Six o'clock. The headlines send electric currents from my soapy, sudsy fingers right down to the chunky soles of my platforms. (I've finally got heels I can walk in.)

There's been another bomb. I don't envy the

237

funeral directors picking up the pieces, pun intended. Some people you can't do much about, not if bits are missing or mixed up. And these terrorist bombs, well, they might not be V-2s but they don't half cause some damage. Thirty years on and it still surprises me it's not the Luftwaffe up to its old tricks. The IRA have had a busy year.

Mick comes in, dusty work clothes, pencil behind his ear, whistling till he catches the look on my face. 'What's up, Betsy?'

'Another bomb.'

He shakes his head, moves behind me, wraps his muscly arms around my waist, my hands still in the water, going cold now, so I'm not altogether sure how long they've been submerged. The spuds are boiling over, the lid of the pan rattling. I have to pull away from Mick to get the tea finished before it's ruined.

'Where's Charlie?'

'Finishing up. He'll be here soon.'

Charlie's still working, alongside Barbara, for the business. He does the embalming, the behind-the-scenes stuff. He also drives the hearse, can squeeze a limousine past juggernauts and market stalls and badly parked BMWs, whatever obstacles lie in his path. He has the stomach for it. The nerves.

Barbara's in the office mainly, front of house. She has a badge that says her name and official title 'Office Manager', though since falling pregnant with Tina by an unknown father she's not so good at managing the office, mainly because she has to bring Tina along with her and five-year-olds are not particularly office-friendly. I give Tina the remnants of the grave clothes for her dollies, like Mum did for Marg and I. Except Tina has no one to quarrel with and I don't actually know if that's a good or a bad thing. Not that she's particularly interested in dollies. She'd sooner look through the funeral catalogues. A Sunshine through and through.

Barbara's got her own place, a council flat up on Dawson's Heights, so she's managing, with a little help from us, but I don't think it's right, all these single parents. It was different in the war. Being a widow's different to being divorced or, like Barbara, an unmarried mother. How she managed to get a baby with no boyfriend is a mystery she doesn't want to explain to us and who am I to question the mysteries of babies. And Mum never says a ruddy thing, which seems unfair when she'd never have forgiven Marg or me for the same sin. *Always a worry having girls.*

As for Charlie, well, after his four-year stint in Donegal, he came home and here he still lives. And here he is now, Charlie, all of a sudden, creeping about in that way of his, washing his hands in the sink, scrubbing and scrubbing with a nailbrush, which makes me think of Lady Macbeth which we did at school, I don't know why. *Out, damn'd spot.*

I plate up the dinner and the three of us sit around the table. Charlie finishes first, quick for once, puts his knife and fork down on the plate like we taught him. 'I've got to go out,' he says.

'I've made crumble.'

'Save some, Mum. I've got people to see.'

'People?'

'Nothing important. Snooker.'

And he's out the door before I realise he hasn't got his snooker cue with him.

Blood will have blood.

I have to drink a hot toddy to stop these chilling feelings. I don't know why I get them. The change, maybe, which I hear is as bad as when you start your monthlies. I wonder if Marg has beaten me to the menopause? She's ruddy well welcome to it if she has.

★ ★ ★

A few days later, Barbara's round with little Tina. They've come for dinner, which is steaming away in the pressure cooker. Not only have I got a pressure cooker, I also have a twin tub, a chest freezer and a dishwasher. All mod cons, but not much good in a power cut, which we keep having.

The power's back on now and we can see the mess Tina has made of the newly fitted carpet. She's been playing with candle wax and so I have to get out the brown paper and iron, one of Mum's tricks. But she's my grand-kiddie, so I don't mind what I do for her. There's this extra bit, I don't know what you call it, between you and your grandchildren that makes you forgive them anything. I leave her with her mother watching *Blue Peter*, the poor girl with no dad so that John Noakes and Peter Purvis and my Mick are her father figures.

Mick's laying the table while I dish up and I'm about to call Barbara and Tina in, when there's this almighty banging on the front door. Mick shouts something, as he hurries down the hallway to see what the commotion is all about, some bogtrotter swear word from his DNA that can still filter its way through when he's annoyed. It involves fecks and Mary-Mother-of-Gods and the next thing I hear is the door being flung back so hard it bangs against the wall and I know there'll be a hole in the plaster because that door has been slammed a number of times — Margie and Charlie being the main culprits with their teenage shenanigans.

It's some bloke, I reckon he's drunk, or he might just be Irish — they're everywhere. Long hair and a wispy beard so you can hardly tell how old he is, he could be Neanderthal, but I think he's young, like Charlie, mid-twenties.

'Where is he? Where's Charlie?' The hairy man is shouting.

'You'd better calm yourself down,' Mick says, all masterly, 'and then we'll talk.'

'Tell me where the feck he is.'

He notices Tina then, my little grand-kiddie, wide-eyed and solemn, standing next to her mother in the doorway of the front room, Barbara holding her daughter close, an aura of lioness about her, and me and Mick standing in the hall, this wild-haired lunatic giving us the heebie-jeebies with his effing and blinding.

'Charlie's on a removal,' I say, firmly as possible, far firmer than I feel inside, which is all wibbly-wobbly like one of Mum's blancmanges.

241

You need to stay calm and poised, I tell myself. Like the Queen. After all, you've handled far worse. Grieving relatives. Corpses too. The Blitz. The bombs.

Nothing's as bad as the bombs. The memory of them makes me feel peculiar, plus the thought of Mum's blancmange, which was never my favourite, it has to be said, sorry, Mum, and thank God she's out at the bingo, her latest hobby, despite her thoughts on it being common.

'What?' He's confused, as though maybe he's turned up at the wrong house, cornered the wrong family in their hallway.

'He's gone to collect a body.'

'A body?'

'He's an undertaker. We all are.'

He looks at Tina. Tina stands up as tall as a five-year-old can.

'And how long will he be?' He's taken a step back, like we'll be burying him if he's not careful. The power has shifted and I'm back at school, me and Joanie Clark in the playground with her posse of snotty-nosed ragamuffins.

'As long as it takes,' I tell him. 'You can't rush Death.'

He stares at us all. Then he turns and bounds out the front door into the street and we're left with each other, lurking in the shadows, wondering what all that was about.

Then the power goes again and darkness wraps around us.

'Shall I fetch the matches?' Tina asks.

★   ★   ★

242

After dinner, we sit in the front room, Barbara and me. We should be drinking our cuppa and watching *Nationwide*. Richard Stilgoe should be singing a song about statutory rights or something. Instead we drink gin and tonic and eat Twiglets, while Mick and the pyromaniac Tina have a game of Frustration by candlelight at the kitchen table.

'I'm worried about Charlie,' Barbara says, in between mouthfuls of yeast extract.

'You're not the only one,' I say.

'Who do you think that man was?'

'I hate to think.'

'Do you reckon Charlie owes him money?'

'Maybe not money, but probably something.'

She crunches away on another stack of Twiglets, and gulps back the rest of her gin, before starting on the lemon pulp, tearing it from the rind with her teeth like she hasn't eaten in weeks when it's only been ten ruddy seconds. 'He's distracted,' she says. 'I mean, he does his job fine and that.' She pauses, the cogs turning. 'It's his manner. He's all distant. I can't reach him like I used to.' She sighs, one of them big ones like an old dog that's tired and resigned. 'We're not close anymore.'

'Have you spoken to him?'

'I've tried, but you know what Charlie's like, never shows his hand. All he says is he's got a lot on. But he keeps sneaking off. A snooker match or a meeting.'

'What sort of a meeting?'

'I'm not actually sure. He's vague whenever I ask.'

I must admit I can be vague when I'm around Barbara. She doesn't half go on and I find my mind wandering to my shopping list. 'Do you think he's seeing a girl?'

'He's always seeing a girl.'

'Maybe this one's married.'

'Maybe.'

'Maybe it's a bloke.'

'Mum. Really? Charlie? He's hardly Danny La Rue.'

'It happens.'

'He's your son. Do you really think Charlie's a homosexual?'

'It's unlikely.' I can't have two of them batting for the other side, which I know is what Barbara's been doing for years, but it's private, up to her, none of my beeswax, but then again Charlie has different genes entirely. 'Maybe he's a ruddy Mason.'

'No. He'd never do that.'

'I'd sooner he was a homosexual than a Mason.'

'Me too, Mum, but there's something, I'm telling you.'

Then the power comes back on and Sue Lawley is saying goodnight to us and it's not so easy to confide in Barbara when she's sitting in those ridiculous flares with her over-tight Led Zeppelin T-shirt and awful Princess Anne hair. Besides, Tina is here now, jumping up and down because she's beaten her granddad and I notice a stream of candle wax all the way down her cheesecloth blouse.

★   ★   ★

So I have a word with Charlie, catch him in the kitchen later that night after closing time, stinking of beer and fish and chips, not the best of times, so it's no surprise it don't go too well.

'Stop worrying,' he snaps. 'Tell Barbara to poke her nose somewhere else.'

I could tell Barbara that, but I don't. There's no point. Barbara has a nose like me. Like my mother. We sniff things out. If something is wrong, we will sniff and sniff, dig and dig until we uncover what it is. And something is wrong. I know it in my bones.

★   ★   ★

It's been a rammed-up week at work. A run of 'flu. A traffic accident. A cancer victim.

Mick and his apprentice have been full on making coffins. I've been organising the funerals and also the draper. I'm still no good with a needle and thread and our old seamstress went off with a man twenty years younger, so I need to check on this new one's work, make sure all's well for Mrs Watkins who's ready for her funeral tomorrow. The coffin's done — oak, brass handles, the works. It was supposed to be a closed coffin, but I have a feeling one of the bereaved daughters will change her mind. I reckon she'll ask for a viewing, only her mother hasn't been embalmed so I need to check on her condition.

When I do, it's not what I'm expecting. Inside the coffin, she looks fine, Mrs Watkins, like she's

245

having forty winks. The draper's done a good job, as have I. It's just that, well, there's a gun tucked into the gown. Now that I really wasn't expecting.

★   ★   ★

I know straight away this is Charlie's doing. It won't be down to anyone else and somehow it makes sense, though it shouldn't. That hairy Irishman that barged his way into my home didn't have an accent like Mick's. It was harsher. Belfast, Mick said. What the hell did a long-haired lout from Belfast want with Charlie? He must have been something to do with the gun. It can't be Charlie's. Charlie must be hiding it for someone. The Belfast man?

I don't get much chance to act on this thought. Charlie and the Belfast man. But I know what it's called. Gunrunning. I've read about it in the papers, heard it on the radio, seen it on the news and none of it adds up to any good. That name, those three capital letters, buzzes around and around my brain like an angry wasp drunk on plums, all through the rest of the afternoon, while I'm pacing up and down the yard, sitting in the chapel of rest, praying that the Watkins daughter won't request a viewing, overseeing her mother put in the chiller to make it less likely.

But I must think about it.

A gun. In a coffin.

Who but Charlie would put it there?

And what do I do about it? Tell Mick? Phone

the police? Chuck it in the Thames?

I can't tell Mick right now because he's out on a removal. I can't phone the police until I know more. And I can't chuck it in the rotten Thames because things have a nasty habit of bubbling back up to the surface. There's not a place you can hide in this world. Or the next.

There's only one thing for it. I need to have it out with Charlie. Only I've just realised I haven't a clue where he is.

'Where's your brother, Barbara?'

She's at the desk, filling in a big ledger, slow and methodical, but one look at me and she knows I mean business. Tina's sitting under the desk, perusing the catalogues, felt-tip pen at the ready for goodness knows what.

'Out the back, Mum.'

'I've been out the back all the afternoon and I haven't seen hide nor hair of him.'

'He said he was going to the stables to fix something or other, I can't remember what.'

'And find that child something more appropriate to do.'

We look at Tina sprawled on the floor in her school uniform, putting moustaches on the undertaker models so they look like mini Hitlers, even the women.

★ ★ ★

He's in the stables, what was once the stables back when he was a little boy but hasn't seen a horse in a long time. He misses them, those solid, dependable creatures. I miss them too and

247

hope one day we can get some more, but there's no money for lavish funerals. Unless you're a big-time criminal.

It's a storeroom now. Coffins, tools, timber. Charlie's sitting on an old chair in the corner, head in his hands. He jumps when I come in, a shot of fear flashing across his pale face, a shadow blocking out the light. He's on his feet now, those feet that used to be so tiny, this little piggy . . . and I haven't realised quite how tall he is or how menacing his eyes are and how I wish Mick was his real dad, his blood dad, but he's not and that's why Charlie has done such a bad thing because I lied, I lied, I lied.

'Don't look at me like that, Mum.'

'I should phone the police.'

'You should. But you won't.'

He's right. I won't. I can't.

He walks up to me, stares down at me, stares long and hard like he don't know who I am, and I want to tell him everything, the whole dirty secret of registrars and birth certificates and foreign ambassadors, but I can't.

I won't.

He raises his hand and I duck, I can't help it, it's a reflex, I'm all on edge, wound up like Tina's clockwork ruddy Noddy. Then I see his face, the disappointment, when I'm the one who should be feeling that.

'I'm not going to hit you, Mum. How can you think that?'

'I don't know what I think, Charlie. Tell me what to think because I don't know.'

'You don't need to worry. It's just this once.

248

Then I'm even and I won't owe anything.'

'Who do you owe?'

'I'm not telling you. You don't need to know. It's nearly over.'

'Did you kill someone?'

'No, nothing like that. I'm just taking care of it.'

'Who for?'

'Some bloke. I have to pass it on.'

'But it's a gun. There's only one reason you need a gun.'

'For a war.'

'War? What the hell are you talking about? War? Are you gunrunning?'

'No, just the one.'

I have to turn away. I am ashamed of him. A gun. A war. What next? Bombs?

'Did you touch it?' he says, urgent, like it's just occurred to him.

'No, I've never touched a gun in my life and I don't intend to start now.'

'You won't have to,' he says. 'I'm sorting it today.'

'You are not giving that gun to anyone. That gun is going nowhere.'

'Mum, they'll kneecap me if I don't.'

'Kneecap? How did you get yourself into such a mess, Charlie?'

He slumps back into his chair, shrunken and hollow-eyed, and I catch a glimpse of Janet lying in that sanatorium all those months. Shut my eyes and breathe.

'What will they do if it's six feet under?' I ask him.

'Wait . . . what?' he says and I watch the cogs turn. 'You can't mean that?'

'Oh yes I ruddy well can. Who'll think to look there?' And I sit myself down next to him and I hold his hand in mine and I look at him straight. 'This is what we're going to do,' I tell him calmly. 'If it comes to it, we will let Miss Watkins see her mum. Then we're going to nail down that coffin and make sure that gun is buried six feet under. Then it'll be safe and won't hurt anyone.'

'But they'll still be after me.'

'Tell them you think you're being followed and that this is the best way.'

He's quiet a moment and I know he's listening to my every word and I've got him on the back foot so I am going to tell him some more. 'And you had better promise me you will give up this Irish nonsense. I mean, you're not even Irish.'

'My father's Irish. I have an Irish passport.'

Before I get a chance to explain myself, and I really am about to explain myself, things take a different course. My hastily made plans fail. There's a God Almighty crash and men shouting and what sounds like little Tina screaming and I wonder if this is it, Charlie's about to get his kneecapping. I tell him to stay put and I'm heading across the yard when four of them burst out the back door of the premises, truncheons raised, rushing towards me, shoving past me, their dark uniforms, their deep booming voices, barging into the old stables. I watch them throw my Charlie onto the floor. I watch the truncheons flail, the thud of wood on bone and I can do nothing to stop them. I have to listen to his screams, listen to their curses, and I know they believe him to be IRA scum and that he doesn't stand a cat in hell's chance. Then they bundle him out, take him away and all that's left are the sirens, a Black Maria and the aftermath.

★ ★ ★

Poor Mrs Watkins. And her poor daughter, coming in to view her mum and being told it's not a good idea, not a good time, not with all the fracas, the uniforms, and the shouting, and little Tina crying, Mrs Watkins, lying peacefully out the back in the chiller, oblivious to the rumpus going on, unless she's watching down on us from above, who knows, I certainly don't. It takes me ages to calm the poor woman down, and by the time that's done, Charlie has been taken away to the police station.

I have to make a quick decision. I look after Miss Watkins, plenty of sweet tea and a ginger snap. Then I ask her if she wants to see her mother, holding my breath, feeling sick that she'll say yes. And she does. She says yes. So I ask for a bit of time while I get her ready. I get Mick to help me, back from the timber merchants so I have to quickly tell him the score. We move the coffin into the chapel of rest. I cover her with an extra gown so it's hidden. The gun.

It's fine. She sits with her mother, a few minutes is all she wants. She's clasping a prayer book, her eyes shut, her lips moving silently so I know she is praying, which is what I'm doing, though I'm not sure if God will listen to me. I worry, worry, every second that she'll find out. But she doesn't. She doesn't touch her mother. She just lays the prayer book gently beside her, and once I've seen her out, me and Mick get to work.

He doesn't say a word. He sets his lips in a straight line. He picks up the gun with a cloth and wipes it clean, puts it back by Mrs Watkins, tucked into the garments. Nails down the coffin.

The next day, the evidence gets buried along with Mrs Watkins and her prayer book. Six feet under the clay soil of south London, far away from Donegal and Belfast and the soft Irish rain.

I should never have let it get this far, but I thought it would be all right. Safe and away from a gunman's trigger finger, but I didn't know this had only just begun.

★   ★   ★

It's a bad year for the bombs. Houses of Parliament, Tower of London, Guildford, Birmingham. Everyone's suspicious of the Irish. Even my Mick gets funny looks when he opens his gob in a place where he isn't known. My Mick who'd never hurt a fly. Mick's dad was a different kettle, a guerrilla fighter back in the 20s, told all his anecdotes to Charlie. No doubt embellished them. Fired Charlie up. Charlie had a good job with good prospects, but it wasn't enough. He wanted glory. He wanted to belong to a tribe other than us Sunshines.

But his tribe grasses him up. The Belfast man

is arrested and dobs Charlie in.

His life is turned upside down. All of our lives are turned upside down, inside out, back to front. He might just as well have planted a bomb in my heart and detonated it.

2016

Bognor Regis

These days everyone's suspicious of Muslims. I've done them too. They wash their own, cover them in a shroud, which was never enough for my dad, not even for paupers, not even during wartime shortages, but you respect their wishes. You respect their ways. We've all got them after all. We've all got a beating heart that will give up on us one day.

They used to say you'd been 'brainwashed'. Or 'caught up with the wrong crowd'. 'Led astray'. Now it's called 'radicalisation'. That's what it was when you think about it. Charlie was radicalised by his grandfather. The four years he spent with that bastard in Donegal, at a time when he was in teenage turmoil, trying to work out who he was, he became a plastic Paddy. I probably should have told Charlie then. Told him he didn't have a drop of Irish blood in him. That he was 100 per cent English. Instead, he got involved in an IRA cell. He claims he never hurt anyone. Not directly. But he did hide a gun in a coffin. No fingerprints, but evidence enough — not that the police were all that particular with evidence. If you were a bogtrotter, you were guilty. And Charlie weren't even a proper one.

But he was guilty. As was I.

We can all see things which we would wish had been done differently or not at all.
Queen Elizabeth II

1975

London

It is a year before I see him. I get a visiting order and, after much debating with myself and arguing with Mick, I go. Mick has been before. He visited him on remand, went to the trial every day at the Old Bailey. It was serious stuff, we both lost hope. At times, I thought I was losing my mind as well, so much so that I couldn't even go to the sentencing. Four years at her Majesty's pleasure. And a fat lot of good he is there, picking up a load of bad habits, as if he doesn't have enough already.

Mick has visited him in Parkhurst and Wormwood Scrubs, he goes whenever he can, whenever the visiting orders haven't been messed with, which happens a lot, because the system has got it in for the IRA inmates of her Majesty's Prisons who demand, in various ways, to be treated as political prisoners. They want to wear their own clothes, they want to be transferred back home (even though Charlie's home is right here in London). They want the right to education rather than penal labour. They want an end to solitary confinement. Reasonable demands if you believe your actions are political. Unreasonable if you believe they have committed murder.

I can handle dead bodies. I can deal with Death. But I can't face visiting my son in prison when he needs me. The reason I finally go is because Charlie's in the prison hospital. He's got a nasty chest infection and something within me stirs, Janet and her sanatorium, like mother, like son, because by now I know that I will never escape Janet's shadow.

I had a letter from Janet after Charlie got sent down. She was in Ecuador at the time. She said how sorry she was to hear of our troubles — an ironic word to choose — and I searched for the meaning between the lines, the accusations and blame, but I couldn't find any. Dear, sweet Janet who still has no children of her own, and is never going to now, not at forty-nine years of age.

I suppose it's her, Janet, nagging the edge of my consciousness, that makes me go. It's not that I've never been in a prison. I've visited Brixton and Wandsworth on removals a few times, accompanying one of the boys. I know what to expect and that's exactly why I don't want to see Charlie in such a place. The 'penal dustbin' someone called the Scrubs, and they're right enough. It's all Dickensian crumbling brickwork, rats, and overcrowding.

Plus, of course, I am still angry. Angry at what he did, the crime he committed. But now I can feel the guilt creep in and settle. The thought of hunger strikes is ever-present. Gerry Kelly who survived sixty days and forced feeding. And Michael Gaughan who died. Now that was a funeral, last year, 3,000 people in Kilburn, before he was taken home to Ballina. The Irish know how to do a funeral, according to Mick. And maybe I should persuade Mum to do the Catholic funerals, but not now. Maybe one day, but not now.

It's not that I don't have sympathy for the prisoners; the stories of mistreatment are horrific, though we don't hear about it from Charlie as his letters are censored, though Mick knows people who know about these things, and while I try not to probe too much, I also want to know the worst, like those rubberneckers who drive slowly by the scene of a car crash. I live in fear that Charlie will want to make a stand, but so far he has kept his head down. But you never know with Charlie. You just never know. And now he's in hospital with pneumonia which you can die from.

★   ★   ★

I get a lift off Barbara. She's been before, from time to time. She's a good sister, has forgiven Charlie his involvement with the gun, the outburst of the Belfast man into our home. She says he was caught up in something bigger than himself, but I can't come to terms with that. There's always a choice, a decision to make. You can always say no. But now I've said yes. Yes, I'll come and visit you, Charlie. Yes.

★   ★   ★

'Hello, Mum,' he says and I hold on tight to that word, Mum. I'm his mum, me. I have to step up.

'Hello, Charlie. It's good to see you.'

He smiles and I think it's genuine, not covering something else, but who knows.

It is a relief to see him, to remember the shape of his head, the fine hairs on the back of his hands, lying by his sides on the hospital blanket, which is scratchy and not at all comfortable for someone who could be dying. He doesn't look good at all, pale, gaunt, stubbly, ever so still, his fingers stained yellow, his teeth too, so much older than he is.

I'm allowed to sit by his bed, a guard standing close by. I want to tell the guard I'm respectable, Charlie comes from a respectable family, but how can he respect us after what Charlie's done. All respect, all dignity, got flushed away when they dug up poor Mrs Watkins, the police, the vicar, all these officials working under cover of night, like grave robbing, like them body snatchers. It used to go on all the time, selling bodies to hospitals so that surgeons could learn their trade. Doctors, vicars, undertakers, we go hand in hand. But us Sunshines weren't allowed to be involved with Mrs Watkins; they needed someone neutral. That duty went to Bob Vickers Jnr, and didn't he just love that, especially once they found the gun, which had no fingerprints as evidence.

Oh, the shame and horror of an exhumation. It's a desecration, rolling up the blanket of death to see what lies beneath. Death hiding a loaded gun, the sick bastard.

Hard to turn the business round after this, Vickers waiting to steal our loyal families away.

But I'm not called Betsy Sunshine for nothing. Six generations and counting.

★ ★ ★

Next time I visit, Charlie's out of hospital. He's on the mend. I wish he wouldn't smoke because that's hardly a help, but he says he has to, he's read all the books and gets bored. It spaces out his day. He's sitting across the table from me like we're having a game of Snap or Beat Your Neighbour. It smells of men. Body odour, testosterone, dirty feet. He notices my reactions, which normally I can hide, part of the job.

'You should've put your Vicks on, Mum.'

'I should, yes.'

He bites his fingernail, rips it off and flicks it across the floor. He used to do that as a boy. I painted that stuff on his nails, to stop him, but it didn't put him off. Maybe it damaged his brain? Maybe something went wrong at birth? Maybe there's something in Janet's family we know nothing about?

'Do you like your job, Mum?'

'Pardon?'

'Do you like undertaking?'

'It's all I know. I was born to it.'

'But I don't feel like that, Mum. I don't know what I was born to.'

This is where I could tell him he was born to an unmarried mother but that me and Mick saved him from all that. We saved Janet too. But I can't bring myself to tell him right now because it's not the time or the place. When he comes

260

out, then maybe I will, but only if I think it's right. Sometimes it's best not to rock the boat. You do what you have to do.

2016

Bognor Regis

Some people might call Sunnydale a prison. No chance of escape from here because our legs don't work, and the staff would've got on well at Colditz. We are told what to eat. When to eat. When to get up. When to go to bed. We're the generation that obeyed. If Winnie said 'jump', you'd say 'how high, sir?'. And you'd try your damnedest. You'd try to jump even higher. The next generation pushed against all that. They wanted change, as if change were a good thing.

I don't know where I went wrong with Charlie, except maybe I shouldn't have done what I did. Janet might've done a better job at motherhood, but I genuinely doubted it when I made that decision. I thought I'd be doing her funeral by the time she turned fifty, what with those feeble lungs of hers, but you know what they say about a creaky gate. So maybe I was wrong. Maybe it was the biggest mistake of my life. Charlie's too.

Charlie was on parole by the time the IRA blew up Mountbatten's boat off the coast of County Sligo, a few months after Margaret Thatcher became Prime Minister. Around this time, there was a rooftop protest by the IRA inmates at the Scrubs. Over visiting rights. (Oh, the irony.) I was so glad Charlie wasn't still in there because these things never end well.

So many years have passed since then. I can't blame him for not coming to visit me here, can I?

My own family often gather round to watch television as they are this moment, and that is how I imagine you now.
Queen Elizabeth II

1979

London

I'm with Mick when we see her. She's getting out of a limousine, arm stretched up straight above her coiffured hair, waving slightly madly as if she's trying to get our attention, a hint of a Hitler salute, standing on the doorstep surrounded by police, her husband lurking behind, a spare part. She's dressed in her trademark blue suit, her handbag seems to be missing, maybe she's left it in the car or it's been stolen with all her speeches and sledgehammers that she'll use to dismantle this country I love over the next decade, all the while trying to sound like my queen:

I'll strive unceasingly to try to fulfil the trust and confidence that the British people have placed in me and the things in which I believe.

There are cheers and there are boos like she's treading the boards in a panto at the Hackney Empire as she quotes from St Francis of Assisi, though as it turns out it's not really his words at all, *where there is discord may we bring harmony . . . where there is despair may we bring hope,* using the Royal 'we' when she's got no right. When she's no Churchill. When I never voted for her even though you might think I'd admire the Iron Lady for being tough as old boots, but no.

265

And at the mention of her dead mate Airey Neave, another IRA bomb victim, my heart plummets to my shoes because I know that the time ahead will be filled with trouble and it'll be no good for my son.

Mick knows it too. He gets up and turns off the box. 'I'll make us a cup of tea,' he says. 'She can't take that away from us.' And he gives me a kiss and I don't know what I'd do without him.

★   ★   ★

Charlie's recently out of prison. He's back at work, embalming and such. He's thinner, still a bit wheezy, so I worry about the sawdust, but at least I know he's safe, hidden away from customers' eyes. Life is returning to a kind of normal. For a while.

But just as I thought, just as I predicted, just as I feared, Charlie gets into trouble again. He's playing snooker down the pub one evening, somewhere in Peckham. He beats this young bloke who won't pay up, so Charlie threatens to thump him one and this lad says go on then, Irish scum, which neither of them can see the irony of. The landlord has to step in and calm the situation and it might have all blown over, except that the young man is the son of Bob Vickers Jnr. And of course Bob Vickers Jnr doesn't like us Sunshines. And Charlie's on parole.

So I do what any mother would do. I deal with it, discreetly. I'm not a ruddy Mason, like Bob Vickers Jnr, but I know how things work in this man's world. I know all will be fine if Charlie humbles himself and apologises. But Charlie has never apologised for anything. So I pay for a new snooker cue for the Vickers boy, seeing as Charlie snapped his in half. I give him a little extra so he can afford to join the snooker hall. And then I go cap in hand to Bob Vickers' office.

I've never been in here, not since it opened when they took over from the Cannings. I used to come in with Mum to get our groceries with our ration books. And then we had to start shopping elsewhere, only that wasn't so easy as you had to register with a particular place.

The cans, the bags of sugar and sweets, the rice and the flour, they've all gone. The front of house isn't so different to ours now, though instead of Dad's big old banker's desk, there's this functional, utility thing that lacks gravitas. And on the wall hang these portraits, not good likenesses, three generations of Vickers, which is over the top, if you ask me, and amateurish. Nothing like our six and we don't need portraits to prove it because we are legendary in these parts. Legendary.

'Betsy Sunshine as I live and breathe,' he says.

I have to bite my lip, accept a seat and a cup of tea before I am able to ask what I have to ask. He says an apology is all he wants off Charlie. But I know he's hoping for something else if that isn't forthcoming.

When I get home, I talk to Charlie. I tell him I've been to see Vickers. I tell him it'll all be squared if he apologises. But nothing's that simple with Charlie.

'I'm not apologising to no one,' he says.

I let him storm up to his room, like the sulky teenager he still seems to be. I've no doubt he was damaged in that ruddy prison. I'll have to work on him gently, make him see he has to do this or he'll be back inside before he knows it. Unless I give Bob Vickers what he's wanted ever since that dance where Marg stole Malcolm the spotty medical student off of me.

Charlie refuses to come down for dinner that night. I leave his food on a tray outside his room. Shepherd's pie and peas. In the morning, the tray is still there. But the plate is empty. As is his bed. But that doesn't let me off the hook with Vickers.

★   ★   ★

I know Charlie is alive because we get these messages passed on by various friends. Why he can't write or phone himself more often is anybody's guess, but nobody's business except mine and Charlie's. And Mick's.

Mick misses him more than I do. I know he blames me for Charlie going, same as it was all down to me that he ever came to us in the first place, wrapped up in his Suttons Seeds shawl. But Mick never grumbles, never says. But every once in a while, something on the news, a piece of music, a memory, and I catch a look cross his face and see those green Irish eyes of his darken to black.

Charlie's been gone a couple of years when Bobby Sands dies. May 1981. Whatever crimes he'd committed, that man was treated worse than you'd dream of treating a dog. I don't know what I would've done if that had been my Charlie.

This is round the time I get ill myself, and I never get ill. I end up in St Thomas' one night after Mick finds me on the bathroom floor, bleeding like all my monthlies in one go when I'm long past the change. It turns out I have a mammoth fibroid and that I'm not dying, though that's what Mick thinks I'm doing.

They patch me up, send me home, and a few weeks later I'm booked in for a hysterectomy. I've never spent much time in hospital personally. I usually pop in the back door to remove the dead, sometimes in the front to visit a friend with some flowers and grapes. And now here I am, lying in pain, on a ward full of women, unable to go to the loo or do much other than sleep.

Morphine is quite a thing. It might take the edge off that pain, and there's a good deal of pain when you've had all your womb and ovaries and tubes taken out of you, but it can leave you to deal with vivid dreams. I'm not one to go on about dreams because dreams don't mean anything to anyone else, they usually don't even mean anything to the dreamer. I've heard the bereaved tell me that their loved ones come to visit them in the days running up to the funeral. They reckon the dead aren't ready to go just yet, they want to watch over their loved ones a while longer, and then when it's time to say goodbye, they leave, who knows where they go but they

269

must go somewhere, else they go nowhere. But this dream of mine, it's like nothing I've ever had in all my life because I don't know if it's a dream or if it's real. I don't know if I am awake or asleep or somewhere in between.

There's someone sitting on my bed. I can feel the shape of them next to my leg, but I can't move my leg or open my eyes or reach out to feel. It's just this presence pressing against me. A smell from a long time ago, one I've forgotten all about, and it's like I've stepped into this room with familiar furniture and curtains, but it's not at all how it should be. And this person, sitting beside me, it's a bloke, but it could be a boy, and he's saying something in this quiet voice, too quiet for me to make out the words and I can't tell him to speak up because I can't speak myself, it's like I'm paralysed, trapped in my body with no movement or sound.

I know who it is. But it could be a dream.

★　★　★

When I'm back home, recuperating, it's hard having nothing to do. I'm not a great one for reading and watching television so I spend more time than I should on my thoughts. And whatever it is I think about, Charlie keeps pushing his way to the fore. Charlie raising his hand and me ducking. Charlie in the dock at the Old Bailey. Charlie lying in that hospital bed with the scratchy blanket. Where did my little boy go? The little chap who used to follow his granddad around, copying him, adoring him,

270

sitting at his desk in the shop, watching him die on the floor in front of our enormous television set while the world watched the coronation of our queen who's still our queen.

⋆   ⋆   ⋆

When the bomb goes off in Brighton, I wonder if Charlie's somehow involved, but I don't reckon he is. I feel like I'd know in my bones if he was part of that plot. And the proof comes through the letter box, a rare postcard, dated 12th of October, 1984. An Indonesian stamp, so I know he was on a different continent at the time. He can't have been in two places at once, he's not ruddy David Copperfield. The postcard says he's working in a bar in Bali and I think of those skills of his going to waste — cocktail mixing rather than embalming, I ask you.

And then one day, not long after, out of the blue, someone else turns up.

⋆   ⋆   ⋆

It's a Wednesday evening, WI night, and I'm just putting on my brooch when there's a ring at the door. Mick's out at the snooker hall, so I rush down the stairs, expecting it to be the Avon lady as I've ordered some Skin-So-Soft. Only it's like seeing a ghost: Janet.

She's still slim, trim and neat, looks younger than she should with those rotten lungs, which have maybe got stronger in the South American sunshine living the high life.

271

'Come in,' I say. 'Come in.'

She comes in, demure and polite, and I show her into the front room like she's never been here when she knows it of old, Mum and Dad's furniture still here, along with Nana's mirror over the fireplace and our Ercol coffee table with its cork coasters which she hasn't seen, nor the flower wallpaper which I'm embarrassed to look at now and must get Mick to strip. And where is he, Mick, playing snooker, I ask you, when I need him here because I feel sick as anything, I don't know why, but I do know.

Janet.

An unexpected guest. My sister who's not my sister. The other mother who's not a mother at all.

'I'm sorry I didn't ring first. It was a last-minute thing. A stopover at Heathrow. I've only got an hour.' She runs out of steam.

'Glad you could fit us in.' I don't mean it to come out like this. I am in shock, that's all. I was expecting my Avon order. I was expecting to go to the WI meeting tonight as there's a woman talking about her career as a meteorologist. 'Sorry, Janet. That came out wrong. I'll put the kettle on.'

We sit in the front room, a tray on the coffee table in front of us. Conversation is stilted. We talk about Mick and Janet's husband, Tony, who is Ambassador for some place that goes out of my head as soon as she's told me because I am too busy looking at her face, trying to remember my Janet, the sister who I robbed of a baby.

'Did you come by bus?' I ask her.

'No.' She hesitates. 'My driver brought me.'

'Is he outside? Ask him in for a cuppa, poor man.'

'No, Betsy, really. He's quite all right out there.'

'Really?'

'Same as a hearse driver. It's his chance for a snooze or to listen to the radio.'

'If you're sure.'

'I'm sure.'

I wish my Mick would hurry back because this is worse than I ever imagined. We live in different worlds. I feel ashamed of my home, my job, which is ridiculous when I have always been so proud of both. And, after all, this is what I wanted. A better life for Janet. A better life for both of us. And of course for Charlie. And I realise that is why she is here. Charlie. So I might as well get it over and done with.

'He's in Bali.'

'Charlie?'

'Working in a bar. It's hot and humid and full of Australians. I was surprised he got a passport.'

'Well, he must have been deemed to have a good character.'

'Really?'

'Of course. He made a mistake and he's paid for it.'

'I don't know.'

'Yes, Betsy. You have to forgive him and move on.'

Then, as we are getting to the nitty-gritty, as I'm about to give her a mouthful of my thoughts, Mick comes in and any further conversation is back to small talk.

Twenty minutes later she's gone, but she knows from looking at me, my body language, my expression, that I'm not best pleased to see her and I don't know why and nor does she, only I expect, deep down, we really do. One word. Charlie.

2016

Bognor Regis

We do get to find out what's in the handbag of the Prime Minister. Battleships, tanks, coal pits, P45s, steel, railways, some islands in the South Atlantic, yuppies, famines, that killer virus, a Hollywood has-been, and the end of society as we know it.

It has always been easy to hate and destroy. To build and to cherish is much more difficult.
Queen Elizabeth II

1989

London

I undertake my first gay funeral — the first I know of anyhow. I've most probably done plenty in the past, confirmed bachelors, lady companions, but this is the first 'out' funeral and it's a tricky one, not because he was a known homosexual but because he died of AIDS.

The funeral's not at all Liberace. It's sombre and dismal and sad. Funerals are of course sad by their very nature; after all, you're seeing off a loved one, saying farewell, cheerio, and you have to understand that they won't ever be coming back. These days it's more fashionable — if that's the word — to view a funeral as a time of celebration and memorial. To remember all the good things the deceased has done in their life and the impact they've had on those around them. But this young man was only twenty-six years old and he ended up with this terrible disease that strips you of life and dignity, layer by layer, bit by painful bit. How can you celebrate that? As I say, tricky.

Things are slightly improving, however, thanks to Princess Di. She's visited a new AIDS Centre in Tulse Hill and they show her on the telly, shaking hands with the patients. Actually shaking hands to show you can't catch this disease by any old human contact. You can't shun them like a leper of old. Put them in a colony on an island in the middle of nowhere where you don't have to see or think about them. They're like you or me, they've just been ruddy unlucky. They say Diana's gesture will help relieve some of the stigma, and maybe it will. And as much as I love the Queen, my twin separated at birth, I know she would never have been able to do this, I can't say why, but Diana has something the Queen don't.

I understand this detachment of the Queen; it doesn't mean she doesn't care. She just can't show it. She has to look strong and queenly at all times, not just when she fancies it. I understand this because you have to be emotionally detached in my line of work, like doctors and nurses, detached but still sensitive and understanding. So it's not often I cry at a funeral, but on this hot summer day when this boy should've been sunbathing on Peckham Rye, having a barbeque, it hits me that he's dead from a killer that is ruthless. He had no chance.

Don't Die of Ignorance, that's what we've all been told. It's like being back in the war when we got leaflets through the letter box giving us orders on the Home Front. *Dig for Victory. If the Invader Comes. Careless Talk Costs Lives.* And not just the war. Some of those public-information films of the 70s and 80s gave you the heebie-jeebies but they proved a point. Pylons, railways, strangers, lakes, rabies, cars, nuclear bombs. Not pleasant viewing but a reminder that there's danger everywhere. *Don't*

Die of Ignorance. Put on a Rubber Johnny. This lad didn't do as he was told and look where that got him. Young people think they are invincible. It won't never happen to them. They won't get caught. They can drink and drive, duck and dive, but something usually trips them up in the end. Even when we get older we still feel we will go on forever, only in my line of work you know it can end any second of any day. There's no escape.

Don't Die of Ignorance.

Most people don't like being told what to do. And most people — Brits anyway, not so sure about the Yanks though, they can be a funny lot (funny peculiar, not funny ha ha) — most people get queasy when they think about Death. They'd rather body-swerve the subject. And as for sex, well, we don't much like to talk about that either. So when you put Death with Sex, it's even more taboo.

But this boy's mum don't care about all that. She just cares that she lost her precious son too young, in such a cruel fashion, with only a few people to send him on his way, mostly young men like him, some a little older. Thank God I undertook the boy's father's funeral a few years back because he wouldn't have liked this, wouldn't have coped with his lad being a fairy, seeing as how he himself was a burly docker. But his mum loved her boy so much. The little lad she used to dress in romper suits, the boy she watched go to Dulwich College on a scholarship, then university, a job as a solicitor. He even found Love with a smashing podiatrist, only it

279

wasn't ever going to last because Death intervened and cut this Love into pieces.

But Love carries on, don't it? Even when you think it's done and dusted, Love picks itself up, puts itself together. If you have staying power, if you're bloody-minded, it keeps on going, even after Death.

And I can see this love play out in front of me, at the graveside, as the young podiatrist stands by his dead partner's mother, clutching her hand. They grieve together and I know a little of that light will shine on through the forging of this new friendship. I only hope and pray this young man wore a rubber johnny, as I'd hate for him to be next.

⋆ ⋆ ⋆

When I get back home, late afternoon, I'm looking forward to a gin and bitter lemon, putting my feet up, and watching some telly. It's mostly rubbish on except for some David Attenborough repeat, which is too hard to watch right now; it's those wretched wildebeests chasing across the screen and you know what always happens to them.

⋆ ⋆ ⋆

I must have dropped off because when I open my eyes, he's there on the sofa, bold as brass, as if he's just come in from work, or school, or playing out, not been gone for years — a handful of letters, the odd card, a few phone calls the only contact in all that time.

'Charlie?'

'Hello, Mum.'

'You're back then?'

'Passing through.' He gives me a meek little smile, the way he used to when he got back late for his tea on a long summer's evening of playing armies on the bomb sites with his school mates. 'I wanted to see how you were.'

'You've waited a bloody long time to do that.'

'Shall I go?' He makes to stand up, a dramatic gesture, so I have to wave my hand at him, though I don't think he's being entirely serious, but I'm not taking any chances.

'Don't you dare,' I tell him. 'Stay where you are and I'll make a pot of tea.'

'You got any beer?'

'Nobody drinks it.'

'Whisky?'

'We're all out of whisky. I'll fetch us some tea.'

He follows me into the kitchen. My legs are that shaky and the world's tilting sideways so I wonder if I'm actually having a stroke, like poor old Miss Bowles running up them stairs, Stan legging it out of there, God rest them both. Stan who turned out far braver than any of us could have ever imagined.

'Mum? You all right? Here, sit down.' He steers me to a chair at the table. 'I'll make the tea. Sorry, I shocked you, didn't I.'

'You could say that.'

He fills up the kettle, crashing around while he checks the cupboards for mugs and teabags. We've had the kitchen done since he was last here. I watch him taking it in — the way we've knocked through to the old scullery and added a side return.

'When did you do the place up?'

'Must be four years ago now. It needs painting again.'

'Must have cost you.'

'Your father did most of it.'

'He's done a great job,' he says. 'How is he?'

'The same.'

He smiles a sad Charlie smile as he hands me a mug of wishy-washy tea, but I don't complain. I thank him and wait for him to sit down and start talking. If there's one thing I remember about Charlie, you can't make him do anything until he's ready, if he ever is.

And I know I should be happy that he's here, in the family home, drinking tea with me, when that poor mother saw her boy six feet under today. I should be grateful I've got him back, but I don't know what I feel except a creeping dread because I don't know this young man — middle-aged man — sitting at my kitchen table, even though he's sat there for so many meals, boiled eggs and soldiers, Sunday roasts, fry-ups, Christmas dinners, breakfasts, teatimes, suppers. Always a picky eater. Always had to be chivvied up to finish so he could get off to school, get off to work. Then one day he left and didn't come back. Only now he has come back. But I don't know for how long. You never know anything with Charlie.

★ ★ ★

282

He asks if he can stay and I say, of course you can stay, this is your home, and he says, well he wasn't sure of his welcome and I say, well enough time's gone by. He asks if he can have a nap, he's knackered, been travelling since yesterday, and I don't ask where he's been travelling from, I'm not ready for that yet and he probably wouldn't tell me anyway.

He gets up from the table, but I stop him, say I need to air the bed first with a hot-water bottle, open the window a smidge as it's not been slept in since Margie stayed a few months back on a whirlwind visit, on her own, in between husbands, though with the next one lined up. I plonk him in the front room, a pot of tea and some ginger biscuits, his favourites that I always get in, every weekly shop, just in case. The television's still on, Murder She Wrote, probably not the best choice, and I know I'm gabbling and faffing and fussing and I suggest he has a bath while he waits for me to cook supper because he looks like he needs a bath, he smells like he needs a bath, and he needs to eat a decent meal, something hot, something nourishing, because he's ever so thin, and I briefly wonder if I do have some maternal urges, unless I'm just worried about my sheets. So I put a hot-water bottle in his bed and a clean towel on top of it and I run that bath, pouring in half a bottle of Radox.

As he's having a soak, I put my head round the door, I know I shouldn't, he's a grown man, but I can't help it. I need to see him, in the flesh, his skin and muscle, which is almost whittled away to nothing. A tattoo on his arm that I've never seen. He has his headphones on so he don't hear me and I stay there for as long as I dare, hardly breathing, praying the floorboards don't give me away with a creak. But when I look at his face, his mouth slightly open, I realise he's asleep. I stay a while longer, remember how he used to be in the bath with Barbara and Mab, the three of them splashing water all over the floor.

What would they say if they could see him now? What about Mick?

★   ★   ★

Mick's home soon enough and I have a cottage pie on the table with peas and carrots, apple pie for afters, browning in the oven. I've already warned Mick; a phone call while Charlie was having his bath. I don't want him having a heart attack when he comes home and sets eyes on him, like I nearly did. Like seeing a ghost sitting on my sofa when I was expecting it to be wildebeests.

Mick's always been better with Charlie, despite the inauspicious introduction into our home when I brought him back from the farm in his Suttons Seeds shawl, and despite the obvious spot of terrorism. It was me that couldn't handle it. Me that went to pieces. I didn't do my duty by him. I was ashamed. I was cross. I was mortified. The mortified mortician.

★   ★   ★

He's gone the next morning, along with the hundred or so quid in the tea caddy, a bottle of Courvoisier and Mick's coat, his favourite sheepskin one, leaving a note on the kitchen table saying one word. *Sorry*. And a kiss. X

I should feel bad that he's gone and I almost have to make myself cry and when I eventually do, when I sit on his bed and hold that hot-water bottle that's gone stone cold, I do cry and then I howl when I realise I'm not crying because I want him to stay, I'm crying because I am so bloody relieved that he's gone. And then I cry some more because I'm such an unforgiving, heartless mother. Who's not really a mother at all.

2016

Bognor Regis

Janet comes to Sunnydale for another visit. *I've got two things to tell you*, she said last time, in the hospital. She told me about the cancer, that was number one. Cancer at ninety. You get that far in life and you reckon you've outwitted the bastard. Even with her lungs, Janet is still here and you don't think it will be cancer. But cancer's not picky, I've done enough of them, young, like Gloria, old, like Janet. But Janet's not dead yet; she's here, come back for more.

She never told me the second thing.

This time she does.

She tells me she's been seeing Charlie.

'You've been seeing Charlie?'

'Yes, that's what I said. I've been seeing Charlie.'

I have to leave this in the air between us for a few moments and, to be fair, she sits and waits too, though for what I have no idea. The Fat One brings along the trolley, gives us a cup of tea each and a soft biscuit, like we're babies. We watch her waddle off, her bottom as big as Desdemona's and I almost laugh when I remember that Desdemona was actually a stallion, not a mare. We're none of us what we think we are. And I shouldn't be thinking of our lovely old horses when I have to know something off Janet and there's nothing for it but to ask her.

'Did you tell him?'

'Did I tell who what?'

I don't say anything, just lob a look in her direction, which I hope she'll catch and she does, with a slight huff.

'No, of course I didn't tell Charlie,' she says. 'That's something you and Mick should've done years ago when he was still a little boy and then maybe all this wouldn't have happened.'

'All this wouldn't have happened? Are you saying it's my fault he got involved with those murderers? My fault he got sent to prison? Really, Janet, that's a terrible thing to suggest.'

She shakes her head at me, her golden locks dull and thin but barely a grey hair, which wouldn't be the case if she'd brought up Charlie. 'Charlie's never seen himself as a Sunshine,' she says. 'That's why he went to Ireland, to see if he was a Delaney.'

'He was looking in the wrong place.'

'Yes, he was,' she agrees.

I have to consider this profound thought but it don't half hurt my head. It's like there's all these jumping beans inside my brain, whizzing here, there and everywhere, so I don't get very far. Janet seems perfectly composed for someone staring down the barrel of a gun. But from that angle, you can say stuff you've bottled up for years. All those famous last words, some more sage than others, come rushing out and there's no stopping them once they start. Other times, you say the most banal things because it's only another moment of your life even if it happens to be your last, because you never know, not really.

Kiss me, Hardy.

I'm bored with it all.

Bugger Bognor.

But I don't like what Janet's getting at. She won't leave me alone. 'You reckon you'd have given him a better life, do you? You'd have been a single mother with a bastard, nowhere to live, no money to your name. You wouldn't have had your globetrotting lifestyle, that's for sure.'

'Your mum would've taken me in. I'd have got a job. But that's not what I'm saying, Betsy. I think we did the right thing, I actually do, but it's the lies that were wrong. Lies trip you up and they knocked poor old Charlie right over.'

'We're all of us in charge of our own destiny. We can't blame stuff on the past.'

'I agree. There comes a time when you have to face up to things and maybe that time has come.'

'What time?'

'Time for you to tell Charlie.'

Janet sips her tea, nibbles her biscuit, crumbs dropping on her lap like a heavy case of dandruff. She's got a ladder in her tights and you can see a varicose vein poking through like a sand worm. She looks at me but says nothing, so I have to pipe up.

'This is what you've waited for all these years, isn't it?'

'What?'

'To take him back.'

'If it was, I'd have told him myself when I visited him in prison.'

'You went to see him in prison?'

'Well, you wouldn't go. I cleared it with Mick.'

'My Mick? He knew?'

'Yes.'

'He never told me.'

'Oh for goodness' sake, Betsy. This isn't about you. This is about Charlie. We need to do something, between us, to make sure he lives out the rest of his life in a good way. We owe him that at least. Don't we?'

She puts down her teacup and it sloshes over the sides into her saucer. There's a pink stain on the china rim. Lipstick at ninety. Will it be me who lays her out one day? Or will I go first? I did Margie. I hope I don't have to do Mab. Mind you, I hope Mab doesn't do me, not with her shocking eyesight.

'Betsy?'

'You've been seeing Charlie?' I ask her. 'How often?'

'Once a week over the past six months, since Tony died.'

Tony. I'd clean forgot that Tony was dead. Sir Tony, Knight of the Realm, Knight of the Shining Ruddy Armour. Janet wouldn't be a dame if she'd kept Charlie. But she's not the only one with honours. I've got my own. Mrs Elizabeth Sarah Delaney Sunshine MBE, but I don't think Janet cares much about that right now, not with her husband gone. 'I was sorry to hear about Tony,' I tell her. 'I would've come to the funeral if I'd been able. Was it a good one?'

'The funeral was fine.'

'Who did it?'

'Stop changing the subject.'

She's got tougher in her old age, like shoe leather.

'Well?' she says, a ring of my mum about her.

'Well what?'

'Don't you want to ask me something?'

'How is he?'

'He's dead.'

'Not Tony. *Charlie*.'

'I thought you'd never ask.'

'I was shocked that's all.'

Janet has another sip and I can't help but notice the little finger sticking out like it's got rigor mortis. She's drunk tea with ambassadors all over the world, even the Queen, but then so have I. That's something Marg never did and I feel a bit sad about that.

'Betsy?'

'I'm listening. Carry on.'

'He's living in sheltered accommodation in Bexley. He volunteers in an Oxfam shop a couple of days a week. He has a sort of . . . girlfriend.'

'What's a sort of . . . girlfriend?'

'A . . . lady friend. I don't think it's terribly serious, but she seems rather nice.'

Terribly serious, rather nice. Miss La-di-da. She'd never have spoken like that if I hadn't taken Charlie off her hands. She'd never have gone into the Civil Service. She'd never have met Tony. She'd never have gone round the world and met all those fabulous people. She'd never have owned a suit like that, or shoes like that.

'Betsy?'

'You've met her, this . . . lady friend?'

'We went out for tea.'

'Tea?'

'Tea and a bun.'

Tea and a bun, like me and my Mick, that first date on Lordship Lane, only this is Charlie and his lady friend and Janet. I feel sick, maybe the rice pudding we had for lunch. The milk tasted off.

'Well, Betsy?'

'Well, what?'

'You've gone rather quiet. You keep drifting off. Are you all right?'

'I keep having these things. These mini strokes, not the big ones like Marg had. She always had to go one better.'

'I'm sorry to hear that, Betsy. It's hard getting old.'

'We're the lucky ones.'

'Yes, I suppose we are.' Janet looks wistful, no doubt remembering her mother and her little brother and sisters, all flattened by that bastard bomb. And her dad in a POW camp. Having to break the news to him when he turned up on our doorstep while we were waiting for *Dick Barton* to come on the wireless, always leaving us on a cliffhanger. She still has a beautiful face, Janet. Good cheekbones. But her suit does look worse for wear. The shoes need a good polish. An undertaker notices these things. You always have to be spick and span. It's respect. It's respect for the dead and respect for the bereaved. The least you can do is press your suit and shine your ruddy shoes.

'Are you down on your uppers?'

'Excuse me?'

'How are you managing without Tony?'

'Well, I miss him, dreadfully, awfully — '

'I mean financially. Saw you all right, did he?'

'Honestly, Betsy. Stop changing tack. Are you going to get in touch with Charlie?'

'Why would I do that, Janet? Can you tell me that? Can you?' I'm getting worked up. I know I'm getting worked up. My feet are hot and sweaty in my slippers and I wish I had on my smart court shoes like Janet, even if hers do need a lick of Kiwi. I feel at a disadvantage somehow.

She puts her hand on my knee and I get a whiff of *Je Reviens* and mothballs. And I try to catch what she says to me. I try to catch those words and hold them tight in my hand. 'Because he's your son,' she says.

Because he's your son.

Only I don't want to hear these words, I want to let them go, put them in the bin and watch the dustcart take them away to be dug over, to be dug right down deep into the earth with the worms and the bones never to be seen or heard of again. Not because I don't want these words to be true but because I don't deserve them. 'He's not my son though, is he?'

She grimaces like she's bitten the inside of her cheek, like she's back in that maths class with numbers swimming all over the shop, like she can remember those birth pains as clear as day. A moment of shock, then it's gone. 'You brought him up,' she says, so kind, so gentle, so generous, so Janet, it makes me want to hurl with sadness.

'I didn't exactly make a good job of it, did I, Janet?'

'Maybe not.' Her hand that's still on my knee gives it a squeeze and it'll probably leave a bruise, but I don't care, because we feel like sisters again and it's been such a long time since I felt like that and I miss Margie, I actually miss her so much. But I've still got Janet, despite the Blitz, despite the TB, despite Charlie, we're both still alive and breathing, though I don't know how long for, but then none of us know the time or the place, which is just as well.

Maybe not.

'I suppose I asked for that.'

She chuckles, young again for a moment. 'But you can put things right now.'

'He's a grown-up.'

'So are you.'

'I'm nearly ninety.'

'So am I. And he's sixty-six.'

Little Charlie. Sixty-six.

Clickety-click.

★   ★   ★

I must have switched off again because Janet's prodding me on the arm. 'When did you last see him?'

'Who?'

'Charlie.' She's getting impatient with me, but I can't help it if I'm not all there.

'Near on four years ago, after the pardon.'

'Pardon?'

'AFTER THE PARDON?'

293

'You don't have to shout, Betsy. I meant, what do you mean, 'pardon'?

'The pardon for Mick.'

'For what?'

'From when he went AWOL.'

'AWOL? When was that? I thought Mick was a war hero.'

'He was. As far as the British army goes anyway. But he was in the Irish Defence Force before that. His daddy was proud of him, wanted him to stay and defend the Irish Free State. But this wasn't good enough for Mick. He wanted to fight for the Allies, but the Irish was neutral. They wanted to concentrate on their own country because they'd only just got rid of the British. They didn't even call it a war — they called it 'the emergency' '.

'An emergency?' she says.

'An emergency.'

Now to my mind, an emergency is when you run out of teabags, not when a megalomaniac is going around killing Jews, gypsies, gays and anyone else that gets in the way of his trumped-up master plan for his 'perfect' Aryan master race.

'So Mick went AWOL,' I go on, because I need to tell her this. I need to tell her about my Mick. 'It was the only way.'

'Oh,' she says. 'I see.'

'And then after the war, he couldn't go home because he'd be severely punished, like one of his mates who went to military tribunal and then prison, where he was treated ever so badly, poor lad, all through a cold winter, no blankets, no warm clothes, beaten and battered, and at the end of all that, no job and no pension. Mick never set foot on his home soil again, apart from a few hours with his mammy and little sisters. He met me instead, on the Number 12 to Peckham.'

'Oh,' she says.

'We went to the memorial, Charlie, Barbara and me, after the pardon was put into legislation. In Dublin. But I suppose he's told you all about that.'

'No, he didn't say anything about that.'

'Poor Mick. He lived with that pain for over fifty years and then by the time the Irish government finally got round to saying sorry, finally got round to issuing a pardon for all the 'deserters', a few years back, it was too late. He was gone.'

'Oh,' she says again, stuck on repeat.

'It would've meant a lot to my Mick. It would've meant a whole lot more had his father apologised, but that would never have happened.'

'Life's not perfect.'

'I should coco.'

Frank wanders into the lounge at this point, shuffling along with a gleam in his rheumy eye, sniffing out lunch. He's wearing two ties and a watch on each wrist. Always smart, never late, not when there's food involved. I bet he gave his wife the runaround, one meal after the other. Washing, starching and ironing his shirts.

Janet looks at him briefly, then back at me, then at her shoes, which still need a polish and buff, only it doesn't seem quite so important now.

'I sometimes think that the beautiful thing about life is its imperfections,' she says, fiddling with her hearing aid so it crackles and squeaks.

'Oh?'

'The wonky nose. The three-legged mongrel. The toothy smile.'

I picture the wonky nose, the three-legged mongrel and the toothy smile and see some truth in it.

'But don't ask me what we're supposed to do with pain, other than live with it and make it part of who we are.'

I have no answer for that, so I pretend to zone out again.

'How did it go with Charlie when you visited Dublin?' she asks, quite loudly, a few minutes later, maybe more, I don't know, time's gone a bit tits-up. 'Betsy?'

'What?'

'How did it go with Charlie?'

'Not so well. I haven't seen him since.'

'I am sorry. I really am.'

'So am I. But, Janet . . . '

'What is it, Betsy?'

'Can you leave it too late to make amends?'

'Not while you've still got breath in you,' she says, and she should know with her lungs.

★　★　★

Janet's gone. I don't know when she left, but it's getting dark now, must be time for tea soon. Eva

Braun is coming round with the tablets, handing them out like sweets, when they could be cyanide for all we know.

I've often imagined seeing Charlie, what I'd say, how I'd act, what we'd do. Maybe a meal out at a Toby Carvery. A boat trip on the Thames. A walk in Dulwich Park where I used to take him and Barbara and Mab to feed the ducks, if Barbara hadn't got to the crusts first.

I even wonder what I'd wear if I was to see him. Once when he was about seven, Charlie said, 'Mummy you look pretty.' I was wearing a summer dress, it would've been the late 50s, it had a full skirt and a flowery print, bold and bright, and he kept playing with the fabric, rubbing it between his fingers which were grimy so I told him to stop fiddling and go and wash his hands. When he came back, smelling of Pears soap, he carried on. 'Why do you always wear black, Mummy?' And I told him about the job, the business, in more detail, and he asked if he could come and look at a dead body and I said yes, because he asked, because he showed an interest, and, after all, you're never too young to know about death, are you. You can accept it once you know about it and then not dwell and wonder. You can accept it's part of life, like Christmas and dentists.

Grief is the price we pay for love.
Queen Elizabeth II

1997

London

The day it happens, I'm having a lie-in after a late night at the Association, when Mick comes into the bedroom to break the news. An accident in Paris and Princess Di is injured. At this point we think she'll survive. Of course she'll survive. The fairy tale has already been broken, surely it won't be smashed up and all?

But it is. An hour later we hear that the Princess is dead. And my first thought is for her boys, left without a mother. I think about my own mother and how lucky I am to still have her. I think of my dad who went too young. I think of all those mothers and fathers and sons and daughters and sisters and brothers that I've prepared for burial. All the grief that's passed through the doors of Sunshine & Sons. All the wreaths, the cups of sugary tea, the scattering of soil, the choosing of headstones, the epitaphs, the poems, the music, all the stop-the-clocks and morning-has-brokens and yea-though-I-walk-through-the-valley-of-the-shadow-of-deaths, all the signing of forms and certificates and the smell of sawdust and chemicals and horse manure and dry-cleaning and all the weather-watching and ham sandwiches and heartbreak. All those tears that if you collected them up would fill the pond at Dulwich

Park ten times over.

Keep Baby with Mother.

And when you see all those flowers lined up outside Kensington Palace, it's not new, it's how grief used to be done — Winston, Victoria, Gladstone, Wellington, Nelson, Elvis, JFK, Eva Peròn, Victor Hugo, Mahatma Gandhi, Ayrton Senna. Not to mention the East End criminals who brought back the horses, though I wouldn't have let Desdemona or Othello anywhere near in case their heads ended up in someone's bed. Rudolph Valentino — now there was an outbreak of mass hysteria if ever there was one. Two of his fans killed themselves when they heard of his death. So this outpouring is nothing new. It's just not particularly British, whatever that is.

You never quite know what you're going to get at a funeral. I mean, you know the details and the format as the undertaker. It's the grief you can only guess at. You might think the distressed widow will fall to pieces, but on the day she might just hold it all together. And this is what takes everyone by surprise, the way Diana's death hits the country hard in the guts. Forget the cynics and the republicans, the commentators and satirists. Think of the ordinary person. The old lady that queued at the town hall to sign the book of condolence. The young man that left a bouquet outside Kensington Palace. The gay man whose hand she shook in a clinic in south London. Whatever you thought of her, she had something special. Some kind of gift. And when that's taken away all of a sudden, you don't quite know what to do with yourself, so you go along

300

with everyone else and somehow the public form a grief that can be measured, mainly in flowers.

This is when the People look to their leaders, to take their cue. Tony Blair does his Prime Minister thing, not a patch on Churchill, but a dignified effort nonetheless. 'She was the People's Princess,' he says. 'And that is how she will stay, how she will remain in our hearts and our memories forever.'

The public looks to the Queen and all. What will she say? Why is she so quiet? Why is she holed up in Scotland? The Queen might be dignified and private, but, here, now, she's put into stark contrast with Diana, who wore her heart on her sleeve, who showed her feelings with a glance or a gesture.

The Queen learns a tough lesson, one her dead daughter-in-law understood only too well. She is queen to a people and what the people think well and truly matters. And so she must mourn in public. We wait with our breath held while she addresses the nation. 'She was an exceptional and gifted human being,' she says. 'In good times and bad, she never lost her capacity to smile and laugh, nor to inspire others with her warmth and kindness. I admired and respected her . . . especially for her devotion to her two boys.'

And on the morning of the funeral, from our front room, where we watched the coronation, where we watched my poor dad die, I sit with my old mum, quiet on the sofa together, holding her hand like a little girl, only I'm not sure if that's her or me. The relief I feel when the Queen bows to Diana's coffin as it passes her by outside the palace is almost more than I can bear. Mick stays in with us because he knows I need him and I reckon he actually wants to watch, from a professional point of view, and because he secretly admired Diana, saw her as the anarchist of the royal family. Mick fought for King and Country, but that was more to defeat the Nazis than to save the British. But who knows how each of us feels, even our nearest and dearest have secrets, sometimes hidden even from ourselves.

Mum and me stay on the sofa all day, watching events unfold, remembering Churchill's send-off, only this one's more tragic, a half-lived life, not even that, as opposed to Winnie's ninety-two years. Mick hovers, bringing us tea and soup and sandwiches and biscuits, like we're invalids, which Mum is, but not me. I'm usually fighting fit, but right now I don't feel able to function properly, watching those poor boys follow the gun carriage that carries their mother's coffin, draped with the royal standard, their flowers and handwritten notes on top. I even weep a little when Elton does his thing. More so when her brother speaks, the ginger one, a moving tribute, the hardest speech he'll ever have to give, summing up the short life of his sister in a few minutes while she lies cold beside him. But I can't take my eyes off the two young princes.

Keep Baby with Mother.

And I don't know why I cry so much.

★ ★ ★

302

The next day I book a cruise and surprise Mick, who by this stage in our married life you might think was beyond surprising. Turns out, he isn't.

'A cruise, you say?'

'Round the Med. Four weeks.'

'A month? But what about — '

'Barbara's got it all under control. She needs to step up if we're going to retire.'

'We're going to retire?'

'It's about time, don't you think?'

'Right. So it is.'

Barcelona, Rome, Venice, Dubrovnik, Istanbul, Athens. All those places I used to dream about, from the films and the magazines,from Judith Chalmers on *Wish You Were Here . . . ?*, from hearing about people's hols, sitting through hours of slides of wonky buildings and neglected animals. All those postcards from Margie and airmail letters from Janet. Now it's our turn.

★   ★   ★

The cruise is probably the happiest time in my life, just me and Mick, no cooking, no washing, no dead bodies and, God forgive me, no children or grandchildren. I love my family, though love's not always easy to talk about, even when you deal with Death every day. And being a mother is not what I expected, it has to be said, and I'm sorry to say it, but there it is. It. Love. Motherhood.

Mick sits in the shade reading his way through the papers and a collection of books. I sunbathe, swim, sunbathe and snooze. I feel like a layer has been stripped off me, peeled back to reveal the woman I might have been if I'd been born somewhere else, like I'm the Queen on her royal yacht and I wonder what she feels when she's out at sea. Does she feel like a mother should feel? Does she feel like a wife should feel? How should we feel?

And the nicest surprise is when we dock at Capri and a certain someone is waiting for us, just as she said she would, but I was never certain she'd actually turn up. As we climb down the gangplank, there she is, in a stylish summer dress, nothing like the orange curtains, looking like a cross between Audrey Hepburn and Fanny Cradock. My beautiful sister, Margie.

★ ★ ★

'So you've done it then,' she asks, cocktail in one hand, cigarette in the other, blowing the smoke over her shoulder in that way of hers that's not changed.

'Yes, we have. You're looking at a retired funeral director and a retired carpenter.' I sip my Campari and lemonade and feel a rush to my head.

Mick shrugs as if to say, *I'll believe it when I see it.*

But right at this moment, sitting at a table outside a pretty café in the Capri sunshine, I mean every word. This is the life I could have been living all those years. The life Margie has lived. The life Janet has lived.

'It's not all it's cracked up to be,' Margie says.

'Two divorces have taken their toll. I never had a good one like your Mick.'

'Aren't you happy with Roger?'

'Happy enough.'

'Isn't that the best we can hope for?'

'Maybe it is, Betsy. Maybe it is.' She lights another cigarette and orders a bottle of Champagne and I think I must be in a film because this is a long way from south-east London and Sunshine & Sons.

★   ★   ★

There's a photograph of that afternoon on my dressing table. Marg and I sitting side by side, smiling at the camera that Mick is pointing at us. He's not the best photographer, but that afternoon he managed to capture something. He captured me and my sister in a rare moment of oneness and I will cherish it always. Even when I want to stove her head in with a bookend. But the opportunities for that are few and far between as we have different lives, on different parts of this big, small planet we call Earth.

2016

Bognor Regis

I often wonder what would've happened to
Diana if she'd got out of that crushed car and
walked away that August night in Paris. She'd
be a grandmother now. She'd probably have
remarried, maybe two or three times. I know it's
silly to think these things. I know she's dead. My
younger self would be tutting at me for being
fanciful, but I seem to be getting more so in my
old age, stuck here in Bognor with a fractured
hip. But you can't help remembering. You can't
help asking yourself *what if?*

I think about the bodies I've done. They pop
up in front of me when I'm eating, sitting on the
stool in the shower, staring out the window at
the giant trees. I dream about them. Night after
night. There's so many bodies in London, layer
upon layer of them, like Nana Mabel's trifle.
Romans, Saxons, Normans. Plantagenets, Hugue-
nots, Cockneys. Plague pits, shallow graves, suicides
buried at crossroads. Men, women, children, babies,
pets. Kings, Queens, paupers and peasants. You
can chart the city's history through its bodies
and burials, its culture, customs, religion and
rituals.

Mum wanted to become part of the earth,
recycled. Dad was cremated; I'm going to be

cremated and all. In the fiery furnace I'll go, ashes to ashes. Barbara can have my wedding ring, not that she'll fit it on her finger. Maybe I could bequeath it to Tom?

And what about cryonics? You can do that in America. (Where else?) You can be stuck upside down and shoved in a freezer in the hope that one day you might be resurrected and made all better. Which is daft in my book. You only get a certain amount of time on this earth. You can't cheat Death. Don't put off your life. Make amends in the here and now. Though it might be one of the hardest things you ever have to do.

The weather plays its part when it comes to funerals. If it's icy or muddy, it can be dodgy for the pall-bearers. Mick would often be called in for pall-bearing duties. In the hard winter of 1961, I remember the hearse slipping in the snow on the way to the crem. We made it through somehow, but it was filthy by the time we got back to the yard. Poor old Stan would've had his work cut out.

This winter it's all rain.

'It's global warming, Nana,' Tom says. He's back for a visit, can't keep away. Anything to put off doing some work, ruddy students. He's making his way through the box of Dairy Milk he brought for me, which I don't mind because he's a beanpole, I'm not complaining.

'We've always had rain, love,' I tell him. 'It's nothing new.'

'But the sea levels are rising and the ice is melting.'

I'm not sure I want a conversation about all

this green stuff right now. I'm more interested in finding out about Jerome. Because he's here too. They've come to see me. Jerome has a car, a Micra. I watched them drive into the car park. I watched them walk up to Sunnydale, comfortable as any couple could be.

'You're not the first to fall for a black man, Tom. I was a little bit in love with this Jamaican trumpet player during the war. He married your great-great-aunt Margie.'

Tom stares at me like I've taken all my clothes off and danced the hornpipe across the residents' lounge. Jerome stares at me like he don't know what breed of person I am. Jerome doesn't look like a gay one. He's nothing like Benjamin either. He's 'mixed race', that's what Tom calls him. I'm not to use that other phrase no more as it's racist. You learn all sorts when you have great-grandchildren.

My husband has quite simply been my strength and stay all these years, and I owe him a debt greater than he would ever claim.
Queen Elizabeth II

1999

London

It's the worst day of my life when Mick goes. One minute you're saying your marriage vows, the next you're saying goodbye, only more than fifty-five years have passed and you're an old woman, a widow grieving for her man. Her lovely gentle bogtrotter.

He gets a cold, never a good patient but never one for doctors either so it's always me that has to run up and down the stairs to his sick bed with aspirin and chicken soup and hot-water bottles because men are no good with illness, men don't have to push a baby out of the equivalent of their bottom. But it's soon apparent that this is not a cold, it's the 'flu. To be more specific, it's the millennium 'flu that is laying siege to much of the country. To be even more specific, this is the Sydney H3N2 virus, brought over from Australia during the Tall Ships race last year, the way we introduced smallpox and the like with our transportation of the convicts back in the day.

It starts when he wakes up with a sore throat and the sniffles the Tuesday before Christmas, but by the end of the day, he's aching all over and running a temperature. By the middle of the night, he's so hot that he's hallucinating, calling me his mammy and all his sisters' names, one after the other, all seven of them. It's burnt out by morning, leaving him weak and dizzy and unable to keep much down apart from a few sips of water. At lunchtime he manages a few mouthfuls of thin broth, but an hour later he has brought it all back up and then it's coming out the other end so that he's having to slump on the toilet seat with a bowl in his hands.

'My head's banging like the devil in a dustbin, Betsy,' he says, a little raspy so I wonder if it's going to his chest. 'Can you get me some paracetamol?'

He sicks all that up too and I shuffle him back to bed, with Barbara's help, and tuck him up in clean sheets and let him sleep.

By the next morning, he's a little better and I think we're over the worst and I start planning the food shopping for Christmas. We've been pushed at work with the old ones going, thanks to this ruddy 'flu, but it never occurs to me to be worried for my Mick. I'm annoyed to be honest, annoyed that he's ill right now what with Christmas approaching in all its glittery splendour and inconvenience. But as the day goes on, Mick deteriorates, rapidly. His temperature soars again and I actually call the doctor, who, thankfully as we're old friends, comes along to check on him.

I know as soon as he puts his stethoscope to Mick's chest that it's not good.

'I suspect pneumonia,' the doctor says. 'His heart rate's very fast and he's having difficulty breathing.' He speaks to me, not Mick. Mick is asleep.

It's Charlie and Janet that have lung problems, that's what I think, but it's the old man's friend, and although Mick's not what I think of as old because he still gets called on for pall-bearing duties, he is seventy-five.

He's not asthmatic or sickly so the doctor is hopeful he'll respond to antibiotics.

'I'll nip out now and catch the chemist before it closes.' I wait for the doc to write me a script, but he's asking to use my phone. So I reach for the telephone by the bed, the phone that's forever on duty, even though we're supposed to be retired, and I watch as he dials 999, which is a little overdramatic, but I don't say anything because doctors know best, at least they think they do, he's just being cautious, he's going that extra mile for a friend in need before Christmas.

Next thing I know, I'm holding Mick's hand, which is all clammy, and Barbara's beside me, flapping and yet unflappable, and then the paramedics are here, a big bloke and a little one so I don't know how they'll manage the stretcher thing between them, you notice these details when it's your job, having to balance the pall-bearers to keep the coffin straight, and now Barbara's got hold of me because I'm shaking like I've got the chills, like I'm coming out in sympathy with Mick, and next thing, I'm in the car, Barbara driving us to the hospital, following the ambulance, which isn't wailing. Not until we get to the top of Dog Kennel Hill when the lights start flashing and then the sirens begin, but we're nearly there, it's rush hour, they probably want to get to the hospital sharpish, they probably want to finish their shift and get off home, and who can blame them, certainly not me.

If I blame anyone, apart from those ruddy sailors who brought the virus from Australia, it's myself. I should've called the doctor earlier. I should've known, all the 'flu cases we've buried over the years. I should've recognised the signs, but they said there was nothing I could've done to stop the septicaemia or the peritonitis that follows.

My biggest regret is that I don't get to say goodbye to him properly. I don't get to hear his lovely, soft voice. By the time I see him he's unconscious, so maybe some of my words get through. Maybe he feels the squeeze of my hand. Maybe he feels the tears that splash on his cheek. Maybe he hears the chants of the hospital priest. Maybe he senses him unpack his bag, like my mum's, only with different tools of the trade: a crucifix, two blessed candles, a bottle of holy water and some oil. Maybe he feels the anointing of this holy oil. Eyes, ears, nostrils, mouth, hands, feet. Maybe. Because he can't speak. He can't confess his sins. He can't take communion. But he can be anointed. He can be pardoned.

At least I have control over one thing. I can keep Mick at home until after Christmas. Nobody questions this. They know that this is my business, the business I've lived all my life, and I will look after Mick at home, same as Nana Mabel and Dad, until the day after Boxing Day when the priest can fit us in. Because I don't hate the Catholics like my mum. I don't hate anyone, because hate eats you up, grinds you down to the bone. And I hope that Mick's not spinning in his grave after the smells and bells and chanting and robes and bling and all. I hope he's happy to have the Requiem Mass, which is so beautiful and painful at the same time.

At least Charlie is here. It would've been better if he'd come home more than a handful of times in ten years and seen his father while he was still alive, but better late than never.

He cries quietly as he sits beside me and I feel the comfort and warmth of his arm around my shoulder. And for a moment, Mick's death is worth this brief moment of peace with our son. Just for a moment.

2016

Bognor Regis

Sunday comes round again with its pre-lunch sherry, post-lunch snooze, and teatime visit from the church. It's one of them free churches, could be any denomination, but they say it's the same God who doesn't judge, though I'm pretty sure he must be miffed at some of the stuff I've done, one thing in particular pops into my mind.

Sunday evening brings Mab's phone call. She has free weekend calls, always watched the pennies and the pounds have certainly looked after her. A holiday home in France (I ask you), not that she goes there all that much these days, what with the wheelchair and eyesight issues.

'I'm worried about you,' she says.

'I'm fine,' I tell her. 'Come for a visit and see for yourself.'

'I can't.'

'Why not?'

'Because of my legs. And my eyes. You could come here.'

'I've fractured my ruddy hip. Can't you get a cab?'

'It's twenty miles.'

'What else you going to spend your money on?'

'I got all my grandchildren and great-grandchildren.

315

They're always skint. Someone's got to help them out and that someone's me.'

'I used to change your soiled nappies, Mabel Winston Sunshine. Worse than embalming that was. Never known anything like it.'

'That was seventy years ago.'

'Never too late to make it up to me.'

'What are you talking about, Betsy? You going ga-ga stuck in there?'

'Like I said, you'll have to come and see for yourself.'

'Maybe I will one of these days. Maybe I will.'

'I should coco.'

The world is not the most pleasant place. Eventually your parents leave you and nobody is going to go out of their way to protect you unconditionally.
Queen Elizabeth II

2002

London

It is not exactly a good year for the Queen, not the infamous *annus horribilis* of 1992, ten years previous, but another dud one all the same. It's not much good for me neither. We both lose a mother and a sister. A few years before, 1995, there they were, the Queen, the Queen Mother, Princess Margaret, out on that balcony, in the brightest of colours, all smiling at the fly-past for the VE day 50th celebrations. And there we were at home, Mum, Margie and me, watching on my new Sony 24-inch. Fifty ruddy years since the day I lost and found my sister in Nana's orange curtains. Now there's only Lilibet and me left.

In February, the Queen loses her sister and, a month later, her mother. But she doesn't wallow. She gets on with it, travels the globe to see the people of the Commonwealth in order to celebrate her Golden Jubilee and to thank them for their loyalty. *Vivat Regina!*

In August, when the flowers are going over and the grass crying out for rain, my mum goes to bed one night, normal as ever, usual routine, cocoa, cold cream, curlers, and never wakes up in the morning. She takes her last breath peacefully and quietly, drifting off to the other side, wherever that might be. I reckon she's simply had enough. She was old and tired and felt she was no longer fulfilling her role in life, which was service and responsibility, same as the Queen. It was like Mum willed herself to die that night. No trouble, no nursing home, no fuss.

So we lay Mum out, like she showed me to do with Gloria all those years ago. Me and Mab and Barbara. In her bed with its dusky pink slippery eiderdown. The room where Nana Mabel used to live with Granddad Bill, who I never met because he was forever young in Flanders fields. Where Mum and Dad lived their married life, and where Mick and I moved in many years later because Mum couldn't manage on her own anymore. I do her make-up, and her hair, the way she likes it, the way she's done it since she was a newly-wed back in the twenties. Mab and Barbara help me dress her in her favourite slacks and blouse. She needs a cardy too. I am, suddenly, sentimental; I don't want her getting cold. Which is stupid because the dead are stone cold. You just have to keep them warm in your heart.

Marg flies in from Dublin, where she is currently living with husband number three. Her only child, Sebastian (I ask you), comes with her. She's walking with a stick and a rattle of pharmaceuticals, but her hair is perfect, her make-up a tad overdone, as per usual.

Janet's on a flight from Switzerland, first-class no doubt, not that I begrudge her that, she'll need all the strength she can get and I'll need her calmness once Marg starts up her weeping and wailing. By teatime, it's all us girls back together again (and Sebastian). This is women's work, as it always was. We've brought Death home. We stay close to him, mark the mean old bastard, because who knows who he'll pick off next, could be any one of us.

Mum's in her coffin by now, in the front room. It's a stuffy hot day. We shut the windows to keep out the flies. We draw the curtains and fetch a fan to keep the temperature down. We switch on the standard lamp, in the corner of the room where Mum used to sit with her knitting and sewing. We take turns, keeping Mum company, rotating in the kitchen over cups of tea and glasses of sherry. All these intimate moments swirl around us, brushing along the carpet and settling on the walls — wedding nights, awkward conceptions, difficult births, nursing babies, feverish children, arguments, jokes, tears, giggles. You can almost see them, like someone's got out an old projector and cine film.

This is what Mum would have wanted, us girls at home with her. She'd have loved it, only she's dead. And on that note, I remember it, the letter. Mum wrote instructions for the funeral and like a ninny I'd completely forgot. I know exactly where it is, in one of the drawers in the sideboard, and so I'm able to lay my hands on it quick enough. I gather the women together — and Sebastian — and read it to them. I'm the oldest after all and this is down to me.

It's a surprise, I'll give her that. Fancy Mum being the one to do the upstaging for once, but if not at your own funeral, then when?

Every funeral demands a whole heap of decisions at a time when you think that the world might possibly be ending and you don't even know if you can manage a cup of tea or a wash. Your emotions are all over the shop, a spilled bag of grief, confusion, numbness, relief, anger, regret. You know these decisions are important but that only piles on the pressure. However, you don't have to make these decisions on your own; that's what your funeral director's for. She should listen to you, support you, guide you through every step of this difficult journey. It's her job. It's her duty. It's her service and responsibility.

You go that extra mile. If I can, I like to visit the bereaved at home, to get them to chat with me in their own surroundings, where it is less formal and scary. I listen to them talk about their loved one, ask gentle questions to bubble up the memories. They still talk in the present tense about the deceased, as if they've nipped down the corner shop for a pint of milk, until they catch themselves and the grief slaps them again, only harder this time because it's maybe beginning to sink in that this person now inhabits their past. I tell them not to apologise; it's perfectly natural to feel they are still here. I dig deeper, probe gently, try to uncover the person that once lived, to get beyond the person that's just died. But Mum's sorted it all out for us; we know pretty much everything there is to know about her. Though I wonder, when I look at Mab and her faded ginger hair. We never really know everything about someone. We don't always know everything about ourselves.

★ ★ ★

A wicker coffin, a woodland burial, Mum, the traditionalist, gone all New Age, a Daimler the one concession, borrowed from Vickers & Sons, seeing as Dad's pride and joy went after the war because he no longer wanted anything German. I go for a second time cap in hand to that premises down the road. Bob's retired now so I deal with his son, the young lad whose snooker cue my Charlie snapped in half. He is all charm and politeness, phones his dad, makes me a cup of tea while we wait for Bob Vickers Jnr to come down. We sit there in the office and we drink tea like we are old friends, me and Bob, when we were never friends. But we're fair and square and time has passed and Death can put a stop to bad things as well as the good. So when he offers his condolences, I take them and put the past to bed.

The wicker coffin does look odd in the Daimler, but it's what Mum wanted. Her wishes. I don't know what Dad would've reckoned to Mum's send-off, but I'm surprised and touched at how lovely it is. Simple, cut back. Mum's very own make-do-and-mend. There are jam jars of sunflowers all up the church path and all down the aisle of St Michael's. We take them back to the house for the do afterwards and then, when the guests have finally imbibed enough sherry and shed enough tears, they take a little jar of sunshine home with them.

322

* ⋆ ⋆

Mum lasted nearly fifty years without Dad — like Queen Victoria without her Albert. I'm lucky I had my Mick so long. My one and only. Never a slip-up. Never a grope or a kiss or even a yearning for someone else — Paul Newman don't count nor my transaction with Bob Vickers Jnr. And I know he never strayed, never wandered, always came back to me night after night. We was always enough for each other. Working together helped. It's serious work but I wouldn't call it stressful. Not so long as you're organised and have all the t's crossed and the i's dotted.

⋆ ⋆ ⋆

Before the year is out, there is another family body. Margie is ill. She's had a massive stroke and is brain-dead. I sit at her bedside in hospital, with Mab. When she's all switched off and her heart is no longer beating, we lay her out and our boys remove her to our chapel of rest. We continue to sit by her, keeping vigil. I do her make-up, plenty of lippy, the way she likes it. Curl her lovely hair. Put on a nice dress. My sister. I cry for all those times we argued and wish we could have just one of them back.

⋆ ⋆ ⋆

Something unexpected turns up in November. I'm having a morning of it, but I manage to get

323

home for a bite of lunch. I pick up the post from the doormat, ignoring the crunch of my left knee, just the one letter, addressed to me, all official-looking, and I think, oh my God it's a ruddy tax bill, even though I'm a ruddy pensioner you can't escape it. (Nor Death, thanks, Mum.) But when I open it I see it's from the Cabinet Office of all places and I think of Winnie for some reason. Only the Prime Minister now is Mr Blair, not that he's signed it; some bloke calling himself my 'Obedient Servant' has done that.

I scan it quickly, and when I assure myself it's not a bill, I re-read it more slowly. I have to sit down. It's not like the time the telegram boy comes; it's the opposite of that. Disbelief all the same.

The Queen may be graciously pleased to approve that you be appointed a Member of the Order of the British Empire (MBE).

Well, I never, is what I think and I let out this strange cry, which is not like me at all, because I like to keep my thoughts inside where they belong. Me and the Queen have that much in common. It's what we've been brought up to do and this letter is what I've been brought up for and all.

For services to the funeral industry and local community.

Well, I ruddy never.

I fill in the form straight away, yes of course I will be graciously minded to accept this invitation, and I grab my coat and hat and nip down to the postbox, the one that's outside

324

Janet's old place that's now a small block of flats. On the way back home, I worry that I've dreamt it, or not filled the form in right. It might get lost in the post and I won't know until I see the New Year's Honours list. So I don't tell a single soul, except I do nip to the cemetery to show my Mick the letter, silly moo.

★　★　★

I needn't have worried. There's my name in the newspaper, the *London Gazette*.

```
Mrs Elizabeth Sarah Delaney SUNSHINE.
   For services to funeral directing
          and the community.
```

It's a shock all right, seeing it in print like that. It's actually happening. I rush to the office and wave it in Barbara's face while she flaps around with surprise and panic and something else, I'm not sure what.

★　★　★

Several weeks later, having received my official letter congratulating me and inviting me to the Palace, the day arrives. I'd have loved to bring Margie, not to rub it in, but because I know how much she'd have enjoyed it. I don't ask Janet because she's in Chile with her husband, and anyway, she's had more Royal meet-ups than hot dinners. No point asking Charlie, even if I knew where he was. Bristol, Birmingham, Bogota. So I take Barbara and Mab. I'm wearing a bright orange Jaeger dress from John Lewis, as far removed from funereal clothes as possible, with a matching small hat. A final check in the hall mirror before we get in our ride. One of the boys is picking us up in one of the limousines, perk of the job.

'You look lovely, Mum,' Barbara reassures me, but I'm not so sure. Was orange a good idea?

We're dropped off right outside the Palace gates. We have our credentials checked by security before we can go any further and are offered congratulations. Everyone's very nice, polite and friendly, making us feel special, which makes a change as you tend to be a pariah in this line of work.

We cross the famous courtyard, the one you see on the telly, and once inside the Palace, we're ushered up this grand staircase lined with fancy soldiers, their uniforms nothing like the khakis and blues of the war. At the top, us soon-to-be-anointed ones are separated from our guests and put in a room to mingle. No booze, just fizzy water, which I don't have because I'll need a wee and it gives me gas something chronic. I get chatting to a midwife, of all people, who's delivered over a thousand babies, like the one who delivered me, and we agree we have a lot in common, opposite ends of the spectrum, hatching and dispatching. Then we have to listen up, oi, oi, saveloy, as Stan would say, God rest him, while we receive instructions from a man with gold braid and spurs who tells us where to go and what to say. Address the Queen as 'Your

Majesty' initially and thereafter 'Ma'am, to rhyme with jam'. I know about all this because I've been told by some of my colleagues from the Association and the WI. And this is when we actually know the Queen herself will be doing the honours and I feel a burst of emotion deep within me when I think I'll be meeting my twin separated at birth.

She's smaller than I imagined. Smaller than me and I wonder if the weight of her Duty has made her shrink because I don't remember her being that small on the telly or in the papers. She shakes my hand, not bothered that it's touched dead people, but then she's wearing her trademark white gloves like Marg used to wear as an air hostess. She gives me a look, that steely-eyed Paddington Bear look — not scary, but intense. 'That's a startling orange,' she says. And I get a flash of Nana Mabel's orange curtains, a crush of crowd, panic over a lost sister, and the kindness of a stranger.

Lilibet.

'Makes a change from black, your Majesty,' I say, hoping that's not cheeky or ungracious, but to be fair I don't really know what I'm saying as all these memories are overwhelming, snatching the breath out of me.

I remember to let go of her hand, ready to take my leave of her, as much as I'd like to drag her off with me for a chinwag, but I don't think she's going to say anything else.

Only she does.

'Younger sisters can be a trial.' She smiles, a hint of mischief.

'They can indeed, Ma'am. Only I'd give anything to have those trials back again.'

'As would I, Mrs Sunshine. As would I.'

And now it's time to go. I can hardly remember how to walk as I make my way from the room, despite all those years processing in public, in front of a coffin. Later, as we have our photos taken, I wish I could spend five minutes alone with her, like we did that day, but without the panic over Marg's innocence or what was left of it. Even though we were surrounded with a great mass of riotous young people, it was just her and me hunting for my sister in Nana's orange curtains. Just her and me. And now I can't get close because she's the Queen, not a princess on a night off.

I don't see her again that day. It's all over bar the photos, which I will cherish forever. I think they might even go to the grave with me, though Barbara might have something to say about that. My daughter was actually a little bit proud of me. Mab too. And that was the best feeling of all.

★ ★ ★

I hope I'm not here to see the Queen's funeral. I want her to go on and on and on as the alternative is not an alternative. Silly beggar. Our longest serving monarch who's spent her life dedicated to her people. And horses. And corgis. (We all need an outlet.)

And she helped me find my sister on the night the country went wild, when all that drunken singing, and congas, and kissing of strangers was going on. There she was, in the midst of the tumult, a picture of calm and serenity. If she was placed on twenty-five mattresses with twenty-five feather eiderdowns, she would feel the pea placed at the bottom and would be black and blue all over. But this day, jostled by raucous servicemen and screaming women, she took it all in her stride. I just wish she could help me find my lost sister now, but poor old Marg is beyond our reach. Rest in peace, you silly moo.

2016

Bognor Regis

Here's a turn-up for the books, a blast from the past. Hiding behind a huge bunch of garish pink and purple flowers is a man I haven't seen since he was brandishing his trumpet in a smoky club in Soho.

'Benjamin?'

'Hello, Betsy Sunshine.'

'I thought you'd be back home in Jamaica, enjoying retirement.'

'I've only just about retired from the road and I've gone home to roost in Peckham.'

'Peckham? Wouldn't it be better for your old bones in Kingston?'

'It's been too long. I think you'll be burying my bones here, Betsy.'

'I'm retired now too.'

'You wouldn't come out of retirement for old times' sake?'

'You trying to tell me something?'

'No, Betsy, I'm doing okay. Just the arthritis in my hands, which means I've had to hang up my trumpet.'

'That must be awful for you.'

'I have me records.'

I remember his jazz collection. He stored those precious vinyl records at ours for a while when he was on the road and they were living out of suitcases, him and Margie, though she should've been used to that, what with being a trolley dolly.

Eva Braun relieves him of the flowers.

'Make sure they go in my room,' I tell her and I could swear she gives her heels a Nazi click, but I don't dwell because Benjamin has sat himself down in the chair next to me, producing a bag of Mint Imperials from the pocket of a dapper jacket, always smartly turned out, and offers me one.

'Don't mind if I do.'

We sit there for a moment. I can see Frank out of the corner of my eye. He's staring at Benjamin. If looks could kill I'd be arranging Benjamin's funeral sooner than expected.

'Do you miss Marg?' he asks.

'More than I ever thought. I don't miss the drama, mind.'

He laughs and almost loses his mint.

'Marg should never have divorced you,' I tell him. 'She should've stuck with you.'

'She broke my heart. But I understand. The captain offered her a better life.'

'Still travelling though, wasn't it?'

He smiles wistfully, makes a clicking noise with his mouth. 'More security as a pilot than a trumpet player.'

'But she left him and all, for that deathly dull banker, Roger the dodger.'

He pats my hand. 'She was always the flighty one, eh Betsy?'

'You're telling me. Always checking over your

shoulder for the next bus to come along.'

Benjamin smiles again, and he looks so young, though he's got to be pushing eighty-eight, hard to believe.

'You got a picture in the attic?'

'Black don't crack, Betsy Sunshine.' He winks at me and his eyes are so full of life I don't know how he does it, like it's the music that's kept him going so long, that's kept the fires burning.

'What? Oh . . . Can you say that?'

'I just did.' He chuckles like a schoolboy and I giggle like a girl, even more than with Frank. This is different. My heart's fluttering and I don't know if it's angina or what. But I do know I haven't felt like this since I don't know when. Then I have a flash of sadness because it's not my Mick. But it's Margie's Benjamin! Now I've got what Marg had. I bet she's spinning. Silly moo. Fancy giving up this one for that sleazeball of a pilot.

'How did you find me Benjamin? Why now?'

'A little bird told me.'

'Would that be a rather plump bird by the name of Barbara?'

'It would.' He laughs, shaking his head at me. 'I went to the shop and we had a catch-up. She told me about Mick. I knew he'd died, read it in the paper, but I didn't go to the funeral because I didn't want to make it awkward.'

'It wouldn't have been awkward. Margie's dead anyway.'

'It seemed like an intrusion, but I thought of you and how hard it must be to live without him.' He reaches for my hand as he says this, his own still rough from playing his trumpet all those years, mine with its liver spots that fits perfect inside his.

'I can't get used to sleeping in a single bed. It's like I'm a kid again.'

'That's the fate of us oldies. Treated like children once we hit a certain age.'

'Put out to pasture like Desdemona and Othello. Do you remember them?'

'Of course. Fine horses. But I never understood their names. I mean they were both black. Shouldn't Desdemona have been white?'

'We needed a matching pair. They were Belgian Blacks. They stood at 17 hands high. I can still remember the smell of them. The feel of their glossy coats. They were so elegant and strong. And so gentle. Barbara's got four of them now. And a whole fleet of cars.'

'She's doing well then.'

'She learnt from the best. As did I.'

'I've always felt so terrible about your poor father, collapsing like that on Coronation Day, finding out his daughter had married a black man. It was like I killed him with my bare hands.'

'He had a heart condition, we found out after. It was no one's fault, though if you want to parcel out blame I'd say it had more to do with Marg who should at least have written or phoned ahead to tell us the situation.'

Silence as we remember the events of that day.

'Why was she called Desdemona?' he asks, startling me as I've popped off elsewhere for a moment.

'Like I said, a matching pair. Though she was actually a stallion.'

'She was?'

'He was.'

He chuckles again, and this time, after a flash of gold tooth, his mint shoots out of his mouth and across the carpet.

'Whoops,' he says.

'It'll have to stay there,' I tell him. 'I can't get out of this chair with my hip and I certainly can't bend down because that's what got me into this pickle in the first place.'

Now we both laugh at the ridiculousness of ageing. It's either that or weeping and, God knows, I've done plenty of that and Benjamin's had his fair share.

'Enough of horses,' I say, once I've caught my breath. 'I heard you got remarried.'

'I did. Hyacinth passed away more than ten years ago. She was a nurse. A ward sister at King's. We had four children.'

'Four?'

'Four boys. Two live in America. The other two in south London.'

'Are they musical?'

'In their own way, not professionally. They're all doctors.'

'Well, I never. Fancy that. Like that hero of yours, what's-his-name. Snakehips Johnson. He studied medicine if I remember rightly.'

'He did, poor old Snakehips. Only twenty-six years of age when that bomb dropped on the Café de Paris. I never got to see him perform. He'd gone by the time I arrived from Jamaica.'

'So many young lives lost.'

And I remember Janet's little sisters and brother and want to heave my heart out.

'We never forget, eh, Betsy.'

'Never.'

Frank appears. Just the one tie today. No watch. He wanders past us, hands clasped behind his back as per, wishes us a good day, tells us he's in a hurry, got to catch a flight to Acapulco when it's clear the only place he'll be going is a nursing home.

'We shouldn't have married, me and your sister.'

'The colour thing?'

'That was hard, of course. She was treated badly. But, no, it wasn't that. It was my job. She liked the idea of it, thought it was going to be a glamorous lifestyle, but there's no glamour in grotty dressing rooms and drab old lodging houses.'

'Everything was grotty and drab back then.'

'She was destined for more comfort.'

'She got that all right, but she missed the excitement. She was bored out of her mind. Once she'd had Sebastian and sent him off to boarding school she was at a loss. Started playing bridge and golf and that's where she met Roger, husband number three.'

'Playing bridge?'

'Playing golf.'

That chuckle again. How can a man listen to all this about a woman he was head over heels in love with once upon a time? Only, I don't expect Marg was the love of his life. That was his second wife, Hyacinth, mother to his children.

'Fancy a walk?' he says.

'I can't walk. I've fractured my hip.'

'Ever heard of a wheelchair? I've got my strength and there's nothing to you, you're all skin and bone, woman, so we can manage a walk between us.'

'There's more to me than meets the eye, Benjamin.'

'I know that, Betsy. Hidden depths.'

'I was thinking more of the roll of flab round my middle but that'll do nicely.'

★   ★   ★

We go for a stroll down the drive and up the road, bumping all the way to the park and I think of our Charlie and Barbara, the pair of them in the Silver Cross pram as I pushed them down Lordship Lane, past the shops, the library, the bomb sites and down to Dulwich Park, round the American Garden, the rhododendrons that Queen Mary used to visit in May (what a mob). The old king, her husband, George V, didn't reckon much to this seaside town. (Bugger Bognor.)

Hotham Park's not Dulwich, but it's all right. We find a bench and Benjamin puts my brakes on, tucks the rug around my knees and I remember I'm an old, incapacitated woman, though I feel like I could be twenty.

'Do you like it here, Betsy?'

'It's all right. I'd sooner be on a Caribbean beach drinking rum.'

'Never say never.'

'I've left the globetrotting a little too late.'

'I know how you feel, Betsy. But all you have to do is shut your eyes and imagine.'

I shut my eyes. I can hear the sea breeze rushing through the trees. Cars zooming up the road. The shouts and screams coming from the water park at Butlins. And although I can remember my pale-skinned Mick reading his *Daily Mirror*, lounging on his deckchair in the shade, I'll be blowed if I can picture a Caribbean beach.

But I can smell the cocoa butter on Benjamin's skin as he squeezes my hand.

★ ★ ★

It's quiet when he drops me back to Sunnydale and heads back off to London. I've told him to phone when he gets there so I know he's safe. I don't want his death on my hands, because I know he (Death) is lurking.

Frank's keeping his distance, which is fine. There's this new resident, an old wrinkled woman, he's been playing cards with her, dirty sod. I'm going to have an early night. I'm very tired, all that fresh air and excitement. Like Marg used to get when she came back from the bomb sites with a piece of treasure of some kind. A button or a scrap of fabric. I didn't like to remind her they most probably came off a dead person, but she knew that already, born to it, as I was. Not that she stuck with it. Two weeks she lasted before going off to be an air hostess.

★　★　★

I can hear the leaves in the big trees because the window's open a crack, the way I like it. Eva Braun tells me off. She says I'll get a chill and I tell her that's fine by me, I'm not bothered about leaving this world because I've lived here long enough.

If I close my eyes, I can smell Desdemona and Othello. Hay and muck and warm sweet horse breath. They had to be stallions, but Dad had it in his head to give them those names. He thought it was serious, the stuff of drama. Shakespeare and England, a horse for a horse, a kingdom for a horse. They had to be black, funereal. The only way to keep a horse black all year round is to keep it as a stallion because once they've had their knackers seen to, they go a browny colour in the summer. But stallions are trickier to handle. They can be aggressive and dominating. My Mick had a way with them. That bogtrotter blood he never quite lost. The soft rain, the Irish Sea, his Holy-Mary-Mother-of-Gods.

He had a way with me too. One look and I was his. But there was one thorn in our relationship. Something we never pruned. And that of course was our son who was never our son but was.

338

For many, the idea of home reaches beyond a physical building to a home town or city.
Queen Elizabeth II

2005

London

It starts off as a normal day. I'm planning to go and visit Mab in hospital because she's had her knee done. I go out to buy some grapes and a copy of *The Lady* and head off for the bus stop as it's only King's College. I know she'll be bored as anything in there, not used to lying around, the worst patient, so she'll be pleased to see me and we can have a catch-up on our families. She's got a whole brood of them, daughters and grand-kiddies, and I still think of Mr Canning and wonder if Mab has any idea, but I doubt it.

Only, by the time I reach the bus stop, there's a bit of a hoo-ha. Something's happened up in town. There's talk of terrorists and I'm overwhelmed with that sick feeling I used to get whenever the IRA or the Luftwaffe got up to no good, but it's been the longest time so why now?

I don't talk to anyone, I make my way to the shop instead. Barbara will be there and she'll be on that ruddy computer, so she'll be able to find out what's going on.

'Mum!' she shouts at me as I go in. 'What's the point in having a mobile phone if you never bloody answer it?'

Well, I don't tell her my phone's most

340

probably still on the kitchen table and it's highly unlikely to have any charge in it because she'll carry on nagging, so I get to the point. 'What's going on? What's happened?'

'There's been a load of bombs go off. On the tube. On a bus.'

'Where?'

'Up in town.'

'Where in town?' I think of Tina, her daughter, my granddaughter, the pyromaniac, catalogue-loving social worker married to a closet Tory with a little son called Tom. Tina who works somewhere near the city and I think that must be where it is, the financial centre, get them where it hurts, like before with the IRA, like the Twin Towers in New York, but it's not there, Barbara says, it's King's Cross and Russell Square, the Edgware Road and Aldgate, which is near enough to where she works, but no, Barbara says, Tina's on a visit this morning in the East End, and again I feel that rush of relief followed by guilt because those bombs will have someone's name on them and maybe quite a few.

I look at my watch. It's five past ten. 'When did this happen?'

'An hour ago. News is just getting through. I can't get hold of Tina, Mum. The phone lines are all jammed, but I know she's all right. She'll be all right, won't she, Mum?'

'Course she will. She'll be all right. A bomb's never got a Sunshine yet.'

★ ★ ★

341

It's three hours before we hear from Tina. All her family are as safe as houses. And all of Mab's too, so I wonder if we have guardian angels or if we are simply ruddy lucky.

Fifty-two people are killed by suicide bombers. Fifty-two people who have names and families, hopes and dreams, and now they've been snuffed out like a candle. Over 700 are injured. All those lives shattered. My city once again enduring a tenor with consequences that'll go on and on, rippling across the Thames.

And I get angry at Charlie. It all bubbles up again and I wonder where he is now and what he feels and if he is ever going to say sorry.

2016

Bognor Regis

Another Sunday evening. Another phone call from the Right Honourable Mab. She's worried about me, she says, again. Don't know why, I'm all right.

'She's bringing me over,' Mab says.

'Who?'

'Karen.'

Karen's her eldest. Four daughters and all of them ginger.

'When?'

'She says she can bring me Wednesday.'

'Doesn't she have a job?'

'She gets the day off on a Wednesday.'

'All right for some.'

'She works weekends, Betsy. She's not a layabout unlike some I could mention.'

She means Charlie, though she won't say it, because the thing about Mab is, she'll always threaten to do stuff but she'll never actually get around to doing it. So chances are she won't be coming on Wednesday and I can watch *Escape to the Country*, because our Bognor Vera Lynn has popped her clogs so there'll be no more bluebirds and no more Jerusalem.

★　★　★

I get that itchy feeling, the one I keep getting, like I want to do something reckless, but the choice is limited in here. Is that what happened to Charlie? He was always surrounded by Death, not least losing his grandfather like that in the middle of the coronation. Was he looking for something with his other grandfather in Donegal? What did he have that Mick and I couldn't give him? Did he know in his heart and in his bones that he was a cuckoo in the nest?

★   ★   ★

I console myself sometimes with the thought that Charlie didn't blow these people up directly. He didn't light the touchpaper, as it were. But he was involved, part of a chain reaction. Whatever choices we make in life, even if we think we're doing a good thing, it can all turn out bad. Fate or Destiny, or I don't know what, but that's the way it goes. The bus you didn't catch might be involved in an accident. The man in a van that gets crushed by a juggernaut might have a victim trussed up in the back, still alive, one he was about to take to some remote place, rape, kill and bury. That job you didn't get, that could have led you to a cocaine habit. Though there's no ruddy excuse for snorting stuff up your schnozz. Dad was bad enough with his snuff. He used to send me down the tobacconist's to get it for him. They wouldn't serve you now without ID. You can get fake ID. Charlie would know about that. Me and all, for that matter.

If Charlie was part of this chain of events, then

I am too. I'm responsible for blowing up innocent people, kiddies even. If he'd grown up with Janet he wouldn't have gone to Ireland to stay with his grandfather. He'd have been a better person. But he was a bastard and we gave him a name, me and Mick, with a little persuasion from the registrar. How was I to know that Janet would survive this long? She could easily have kicked the bucket when Charlie was a nipper and then he'd have ended up with us anyway most probably. It's a fool's errand, this picking over the past. What's done is done.

★ ★ ★

'Betsy? Are you still there? Betsy?'

I wish my sisters would give it a rest.

And Winston? What would he think of me?

Charlie said Churchill was a racist. He was responsible for the first concentration camps, in the Boer War. He treated the Irish like dogs, unleashing the Black and Tans on the Roman Catholics. I thought it was Charlie spouting his bogtrotter propaganda, but then last time Tom came for a visit, he lent me this book on Churchill and the empire. (He's doing history at Brighton.) I can only read a bit at a time. Because of my eyes. I get headaches. But I keep coming back to it. Stuff Charlie used to go on and on about. Bengal, Kenya, Iraq. Even the mess of Israel. They blame everything on Winnie.

I wouldn't listen to Charlie. I wouldn't have a

bad word said about the man who got us through the dark nights and the grey days when we was on the verge of giving up like the Frogs (sorry, Mum). He gave us strength, tenacity, bloody-mindedness.

He saved our freedom.

Charlie used to say one person's freedom is another person's prison.

Now the itchy feeling's reached my brain, bad thoughts wriggling around it. And the worst question of all: Did Churchill see Hitler as a rival to the British Empire?

Not my Winnie, no. After all, nobody's perfect. Dig deeper and we all have faults. Even the Queen. She's a person, same as you and me, works hard, does her bit, only she has a few extra quid and some very nice jewels.

'I'll be there on Wednesday, Betsy.' Then the line goes dead.

I have to be seen to be believed.
Queen Elizabeth II

2006

London

You know that thing about waiting for a bus? How I waited for a baby then got Charlie and Barbara within six months? The same happens with the Queen. Four years after my trip to the Palace, I get invited back, only this time it's even more of an honour, even more special.

The gold-embossed invitation is for a lunch and reception to celebrate Queen Elizabeth II's 80th birthday. And, of course, it's the same day as mine. So along with another 98 people born on the same day, I'm invited to the Palace on the 19th of April. I have no idea until the letter comes. Barbara went and put my name forward into the ballot and, would you believe it, I'm one of the lucky ones. So I ask her to come with me as I can have one guest. I would've taken Mick or Marg if they hadn't gone and died. Or Janet if she wasn't still globetrotting. I would've taken Mab, only she's forever crashing into things even though she's only sixty-three.

I don't tell Barbara she's fifth in line to the invite. I'm not that stupid. So, two days before our actual birthday, off we go to Buckingham Palace, in one of the limousines again, driven by one of the boys, they have their uses, all done up proper, but no hats, which is all right because

I've spent most of my life wearing a hat of some sort or other, usually black.

We assemble in the Picture Gallery for a sherry, and of all the glasses of sherry I've drunk over the years, I never expected to have one here, in a room full of almost-octogenarians, including the Queen. And yet here she is, a little vision in pale green, a double string of pearls to match her brooch, smiling and relaxed, and I wonder if she is genuinely enjoying herself, knowing she's in a room of her subjects who've lived through what she has lived through, the war, the end of the empire, bombs and bombs and bombs, and even though she was born with a silver spoon in her mouth, it's fine because today we all get to dine off of silver plates usually reserved for state banquets, which must be a nightmare to clean as you can't exactly put them through the dishwasher. We could eat fish and chips from the paper for all I care, but it will be nice to be waited on in such grand surroundings.

Then it's time for lunch, in the Palace Ballroom. Twenty tables of ten, like a big fat wedding, and would you believe it, Barbara and I get put on the table next to Her Majesty's, so close you could spit on her and I have this urge to do just that, which is ridiculous as I have never spat in my whole life, only when I'm cleaning my teeth, and why would I spit on the Queen, of all people, my heroine, my majesty, but it's that urge I get sometimes to shout out 'knickers' in the middle of the crem, to do a cartwheel down the aisle of a church, because all my life I've had to be good, I've had to toe the line, and I reckon the Queen must get these urges too, but, like me, she can suppress them, and I know I'm only getting this outrageous desire now because I'm as nervous as anything. And for some reason Joanie Clark pops into my head, dropping me a sarcastic curtsey in the playground with her posse of snot-nosed ragamuffins. If only she could see me now.

'You all right, Mum? You've gone bright red.'

'I feel a bit overwhelmed all of a sudden.'

Barbara pats my hand and I can't remember her ever doing that and I realise that's because she's all grown up now at fifty-eight years of age, about ruddy time.

The food is smashing, a three-course meal, all in French, but basically posh beef and mash with some lovely wine. And we're accompanied by a wonderful orchestra who play the show songs and I get a vision of a trumpet player with a smoky voice.

The Queen gives a short address, short but very, very sweet.

I doubt whether any of us can say that the last 80 years has been plain sailing, but we give thanks for our health and happiness, the support we receive from our family and friends, for wonderful memories and the excitement that each new day brings.

She tells us we're her 'exact twins' and I notice that half the room are reaching for the hankies up their sleeves. We all share something with her. And I feel this connection, like I know a bit of what she's had to do, a bit of what she's had to live through, because both of us got burdened with a job for life. She was the accidental heir to the throne, same way as I was the accidental heir to the business, for I know without a shadow that Dad would have passed the business to a son if there'd been one. She and I have shown that women can do it. We don't just talk about it, we get our hands dirty and we ruddy well do it. Barbara too. She might be a feminist and spout her man-hating stuff, but she does run a business. Never married though, never known what that's like, not like Lilibet and me. Had Tina on her own, and Tina may have got married to a closet Tory, but she's just got the one kiddie, Tom, the gay who's at university. So who is there to carry on the family business? Unless I can persuade Margie's boy, but I can't see Sebastian working with corpses somehow, though there could be one of Mab's litter going spare, so who knows.

A nice chap stands up on our behalf and responds to her Majesty's speech. He's a Methodist pie and liquor and a gracious gentleman, which doesn't surprise me as I never minded the Methodists. What does surprise me, though, on this most surprising of days, is that I get the chance to chat with her, my Queen, and it's like chatting to someone I went to school with, only a lot posher, and I try harder than ever to mind my manners and enunciate properly just as Mum always nagged Margie and I. She asks me where I've come from and I tell her from south of the river. And then, before she asks the other obvious question, I tell her what I've done with my life and she looks at me curiously, that Paddington Bear stare, and there's this click of recognition.

'Mrs Sunshine.'

'Yes, your Majesty.'

'How lovely to see you again.'

'The pleasure's all mine, Ma'am.'

We talk for a bit, a proper chit-chat, because we are exact twins and all of us in this room have this connection that can't really be explained, so I tell her about losing the love of my life, my Mick, and I tell her he fought for the Allies, an Irishman, and she said he must have been a brave man. Other than that, what is said in the palace, stays in the palace, same as the mortuary. Not that there's much talk in the mortuary, but you get the drift.

I know this is the last time I will see her like this, but she will be my Queen forever.

Vivat Regina!

2016

Bogor Regis

A man who is tough is a woman who is a bitch. A man who is assertive is a woman who is aggressive. A man who doesn't suffer fools gladly is a woman who is up herself. A man who is strong is a woman who is bossy.

You can't beat that so you have to get on with it. I was lucky to be given a role in life. I was lucky my dad thought differently to other dads and that he listened to Mum. I was lucky I married a man who let me be the person I was meant to be. But there's always that nagging feeling, that itch to shout and spit at inappropriate times that cries out to be scratched, but it's an itch worth putting up with because we can't all do what we ruddy well like.

Eleanor of Aquitaine was all of those things, according to the history books. Barbara's been researching our family history, one of those websites she belongs to. She reckons I'm a twenty-fourth generation direct descendant of Eleanor of Aquitaine, which she says explains a lot, cheeky so-and-so. But what we never know from a family tree or from records, despite what my mum said about the importance of registering births, christenings, marriages, and deaths, what we never know is the truth of who we are, the validity of the bloodline. Because women sleep with men who aren't their husbands. Women have babies off the bread man. History is littered with bastards. Charlie's parentage is nothing unusual in that respect, so he can't blame his criminal activities on a decision I made back before he was born. Once you're a certain age you have to take responsibility. Though by the time you reach sixty-six it's possibly too late, never mind nearly ninety.

I might have royal blood running through my veins, but that still doesn't make me the ruddy Queen, God save her.

2012

Dublin

The last time I see Charlie is at Islandbridge war memorial in Dublin. The Queen came here a couple of years ago and laid a wreath of poppies, the first time she'd ever visited Ireland. And this is my first time.

It's a cool June day. We gather together, a small group of families and supporters, including one of the last surviving veterans, to mark the pardon for all those Irish servicemen, which is now official. Barbara and Charlie are with me as we do this on behalf of Mick. It can't go any worse than Churchill's funeral when Charlie went to Ireland the first time. I track him down and suggest he comes along now because I think it might help lay that particular ghost to rest; if Charlie can see the bigger picture, because there's always a bigger picture if you stand back far enough, this might soothe his troubled soul and he might understand the solid, decent principles surrounding his father's decision to fight the Nazis.

And it all seems to go off all right. I think we've done it, we've built some bridges, now can we get on with life, what's left of it. I don't say that, I bite my tongue, which is what annoys Charlie, because when we're in the café afterwards, he starts quizzing me about Mick.

Why did he desert?

Why did he support Churchill?

Why did Mick do this and that, when I thought Charlie was now of an understanding, that he'd long ago put all of this aside, but no. He stands up in that café and he bangs the table with the palm of his hand, and he marches off, slamming the door, leaving Barbara and me staring into our cups of tea wondering what that was all about.

'Is there something you want to tell me, Mum?'

'No,' I say. 'I've got nothing to tell you.'

'Only,' she says, 'Auntie Janet said you might want to tell us something today.'

Ruddy Janet when it's none of her beeswax.

★   ★   ★

We find Charlie later, at the gates of the memorial of all places. He's smoking and coughing, but I don't nag. I ask him if he's hungry, shall we get fish and chips, and he says, Yes, Mum, let's do that. So the three of us find a chip shop, like in the old days, and we eat them on a bench, in the dusk, out of the paper, using wooden forks, looking over Dublin, and it's the best fish and chip supper I've ever had, despite the soft rain that starts to fall, in June, I ask you.

★   ★   ★

When we return to London, there's someone I have to write to. There's someone I have a bone, to pick with. But before I have time to get out the Basildon Bond, there's a phone call, long distance from Washington.

'How did it go?' Janet asks me. 'There wasn't much mentioned in the news, but then this is America and they're not terribly interested in the rest of the world, especially Britain, unless it's to do with the Queen and so that pretty much rules out Ireland.' She catches her breath. 'Anyway, I'm so glad for Mick.'

And I say something wicked because she's stumped me, still getting involved after all this time.

I tell her to eff off and mind her beeswax and I slam the phone down so hard I make a crack in it, which is all right because we need a new one.

2016

Bognor Regis

'I read your book.'

'That was quick, Nana,' Tom says, surprised, ruddy cheek. 'Did you get through all of it?'

'I had nothing else to do. There's only so many property programmes you can watch. It's times like this I wish I could knit.'

'You could do some of that colouring for adults.'

'Do what? I'd sooner get my nipples pierced.'

'Nana!'

'Sorry, love. Don't know what came over me. It's like I can't help saying things these days. I used to think bad stuff but I'd never say it. I was brought up to keep my mouth shut. All those years I had to be dignified and serious. Even us funeral directors, retired or otherwise, have to have fun every once in a while.'

'Right, Nana. So what did you reckon to it, the book?' Tom shifts in his chair, as he ruddy well should.

'I don't know really, if I'm honest with you. I do know your Uncle Charlie would agree with it all. But it makes Churchill sound like some kind of fascist and how can he be that when he was there with us, in the War, fighting fascism? That's what we were fighting against. That's what

358

Granddad Mick gave up his country for. God knows what would have happened if Winnie wasn't our leader. We'd be dead, or German, or I don't know what. They'd have put you in a gas chamber for a start.'

Tom raises an eyebrow. I think he's been plucking it. I used to do that to some of the corpses, tidy them up. 'Why's that, Nana?'

'Because you're a gay.'

'I'm gay, Nana. Not a gay.'

'That's what I said. You're a gay.'

He shakes his head at me, his blue hair flopping about. You never know quite what to say these days. I used to have the right words and knew the right times to say those words, but now it's all too easy to put my foot in it. I'd blame it on dementia if I could, but they might boot me out of Sunnydale.

'Do you think we can learn from the past, Nana?'

I wasn't expecting a philosophy session today, but Tom's always been a thinker. Used to stare at the contents of his potty as a toddler, as if he could see the future in a poo, when what you could actually see was whatever he had shoved in his mouth and not digested, buttons, flowers, crayons. And right now, with his parrot hair, he's waiting for me to answer him, so answer him I do. 'I don't honestly know if we're capable of it, Tom. We do the same stuff over and over. Sometimes we get better at it, sometimes worse.' Which is not very philosophical, I know, but it's all I can come up with when put on the spot by my gay great-grandson, Tom, who I love very much but who's a know-it-all now he's a ruddy student.

He's quiet for a moment, which is more than his grandma and mother can manage with their big fat cakeholes. 'Maybe you need to see Uncle Charlie?'

'What's your grandma been saying?'

'Just that it makes her sad you two don't see each other.'

'Does she see him?'

'You know she does, Nana. Not often, but she does go and visit him.'

'She won't tell me anything.'

'Nana. You won't *let* her tell you anything.'

'You can be a cheeky so-and-so.'

'You're my great-grandmother and I love you. I think you've led an amazing life and that you should make it up with your son.'

'But he's not my son.'

'You can't disown him, Nana. He'll always be your son.'

'But he's not. Don't you see? He was never my son.'

'What d'you mean?'

'He was Janet's. She fell for him off a married man and Mick and I took him on.'

'Auntie Janet?'

'Yes, your great-great-auntie Janet had a child out of wedlock and I took him on because we couldn't have kiddies, me and Mick, and it solved all our problems.'

'But you had Granny Barbara.'

'She was my lucky egg.'

'An accident?'

'A surprise.'

'And does Uncle Charlie know this?'

'No, he doesn't. We thought it best not to tell him. I know they want you to tell your adopted kid everything these days, but we didn't adopt him as such. We put our names on the birth certificate, told everyone he was ours, and no one ever questioned it.'

'Except maybe Charlie?'

'You think he knew?'

'Maybe on some level of consciousness.'

'Ruddy hell.'

'Ruddy hell indeed, Nana Betsy.' He smiles this lovely warm smile and a thought occurs to me, so I tell him. He's got that kind of face.

'You'd make a smashing undertaker.'

★　★　★

Another Sunday.

'Was Dad my father?' Mabel has asked the question I've been waiting for her to ask for a very, very long time.

'What?'

'You heard.'

I never knew how I would answer this, so I answer with a question, a technique learnt over the years to get the most out of clients. 'Who do you think's your father?'

'Mr Canning.'

'Mr Canning?'

'The grocer.'

'I know who you mean, but I don't know where you got that idea from.'

361

'Because I heard Mum and Dad have one of their whispered arguments. I must've been six or seven and Mr Canning had been round with a present for my birthday, a dolly, and Dad had pushed him out onto the street and mortified Mum.'

'She didn't like a show. Undertakers are not supposed to make a show.'

'I reckon us Sunshines have all put on a show from time to time,' Mab says.

'Speak for yourself.'

'Don't you think it's time for the truth, Betsy?'

'Are you talking about Mr Canning?'

'I'm talking about Charlie.'

'Not you and all.'

Why's everyone talking about Charlie?

★   ★   ★

The following Sunday evening she calls me again while I'm half-asleep and muddled.

'Well, Betsy?'

'Well, what?'

'You know.'

'Do I?'

'You know what you have to do.'

'What's that, Mab?'

'You have to make amends.'

'How the ruddy hell do I do that?'

'You give him back his mother.'

Keep Baby with Mother.

It has been women who have breathed gentleness and care into the hard progress of humankind.
Queen Elizabeth II

2014

East Dulwich

It's time to say goodbye to the old house, to Lordship Lane and SE22. I've lived here all my life. Thought I'd die here too, but it's time to go. I've had enough. I want the seaside.

★   ★   ★

I think I've made a ruddy mistake when I move into Sunnydale. It's like my first day at school all over again, but I can't cry because I'm not a kiddie, though I might as well be. Most of the first week I sit on my Jack Jones, watching telly or reading a magazine. I even take up word searches, which I never saw the point of, but there's this quiet satisfaction when you complete one, all those found words.

It was before the Fat One and Eva Braun. There was this nice young Filipino girl. She was smashing, can't remember her name, Emily or something. Yes, Emily. She told me about her family back in the Philippines. She had a little boy, four years old he was. He lived with her mother while she was over here, sending money back. Halfway across the world to look after some old people while her mum looked after her boy. Now that's hard work. Some of the

364

residents judged her. Said she shouldn't go off leaving her little kiddie behind, but I told her, good for you. You do what you have to do. Sometimes it works and sometimes it doesn't.

'Tell me about your life,' she says to me one day. And she means it. She wants to hear all about everything.

'I was an undertaker.' I look at her, wait for the reaction.

'Is honourable job,' she says. 'Very good.'

'Yes, it is,' I say. 'Thank you.'

She smiles at me and holds my hand. 'It's my welcome.'

After that she sits with me for five minutes when she can. She gets me into armchair athletics and Vera Lynn's sing-alongs and I begin to make some friends so I don't feel such a wallflower, though I've been a wallflower all my life, it goes with the job, so maybe it's not too late to change.

But I watch the old ones leave, one by one, in an ambulance or a hearse. Nursing home or hospital or morgue. They don't come back.

Better late than never.
Betsy Sunshine

2016

Bognor Regis

She's gone now, Emily, the Filipino. She hooked up with a local, the son of some old dear who was a resident here, before she got demoted to the nursing home. Dead now, I believe. Emily married the chap and they moved to the Philippines, opened some café or other. She sends a postcard every now and again and the staff pin it up on the noticeboard in the hall, but most of them don't even remember her. But I do. That little boy of hers will be getting big and she'll be there to see him getting bigger, which is nice.

★ ★ ★

The new resident, the one that Frank's taken a shine to, is getting on my nerves already. I've managed to avoid her the first few days. I've been spending a lot of time snoozing, but she keeps waking me up as she's a loudmouth. Shouts like a fishwife. It's only today that I realise something. I know her. But I don't reckon that can be right because why would she end up here of all places? Of all the nursing homes, in all the towns, in all the world, she's wheeled into mine, ruddy Joanie Clark.

'Oh my, God! It's the Queen!' she says when she clocks me properly for the first time.

Benjamin's been for a visit and brought me some Mint Imperials and I can see that she and Frank are talking about us, huddled together over the other side of the room. When he's gone, I'm feeling a bit low, tired as anything.

And there she is, in front of me, with her Zimmer. 'Sorry I can't curtsey, but my knees don't work.' She cackles and I feel all the violence of a five-year-old's anger and no mother to rein me in.

She can't bully me now. I'm the one with friends here. Where's her posse of snot-nosed ragamuffins now? All dead. I know that because I've buried each and every one of them. Just Joanie Clark that's left and she's not aged well, looks at least a hundred, all wrinkled round the lips from smoking and frowning and too much Spanish sunshine. How come she's avoided cancer? Some people do everything they can to avoid it, but it don't care what you think or what you do. If it's got your name on it.

'Who's your fella?' she says.

'Which one you talking about?'

' 'Which one' ', she says. ' 'Which one?' ' Joanie cackles again, nails down a blackboard. 'The coloured one?'

'If you're referring to the black gentleman, he's Benjamin. Used to be my brother-in-law.'

'Which sister? Marg or Mab?'

'Who do you think?'

'Lucky Marg.'

'She left him.'

'Whatever for? Did she get dog mess though the letter box?'

'Dog mess? Oh, you mean from the racists?'

'Dirty scum.'

'The blacks or the racists?'

'The racists, Queenie. The racist scum. I once chased one of them National Front hooligans all along Lordship Lane with only a dead turbot to hand.'

I must look surprised. I assumed Joanie Clark must be a racist herself because she was a bully. Maybe I got her wrong. Maybe I should have dug deeper. She had a rotten childhood, after all. Her dad was a drunk, a bully, and he stoved her mum's head in for all we know. She had to leave school and start earning to help feed her siblings who got farmed out to aunts and anyone who'd have them. No wonder she ended up getting married so young to the fishmonger's apprentice. Imagine that: stinking to high heaven of haddock and pollock. Never had kiddies of her own — reckon she'd done enough caring of little ones to last a lifetime. No one to take care of her now though. Who's going to visit her here?

'You got family?'

'Nieces and nephews. All got money and jobs but none of them have much time.'

'Isn't that the way.'

And I can't believe I'm chatting to Joanie Clark like we're old friends, when she was never my friend, but you don't know what's round the corner. Though, I can hazard a guess what's round the next one: Death, waiting in the shadows, wearing a cloak and wielding a dagger. Though I might dodge him a while longer, the ruddy bastard.

★ ★ ★

Charlie would have been a bastard had me and Mick not taken him on. It doesn't matter these days, there are bastards everywhere, but it mattered then. You were nothing without a dad, unless he'd died in the war, and even then he had to be married to your mother. That's how it was. I'm not saying it was right. I'm not saying it's right to go round having bastards all over the place either. Different dads for different kids, all living as a family under one roof. All those double-barrelled names that used to be posh but they're not any more because they mean you've shacked up and had a kid without tying the knot. Mum and Dad wouldn't have liked it, but they wouldn't judge. When you're dead you're dead. It doesn't matter if you were married or not. It's how you live your life that counts.

★ ★ ★

'I had an affair,' Joanie says.

'You did?'

'Don't sound too surprised. I used to be a looker.'

I ignore that comment and focus on the important details. 'Who with?'

'Bob Vickers,' she says, sharp as a knife, like

370

she's on Mastermind.

'Senior or Junior?'

'Ha, ha, very funny. Junior, thank you very much.'

Joanie, the fishwife, laying with a layer-outer.

'You used to tease me about dead people and there you were all that time.'

'Only a few months,' she says.

'Even so.'

'I s'pose I was sort of mean to you at school. But you was always Miss Snooty. Princess Betsy.'

'I was a little girl, same as you. And I got a wallop — two wallops — for standing up to you and your rotten bully girls.'

'What doesn't kill you makes you stronger.'

'Not if you've fractured your ruddy pelvis, it don't.'

'True, Betsy. True.'

★ ★ ★

'Bob Vickers got me up the duff.'

'He never.'

'Oh yes he did. Then he made me see one of them backstreet women. You know the ones. Nearly killed me she did and there were no kiddies after Harry and me got hitched.'

'Might've been Harry firing blanks.'

'Might've. Or that witch might've ruined my insides.'

'More likely.'

And I want to tell her about Charlie but I daren't. It is Joanie Clark after all. I'm not that daft.

But, as I said, her posse of snot-nosed ragamuffins are all dead now. Our husbands and lovers. Our fathers and mothers. All those people we once knew. Joanie's got her nieces and nephews. I've got Mab and Janet. Barbara, Tina and Tom. But I don't have Mick no more. Or Margie. Or Charlie. Though Charlie was never mine to have. Never mine to keep. No wonder he can't bear to be within spitting distance of me. And no wonder I'm relieved. Only, there's this nagging feeling, this gnawing in my guts that makes me nauseous. I must ask Eva Braun if she can get hold of some Andrews Liver Salts. There's not much a dose of that won't cure.

It's not all bad news. I do have something Margie used to have — not that she wanted him no more because the next bus had come along with a pilot driving it. I've got Benjamin. Three times he's been to see me now. Still driving at eighty-eight. Mick never learnt. All those years and he never learnt. So he could never drive a hearse. Though he knew how to handle the horses and he could carry a coffin along with anyone. I miss being able to get in a car and just drive off. Getting old means you lose your freedom. You lose your choices. It's like going back in time, being a kiddie again, only without the fun. But seeing Benjamin has reminded me what fun looks like. How it feels. I'm not dead yet. And Joanie Clark had better keep her hands off of him.

★ ★ ★

'What happened to Bob Vickers?' I ask Joanie later, teatime, jam sandwiches and jelly, a kiddie's birthday party but without the balloons and tears.

'Dead,' she says.

'I know he's dead. I mean what happened to the pair of you after the youknowwhat?'

'Oh that. Well, it was all over. I didn't want nothing to do with him no more. Couldn't even look at him 'cos all I could see was the dead baby that was never a baby. All I could see was a mess of blood and gore. I hated him.'

'Nasty piece of work. Hands everywhere, like an octopus.'

'He knew how to turn on the charm.'

'He certainly knew how to get what he wanted.'

She nods her head in agreement. Then puts on a wistful smile. 'He rocked my world, for a time. Which was more than my Harry ever did.'

'Your Harry was a good 'un, though, weren't he?'

'He was. He was never going to light up the sky, but he shone enough for me and him. He was my safe pair of hands.'

'Nothing wrong with a safe pair of hands.'

'Now tell me about this Frank. Is he a goer?'

'Really, Joanie. Your Harry's barely in the ground.'

'Don't matter, does it? He'd want me to be happy.'

'You think Frank will make you happy? Look at him, snoozing in his armchair with his mouth all slack, catching flies.'

'Well, he's alive, unlike my Harry, so that's good enough for me.'

'Barely. I'm not actually sure if he's still breathing.'

She cackles then, but I don't mind. I even find myself smiling. Smiling at the way life turns itself inside out.

'Here, Betsy,' Joanie says. 'You got your undertaker's bag of tricks? I used to watch your mum going into people's houses with hers. What did she keep in there?'

'A mirror, some Vaseline, Vicks, a comb, a handkerchief, needle and thread. I've still got it.'

'I reckon we should fetch it and test them out on Harry Two Ties.'

I have a go at cackling myself.

★　★　★

Mum had all sorts in her bag. Sometimes I lie awake and reel off the contents like a memory game. As well as the obvious, and what I told Joanie, she kept rolls of cotton wool that she'd douse with cedar wood oil to keep the flies away from the deceased because you really don't want maggots. Shaving stuff. Eye caps. A towel. Strips of sheet. An apron. It was the Mary Poppins of bags. Mum could make a corpse so good you'd think it could get up and dance.

The Queen has a bag too. Not sure we'll ever know what she keeps inside it. A mobile? Lipstick? A hanky? A small hand grenade to throw at her husband when he gets too much?

***

'You used to call me horrible names,' I tell Joanie.

'Sticks and stones, Betsy. My Harry used to say I don't care what you call me as long as you don't call me late for dinner.'

***

Joanie's got me into bingo. I always thought it was common till Mum started going in her latter years. It's right up Joanie's street, but it's good for the old brain. Use it or lose it, Joanie says, and I don't think she's just referring to the old grey matter, not the way she cackles, dirty cow.

Frank has definitely taken a shine to her. He's given me a wide berth since my visit from Benjamin. Joanie's welcome to Frank with his two ties and watches.

'Do you remember that Malcolm, the doctor?' she asks me after she's beaten everyone at housey-housey.

'The medical student?'

'He told me he was a doctor,' she says, indignant. 'The randy bugger.'

'Oh don't tell me you went with him and all, Joanie Clark.'

'Just the once,' she said. 'After some dance down the hall. Your dad brought your Margie home in disgrace, so I felt sorry for him, left high and dry.'

'My dad?'

'He turned up during the last number and

gave her a right earbashing.'

'Well, I never knew that. I was out with Mum. My first body.'

'Who was that?'

'Gloria Bannister.'

'Gloria? From Infants? Lived down Pellatt Road?'

'That's the one.'

'She weren't half a good footballer.'

'She was, Joanie. She was ruddy good.'

'Bloody shame. That Hitler had a lot to answer for.'

'It was cancer.'

'Cancer has a lot to answer for and all.'

'Besides, it was after the war when she died.'

'Was it, Betsy? It all gets a bit blurry.'

'Doesn't it just.'

'And we never learn, do we?'

'No, Joanie. I'm not sure we do.'

★ ★ ★

'I used to work in a chemist,' she tells me later.

'Did you?'

'Down the road from you, Lordship Lane. I worked there on Saturdays. It got me out the fishmonger's. We had a Saturday boy that covered for me.'

A chemist. A cow of an assistant with a sleazeball for a husband. Mr Trigg and his ruddy wife.

'I worked with this old bat.'

'Elsie Trigg?'

Joanie nods, her glasses skew-whiff, her cheeks reddening. 'Now *she* was a nasty piece of work.'

376

'I thought you got on with her?'

'What made you think that? She used to put pinholes through the sheaths, thought it was funny, playing Russian Roulette.'

'That's awful.'

'She was a cow.'

I want to say that's the pot and the kettle but I don't because I actually like Joanie, words I never expected to fall out of my mouth. She plays bingo with me and keeps me company. She's a breath of fresh air in this waiting room. She's my ally against Eva Braun and the Fat One with the name I can't remember because it's made up. She's given Frank a new lease of life and she's kept her hands off of Benjamin, who, so it happens, has been for another visit, can't stay away, even played dominoes with my Tom.

It's all go here. Better than school. I'm enjoying it more this time round, but I don't half miss my sisters. Mab still hasn't been. She came up with some excuse. A hospital appointment or the dentist's or Specsavers. But any road, she says she's coming next Wednesday, which we'll wait and see.

★   ★   ★

'Betsy? I was going to tell you about Elsie Trigg. It's important . . . '

I'm tired now. I wish Joanie would ruddy shut up and let me have forty winks, then I'll be ready for *Pointless* and that lovely Alexander Armstrong who sounds like he could be a prince with that voice of his and the bald spot.

'I remember something, Betsy.'

'Bully for you.'

'To do with that Mr Trigg, the registrar.'

My heart shudders and I turn quite cold all of a sudden.

'He was having a thing with Janet.'

'Janet?'

'Your Janet. Didn't you know?'

'It was a long time ago. Like you said, things get blurry.'

'Not that blurry. You must've known. You two were bosom buddies.'

'I don't remember.'

'Well, I remember this. I heard that Trigg woman say something to him. They was having an argument in the shop — I was out the back and they didn't know I was listening. She said something about a baby. He was begging her to take it on. He'd got someone up the duff and I reckon it was Janet. Only Janet never came back.'

'She joined the Foreign Office. She never had children.'

'Only, I seem to remember you coming back with a baby, Betsy. And six months later you've got another one. Now, I might not be the brightest, but I can do my numbers and they don't add up.'

★ ★ ★

I'm too ruddy tired for this. I ask Eva Braun to help me to bed. My head's banging.

★ ★ ★

Next thing I know it's morning and I'd be quite happy to stay in bed today. I will stay in bed. I'll tell them I'm poorly. I think I am poorly. I'm nearly ninety, for flip's sake.

'Would you like me to phone your daughter?'

'I'm not dying.'

'I'll let her know you're not feeling too great.'

So I get Barbara phoning me up, fussing. 'Mabel's coming to see you today,' she says, like it's the ruddy Queen not my little sister.

'Today? It's Tuesday.'

'So?'

'She said it would be a Wednesday.'

'Tuesday or Wednesday, it makes no odds, does it, Mum. Perk of being retired. You can please yourself.'

I wish.

'I'm tired today, that's all. Can you put her off?'

'They're already on their way according to Karen.'

Karen, the oldest ginger with a face full of freckles. Drives a BMW and lives in Chislehurst. Drives me mad when she talks about her grand-kiddies, all at private school with an armoury of cellos and tennis rackets.

★ ★ ★

I'm snoozing in the lounge when they turn up. Karen pushes her in, little Mab in a wheelchair, and I remember her on that bike Dad bought her, Queen Boudicca. Mab is wearing spectacles that make her eyes appear like they belong to a fly. She looks tiny, like she's shrunk into herself, but we all do that as we get old. We become so small we end up practically invisible.

'Hello, Betsy,' Mab says. She's on a level with me as we're both sitting down, me in my wee-resistant armchair, her in her chariot. She rubs my knee because we neither of us can manage to reach in for a kiss, and besides, we're not that sort of family, never have been touchy-feely. My Mick more than made up for that, God rest him.

'How are you, Betsy? You all right?'

'Can't complain. Who's this you've got with you?'

'This is Karen. My oldest. You remember Karen?'

'Hello, Auntie Betsy,' Karen says, not so ginger now, more of a washed-out peach. With a bum to match.

'Course I remember Karen. I'm not doolally.'

'I never said you were. You just looked a bit blank for a moment.'

'That's these things I keep having. My mind wanders off but it usually comes back.'

'Well, that's all right then.'

'If you say so.'

We're saved by one of the new assistants, looks like she should still be at school, bringing us a tray of tea and biscuits and I notice that Karen helps herself to two custard creams and a digestive when she drives a BMW and lives in Chislehurst.

'Thanks for coming to see me, Mab. I'm too old to be gallivanting around and Barbara's too busy to drive me to see you.'

I ignore Karen's look of disgust when I mention my daughter, as if they don't have Death in Chislehurst.

'How is Barbara?' she forces herself to ask.

'Doing very well, thank you, Karen.'

'Does she have a boyfriend?'

'A boyfriend? She's ruddy fifty-eight, what do you think?'

'All right, Betsy. No need to be like that,' says my little sister and she's probably the only one I can take this off, so I leave it be.

'Sorry, my head hurts.'

'Maybe we should go, Mum.'

'Tell you what, Karen, pop to Marks and get us some of those nice prawn sandwiches and we can stop off on the way home, up Bury Hill or somewhere.'

Karen's out of here like a shot.

'Sorry about her, Betsy. She's just found out Simon's having an affair.'

'If that's how she behaves who can blame him.'

'She's actually very sweet-natured. You've caught her on a bad day.'

'All right, then, well, I know those only too well. Don't have many good days myself anymore.'

We sit and chat for a bit and it's nice being with my sister because she knows stuff nobody else knows.

'I think Mr Canning was your dad, but it doesn't matter, does it. My dad was your dad and that's all there is to it.'

'It would've been nice to have been told. To

stop the wondering.'

'Would it have made a difference to your life?'

'I was lucky I got into Country and Western, rather than gunrunning like your Charlie.'

'What are you saying?'

'I know he was Janet's. We could all work it out.'

'So why did none of you say anything?'

'Because that was up to you.'

'And Charlie?'

'You'll have to speak to him, won't you.'

'I suppose I will, Mab. I suppose I will.'

★   ★   ★

My Granddad Bill was one of eleven children, seven boys, four girls. Three of the boys were killed within a month of each other at the Somme, including Granddad Bill. His younger brother, great-uncle Percy, his playmate, too young to join up, could never have the war mentioned without him having to leave the room. Nana said he didn't want anyone to see him cry. I never knew men could cry until she told me that. I know it now. I've seen many a hard man cry at a funeral. I saw my dad cry when the next war was announced on the wireless. I saw Mick cry a few times. I never saw Charlie cry, not since he was a baby when that's all he'd do.

If I could see him cry. Just once. Then maybe.

★   ★   ★

I've dozed off again. When I wake up, she's gone. An empty packet of prawn sandwiches lies next to me on the table, which the young assistant is clearing.

'How are you doing, Mrs Sunshine?'

'I'm tired. Do you think you could help me up to bed, only I feel a bit washed out.'

'Course,' she says. 'That woman was a bit bolshy wasn't she, the one with the ginger hair.'

'She was. I think it runs in the family.'

* * *

They're having a party for me next week. Ninety years and I still have friends and family alive, so I'm not doing too badly. It's going to be a bit fancy, more than the usual cake and glass of sherry, because I share the day with the Queen.

On today's visit I tell Barbara to ask Charlie and his lady friend if they'll come. She says she'll see what she can do and before she leaves she gives me an early birthday present. A ruddy mobile phone.

'You're never too old to learn new tricks,' she says. 'This one's got big buttons and couldn't be easier to use. You can text.'

'Why would I want to do that?'

'To keep in touch,' she says with a sigh. 'Charlie has a phone. I've put his number in your contacts. And mine.'

She shows me what to do but I fall asleep and when I wake up she's gone, the phone all warm in my lap.

'Do you know how to work one of these?' I ask
Eva Braun later. She's growing on me. Turns out
she's from Lithuania and her grandparents died
in the war, so I should try and remember her
name.

'Of course,' she says. 'Let me show.' She has it
out of my hands and fiddling with it, her red
nails flashing. She spends ten minutes showing
me how to do a text, but my head hurts so I ask
if she can do one for me.

'Of course. Who to?'

'My son.'

'You have son?'

'I have a son, yes. He's got a lady friend.'

'Like your daughter.'

'Pardon?'

'She has lady friend.'

'She told you that?'

'Wendy. She waits in car park sometimes.'

'Next time, get her to come in and see me.'

'Okay. I do text now?'

'Two texts. One to each of my children. I want
to ask them both to my party and I want them
both to bring their lady friends.'

'Okay, Mrs Sunshine,' she says.

'Call me, Betsy.'

'Okay,' she says. 'And you call me Maria.' She
winks at me, cheeky moo, and I have a quiet
cackle because she's caught me out and fair's
fair.

Tomorrow's the party. It would be awkward if I was to slip off tonight, though they could still celebrate the Queen. (*Vivat Regina!*) After all, Death's had a right busy time of it this year, taking out the famous people. That David Bowie who Charlie and Barbara used to like. Victoria Wood who made me laugh with her trolley and *Woman's Weekly*. Little Ronnie Corbett with his long-winded stories and fork handles. And the other little American one, that was all purple, the little Prince. And then Muhammad Ali, Mick's hero, so many people's hero, so funny, so clever, and honourable. And Terry Wogan who made me laugh with his soft Irish rain chat, just like my bogtrotter husband who I miss every hour of every day.

And that's not forgetting all the other famous people and ordinary people who die every day of every year, because that's what happens, that's life and you can't fight Death forever, even if you're stuck in a ruddy freezer, you won't ever come back to life, like Lazarus, like Jesus. No one knows what happens next, so you have to make amends don't you, before you go. You have to put things right.

★   ★   ★

I'm going to wear a yellow dress because I am a Sunshine after all. Barbara and I went to Marks and Sparks with her friend who's called Wendy. Wendy is a retired solicitor and has a few bob, so I reckon Barbara's done well for herself. She gazes adoringly at Wendy the way she looked at

Pam from Cirencester in the middle of the boating lake at Butlins, just down the road from here, so close I can see the white turrets from my first-floor bedroom. And, beyond those white turrets, a peep of blue-green sea.

They used to have the Birdman of Bognor here. All those ridiculous men dreaming up designs to see who could 'fly' the furthest off the pier before splashing into the waves below. Then it moved to Worthing, for some reason or other, and now Worthing can't do it no more because they can't get the funding or health and safety or some such.

We used to make our own fun. Marbles in the gutters when we could get away with it, as long as Marg behaved and didn't show her knickers to the rag-and-bone man's son. Stan and the lads would play Knock Down Ginger and get a clip round the ear if they annoyed anyone and no one phoned the police or social services. They should've done more of that in the 70s, with those celebrity kiddie-fiddlers. It's not right. I had to do the funeral of a kiddie-fiddler once. You're not supposed to judge. But I wanted to do something wicked. I wanted to cut off his penis, deep-fry it like a saveloy and feed it to the pigeons. Nobody would ever have known. Except for me. And I was better than that. But I did speak to him and I told him exactly what I thought of him and where I hoped he was headed next. And as he disappeared behind the curtains, I imagined all those pictures of hell we used to see in the old books at Sunday school, and I imagined his nasty body burning in the crem and I thought of his evilness burning for eternity, but I knew it was a false dream because hell isn't a place you go to when you die. Nor is heaven, for that matter. Heaven and hell are a whole lot closer than you think. They are all around us, everywhere, all of the time.

★   ★   ★

Barbara arrives early (for once) to help me get ready, while Wendy is out at Tesco's buying Champagne, I ask you, but I'm not complaining.

She helps me get dressed, zipping me into my frock and fussing with my uncontrollable hair. She even clasps my string of pearls round my neck because she knows they are the ones that her dad, my Mick, gave to me when we were on that cruise. He bought them in Capri while I was drinking cocktails with Margie, the crafty so-and-so, God love him.

'A ray of sunshine,' Barbara says to me, while she snaps a picture on her phone and I do want to tell Barbara that I'm proud of her, because I am, but I don't know why I find it so hard, except that my generation don't tend to go all gushy with their kids.

'You're my girl,' I tell her, that's the best I can come up with and I have to dig deep to manage even that, but it does the trick because she says, Yes, Mum, yes, I am, and then she suffocates me in her generous bosom.

★   ★   ★

There's red, white and blue balloons all over the residents, lounge. There's even a familiar-looking banner strung across the picture rail of one wall. God Bless the Queen, made by my very own mother.

I've had a telegram, not from the Queen as I have to live another ten years before that happens, as does she. But from Janet, who's the next best thing to royalty.

'Happy birthday to my dear sister. Sorry not to be there but I'm swimming with dolphins.'

She has a sense of humour after all, poor Janet, with her cancer of the bum.

Mab is here with ginger number two who's altogether much nicer than number one, which is why her husband isn't having an affair. Denise she's called and she brings me a huge bouquet of flowers that I ask Maria if she will put in the hall for everyone to see.

Tina, the Tory and Tom are next to arrive and they bring Jerome who is now watching Benjamin play a game of dominoes with Frank, until Joanie asks him to play cards with her, which he obliges, only looking a little bit scared, but who wouldn't, she's still Joanie Clark. And Tom sidles up to me and says that he's leaving Brighton because there's only so much you can learn from history books and he wants to join the business so that he can learn from real life (and Death, obviously) and that he thinks he'll be good at it because he's big on the little details which is just what you need for undertaking, though he'll have to sort out that hair of his. And I tell him I'll miss his visits, but he says not to worry, he'll come whenever he can and in between he'll send Jerome along.

Barbara is getting twitchy. Wendy is pouring fizz for a toast and the cake is being wheeled out, a mass of fire like the Blitz. Ninety ruddy candles.

And then there he is, in the haze, like he's walking out of a mirage into real life, walking towards me, one step after another, until he's bending down and kissing me and I think he is only six years old, my boy, even though he's sixty-six.

The song is sung and the cake is cut and distributed and he sits by my side all the while, with his lady friend on the other side and I reckon he's done all right for himself, punching above his weight.

'I came to see you in hospital,' he says.' Do you remember, Mum?'

'Was that you, sitting on my bed?'

'Yes, Mum.'

'I couldn't speak. I wasn't being rude, I just couldn't speak.'

'I know, Mum. I don't know if you heard me say sorry, but I am. I'm sorry.'

'Thank you, Charlie. That means the world, only I've got something I need to tell you. About your Auntie Janet.'

'I know all about that, Mum. I worked it out long ago. But you're my mother. You always have been. I'm sorry I've not been a better son.'

Keep Baby with Mother.

And that breaks my heart, all those missed times, missed moments, missed opportunities, but you can't change the past, I should coco.

'I'd better live a bit longer then, hadn't I, so we can make some better memories.'

'Do you reckon you can reach a hundred?'

'I've outwitted Death so far. What's another ten years between friends?'

'So Death's your friend now?'

'He has his moments.'

'As do you, Mum. Our Betsy Sunshine.'

Acknowledgements

Many thanks are due to the following people for their generous feedback, encouragement and support: to everyone at Legend Press, especially Lauren Parsons; to Broo Doherty, my lovely agent, for her continuing faith in me; to my writing buddies, Margaret James and Cathie Hartigan for their sharp early eyes; to Paul McVeigh for his input with That Killer First Page; to Hilda Sheehan for challenging my pelvic floor with her antics and words; to my war baby mum, Mary, Queen of Make-do-and-mend, and to her mother, Barbara, who lived life fully until her 91st year despite her birth weight of 'three and a bit pounds' and the Bristol Blitz; to my great-aunt, Ruth Gillespy, born during the same year as Princess Elizabeth, who worked on Enigma as a teenage Wren. Also to all the funeral directors who serve behind the scenes, unsung heroes all. And, of course, to the unexpected Queen, Lilibet, for doing her duty and for outliving all those politicians, prime ministers, archbishops and heads of state. Finally, special thanks as ever to Niall, Johnny, Eddy and Izzy who continue to put up with this writer.

We do hope that you have enjoyed reading this large print book.

Did you know that all of our titles are available for purchase?

We publish a wide range of high quality large print books including:
Romances, Mysteries, Classics
General Fiction
Non Fiction and Westerns

Special interest titles available in large print are:
The Little Oxford Dictionary
Music Book
Song Book
Hymn Book
Service Book

Also available from us courtesy of Oxford University Press:
Young Readers' Dictionary
(large print edition)
Young Readers' Thesaurus
(large print edition)

For further information or a free brochure, please contact us at:
Ulverscroft Large Print Books Ltd.,
The Green, Bradgate Road, Anstey,
Leicester, LE7 7FU, England.
Tel: (00 44) 0116 236 4325
Fax: (00 44) 0116 234 0205